Falling For Nick

JOLEEN JAMES

FALLING FOR NICK

Printed in the United States of America

ISBN: 1489536884
ISBN-13: 978-1489536884

Other Titles by Joleen James

Hometown Star

Under A Harvest Moon

Hostage Heart, *a short story*

For Ray, the love of my life.

CHAPTER ONE

Port Bliss, Washington

A pitiful handful of mourners had gathered to bury Maude Lombard.

Clea Rose still had no idea what had compelled her to attend the funeral. Her black heels poked into the soggy grass like stakes in the ground, holding her prisoner to the macabre scene before her. Tangy sea air, thick with unleashed moisture, threatened to drench the sad group at any moment. The tension built in the air as a storm brewed both overhead and at the Port Bliss Cemetery.

She didn't belong here, knew she should leave, but she couldn't go, not yet. The wind picked up, and the birch trees lining the perimeter of the cemetery shivered, sending an ominous whisper around the mourners. Clea shook off the feeling of foreboding and focused on the people encircling Maude's casket.

Dick and Andy Bower, the town drunks, stood to Clea's right. Dick and Andy were Maude's best customers at the Port Bliss Tavern where she'd worked as a cocktail waitress for close to thirty years. To Clea's left stood DeAnn Schemer, Maude's best friend. DeAnn owned the local beauty parlor, affectionately called DeAnn's Doos. Next to DeAnn stood Bernie Cottenheimer. Bernie had been Maude's current boyfriend and best drinking buddy. His normally red eyes appeared even redder today. He'd been crying, and that surprised Clea, making her wonder if he'd actually loved Maude. Next to Bernie stood Maude's youngest son,

Billy.

At one time Billy Lombard had held all the promise for the Lombard family. Two years younger than Clea, he hadn't changed much in the ten years since she was in high school. His jet-black hair still stuck up in all the wrong places. Dressed in what had to be a new black suit, he stood beside Maude's casket, his head bowed. Clea knew first-hand that Maude had been a rotten mother, yet her death would cause great sorrow for Billy. He'd always had a soft heart, a beautiful soul, and a sharp mind, a mind he'd wasted here in Port Bliss.

As Reverend Parrish began the service, Clea focused her attention on the spray of red roses and baby's breath covering the casket. The Reverend's words blended into the soft shuffling of bodies around her. Clea's mind went back to the moment she'd arrived at the cemetery. She hadn't missed the light of surprise in Billy's eyes when he'd noticed her walking toward the gathering. Something had brought her here to say good-bye, to show respect for the grandmother of her son, despite the fact she had a silent agreement with the Lombards not to speak of the connection between them. Maybe the need for closure had brought her here, closure she'd never had with Nick.

She couldn't help but think of Nick today. He'd been out of prison for close to three months. Did he know his mother had died? Would he care? Clea didn't know. She did know he cared about Billy. Nick would do anything for his kid brother.

Bernie said a few words about his love for Maude as DeAnn sobbed quietly beside the casket.

"Maude leaves behind two sons, Nicholas and William," Reverend Parrish said, "and a grandson, Johnathan Rose."

All eyes turned to Clea. Pride and her high heels kept her rooted where she stood. Her eyes met Billy's and he gave her a nod, a respectful nod. After all this time, she wasn't sure how she felt about a nod from the Lombard family. They'd given up their right to know her son years ago.

The unmistakable roar of an approaching car distracted the mourners, and everyone turned toward the road. Glad all eyes were off of her, Clea also sought out the car. Her breath caught when she recognized the yellow and black '69 Mustang Boss racing toward them. Only one person in Port Bliss had a car like that. Her heart lurched. It couldn't be.

The Mustang braked to a stop at the edge of the grass. The door swung open and Nick climbed out - all six foot four inches of him. Wearing black jeans and a black leather jacket, he looked every bit as dangerous as he had in high school.

Clea's chest tightened with panic. She'd always imagined meeting him again, but not like this, not at a funeral.

Beside her DeAnn said, "Well don't that beat all? Nick's come home."

Clea tried to move, but her heels remained stuck in the grass. Unable to make a quick exit, she turned to face the casket, hoping Nick wouldn't notice her. She felt like an animal snared in one of old man Patenski's iron beaver traps. Her heart beat so loud she could hear the echo in her ears, the roar blocking her ability to think clearly.

"Go on, Reverend," Billy said as Nick stepped into place beside him.

"Nick," the Reverend greeted before continuing. "And so we say our final good-bye to Maude Lombard…"

Clea didn't hear any more. A powerful force she didn't understand pulled her toward Nick and she found herself held captive by his stare, a stare so compelling every nerve in her body began to hum. The intensity in his eyes made her remember every reason she'd been attracted to him, every reason she had to fear him.

"May you rest in peace, Maude." Reverend Parrish concluded the service, then extended his hand to Nick.

Clea made her get-away, dislodging her heels from the earth. She was halfway to her car when the rain started. Fat, angry drops, and for some reason the saying, "Raindrops are tears from God," ran through her head. Was God crying for Maude? Or was He crying for them all? The rain soaked her as she fumbled in her purse, looking for her keys.

"Clea."

"No," she said sharply. She needed time to get her emotions under control. She couldn't talk to Nick, not yet. Locating her keys, she inserted the key into the lock. The late model Honda clicked, all four doors unlocking. She reached for the handle. Nick's fingers closed around her arm.

"Aren't you going to say hello, Princess?"

The smooth sound of Nick's voice brought back every ounce of physical hurt, every shard of mental anguish she'd felt the past ten years. "Let go of me, Nick." She kept her eyes on the car. She didn't owe him a thing, not anymore.

"I don't want to fight, Clea."

Regret softened his words, and awakened her own regrets. Clea glanced at him. Close up, he was even more handsome than she had remembered. It wasn't fair. He still wore his black hair longer than fashionable. The dark stubble that had felt like sandpaper against her skin shadowed a jaw that had grown stronger and leaner with age. Blue eyes the color of a hot summer sky glowed with a promise she'd tried to forget.

He let go of her arm, but his stare kept her pinned to the side of the car. As much as she wanted to she couldn't move.

"I'm sorry about Maude," she offered, not knowing what else to say.

"Don't be. I'm here for Billy."

The hard tone of his words stirred an ache within her. "Yes, well, I'm sorry for Billy, too."

"He's had a tough time," Nick said, "but he's back on his feet now, working at Mullin's Garage."

"So I hear," Clea said. "Look, I need to go."

"How's my son?"

For a moment she had trouble thinking, let alone speaking. With an effort, she cleared her throat. "Don't confuse him, Nick."

A hard glint darkened Nick's eyes, and she remembered the lightning fast way his moods could change.

"He's my son, too, Clea."

She turned away from him, toward the car. "You made it clear a long time ago that you wanted nothing to do with him. You've never even seen him." With shaking fingers, she pulled the handle open and slid inside the car. When she tried to close the door, Nick caught it.

"I'm John's father," he said. "I have questions."

A chill ran down Clea's spine. Was Nick here for more than just the funeral? Had he come home for John? "I'm sure you have questions, but I'm not sure I'm inclined to answer them. Especially not here, and not now."

The muscle near his jaw tightened. "Then when? Just say the word and I'll be there."

"I don't know." A terrible tightness had taken hold of her chest.

"Nick," Billy called from the graveside. "Come on, man. We're waiting for you."

"You better go," Clea said, the words a whisper.

"I'll be in touch."

He started to reach for her arm. Clea's heart skipped a beat. At the last minute he pulled away. Turning, he walked back to Billy, placing a comforting arm around his brother's shoulders. At one time she would have given anything to have Nick comfort her, but those days were gone.

Clea yanked the Honda's door shut and flipped the switch, locking Nick out of her car, her heart, and her life. She started the engine and drove off. She didn't look back.

* * *

"You'll make a beautiful bride, Clea."

Clea stared at herself in the full-length mirror. On the outside she looked composed, but inside her world was crumbling. Thoughts of her encounter with Nick yesterday twisted her nerves into tight knots. Last night she'd put off telling her mother, and her fiancé, Robert, about Nick. She'd needed time to adjust to the news herself before having to deal with their comments. At this moment, she wanted to be anywhere but where she was, in Elizabeth Spencer's Clothing Shop, trying on her bridal gown.

"The dress is worth every penny," her mother said with a satisfied nod. "You look like a princess."

"I'm not a princess," she said, remembering Nick's words yesterday. "I'm far from it."

Vivian Rose walked a slow circle around her daughter. As usual, her mother had dressed to the nines in a powder blue Chanel suit. At age fifty-nine Vivian appeared years younger. Her blonde hair, born from a bottle now, was cut short, chic, with soft layers framing her face. Clea wished she had her mother's sense of style. Her mother looked elegant, put together, in control. Clea had never been in control, not once, and lately that thought bothered her more and more.

Vivian tapped one French-manicured fingernail against her chin. "This dress needs a tiara. You could wear your hair up."

"A tiara?" Clea said. "I don't know. It sounds pretentious. I thought it might be nice to keep it simple and have some flowers woven into my hair."

"Flowers? Really, Clea, you only get married once." Vivian

smiled. "You're going to be the daughter-in-law of a United States senator, the wife of a prestigious attorney. You need to look the part. Everything's going your way, both personally and professionally. Winning the internship for your photography means a fresh start for you, Robert, and John. New York is waiting for you. It's your time to shine, honey. All your dreams are about to come true."

She fussed with Clea's skirt, straightening the line of the creamy white satin. "With a sleeveless dress like this you need gloves, elegant satin gloves that come above your elbow." Vivian gave Clea's arm a pat.

Clea forced a smile. She willed herself to be happy, to catch her mother's enthusiasm for the wedding. She loved Robert. They were going to have a wonderful life together. Nick's return wouldn't change things. What worried her was Robert's reaction to the news. He hated Nick and time hadn't eased Robert's anger.

For the first time in her life, she wished she'd listened to her mother when she'd suggested Clea have Nick sign away his parental rights, but she'd been so young, her heart broken. A part of her still ached at Nick's betrayal of the young love she'd felt for him. Seeing him yesterday had opened the wound in her soul; a wound she thought had healed years ago.

"What do you think about the length of the gown?" her mother asked, breaking into Clea's thoughts.

Clea glanced down at the hemline. "It's fine."

Her mother frowned, the action stealing some of her beauty. "Darling, you could be more excited about the dress. It's costing me a fortune."

"I do love the dress. You know I'm excited for the wedding." Clea ran her hand over the satin skirt. "The hemline is just right."

"Now there's the Clea I know," Vivian said with a smile. "Having two months to plan this wedding is ludicrous. I'm not a miracle worker."

"No one expects you to be," Clea replied. "You and Robert wanted a big wedding. I wanted to elope, remember?" Clea tugged at the bodice of the gown. "I would've been happy in a simple off the rack dress."

"Don't insult me, Clea. I've waited my entire life for this wedding. Elizabeth." Vivian turned toward the shopkeeper. "Will you be able to handle the tiaras and gloves?"

"Of course." Elizabeth Spencer, the owner of Port Bliss's one and only clothing store, rushed forward.

"The gown fits like it was made for you," Elizabeth said. She used a special buttonhook to unfasten the tiny satin covered buttons that ran down the back of the gown.

"Thank you." Clea lifted her hair out of the way, allowing the shopkeeper better access to the buttons. In a matter of minutes Clea stepped out of the pool of satin. While Elizabeth saw to the dress, Clea pulled on her dark denim jeans and white T-shirt. Unlike her mother, clothes weren't important to her - comfort came first. Her one concession to style was her Anne Klein black leather boots.

When she rejoined her mother, Vivian was at the counter with Elizabeth, giving the woman instructions on how many tiaras they wanted to see, and the different styles of gloves.

"Thanks for all your help, Elizabeth." Clea smiled. "You've done a wonderful job."

"It's my pleasure, dear." Elizabeth returned Clea's smile. "I'm happy to help. I know this can't be an easy time for you with Nick Lombard back in town."

"What!" Vivian gasped, her eyebrows shooting up somewhere near her hairline. "Nick's here? In Port Bliss?"

Elizabeth glanced between mother and daughter. "I heard over at the café that he came home to attend Maude's funeral." She looked at Clea. "I'm sorry, Clea. I thought you knew. I just assumed with him being John's father..."

"I did know," Clea admitted. "I saw him yesterday."

"Clea! Why in heaven's name didn't you say something?" Vivian took her daughter's arm and propelled her toward the door. "Thank you for everything, Elizabeth."

"You're welcome." Elizabeth came around the counter, her forehead wrinkled with concern. She followed them to the door. "And again, I'm awfully sorry if I've upset you, Vivian."

"It's not your fault." Vivian gave Clea a stern look. "I appreciate the information. God knows when my daughter was going to tell me."

"Well, good afternoon then." Elizabeth held the door open.

When the shop door shut behind them, Vivian said, "How dare you keep news like this from me? Do you know how embarrassed I am? Does everyone in town know?" She led Clea down the sidewalk.

Clea bristled. She pulled her arm from Vivian's grasp. "I needed time to digest the news myself. I was going to tell you right after the fitting. I knew you'd be upset."

"Of course I'm upset." Two bright spots of color highlighted Vivian's cheekbones. "We don't want that man anywhere near your son. He almost ruined your life once. I won't let him do it again. What if he's come back for John?"

Her words awakened Clea's fear for her son. She'd felt a lot of things for Nick over the years - everything from love, to lust, to hate, but she'd never been afraid of him. She'd never expected him to come back to Port Bliss. What had happened between them had been a terrible mistake. She didn't want her son to pay for that mistake.

"Robert isn't going to like this." Vivian zeroed in on Clea. "He does know, doesn't he?"

Clea glanced away. "No, I haven't told him yet. I didn't see him last night. This isn't the kind of news you deliver to your fiancé by phone."

"Oh, for God's sake," her mother snapped. "You need to tell him. He'll protect you this time, Clea. He's a powerful attorney. He has connections. We'll have him draw up papers to keep Nick away from John. Nick Lombard doesn't belong here. He never did."

* * *

Clea checked on her son for the tenth time since putting him to bed. She crept to his bedside. The light from the hall gave off just enough illumination to see his small body nestled under his navy bedspread. Unable to help herself, she touched his dark hair. Hair the same color as Nick's. Both had black hair and blue eyes the exact shade of a robin's egg. Both had a dimple in their left cheek and a smile that could melt a woman's heart. From the moment of his birth there'd been no denying that Nick was the father of her child, as much as her parents had hoped otherwise. In those days she'd been an idealist, full of hope that Nick would want her and John, that one day they'd be a family, but as the years passed, her hope had faded, until nothing remained but her determination to raise her son alone.

Clea bent down and kissed John's soft cheek. "Sleep well, my angel," she whispered. John might have been an accident, but she'd never regretted his birth, not once. She'd fallen in love with him on sight. She couldn't bear to be parted from him - ever. Satisfied he was safe, she left his room, closing the door.

Since the funeral she'd been on edge, waiting for Nick to show up, demanding to see John. So far, he hadn't contacted her, and his silence unnerved her. He'd told her once that he didn't want to be a part of John's life, yet Nick had come back to Port Bliss. Had he come back for John? He'd said he wanted to meet with her. With each hour that passed Clea's anxiety mushroomed.

The minute Robert had heard the news of Nick's return, courtesy of Vivian, he'd rushed right over to comfort Clea, and she had to admit his presence tonight had done some good. He'd assured her that he would do everything in his power to protect John from Nick.

"Is he sleeping?" Robert asked when she joined him in the living room.

"Yes."

Robert sat on her black leather sofa, a crystal tumbler of Glenlivet in his hand. He usually didn't drink, but tonight he'd asked Clea to pour him a Scotch.

Nick's return had upset him more than he let on. Robert was so different from Nick, and it was more than that they were from different parts of town.

Clea couldn't help but compare the two men. Dressed in khakis, a crisp white shirt, and expensive brown leather shoes, Robert looked every inch an up-and-coming attorney, right down to his perfectly styled blond hair and professionally manicured nails. Clean-shaven, he oozed respectability and charm. The right mix for his profession.

Where Robert was smooth, Nick was rough. He was all black leather and denim. She'd been attracted to him since she was seventeen, and eleven years later, she still felt the physical pull of that attraction. Only now she was older and wiser. She wouldn't repeat history. This time she had to think with her head, not her hormones.

"I wish you'd brought John to my place," Robert said. "I don't want to leave you two here alone tonight." He patted the seat next to him. "Sit down. Have a drink. It will help you relax."

"I don't want a drink." Clea sank down on the sofa. The leather felt cool through her clothes. A fire burned in the gas fireplace, but its cheery glow couldn't chase away the dread she felt. "You know I don't want to upset John. He has school tomorrow. I want to keep his routine normal." Robert stretched his arm across the back of the sofa and she settled against him. "You could stay here, Boomer."

Robert grimaced. "Clea, I've asked you a thousand times not to use that silly nickname anymore. No credible adult goes by the name Boomer. And I can't stay. I wish I could, but I have a nine a.m. meeting with a client. All my notes are at my place." He took a sip of his drink. "Maybe you should think about staying with your mother until this all blows over."

"I like living here in town above The Coffee House. It's convenient for me. John's bus stop is out front. I love being near the canal." She smiled. "Besides, how many people do you know who are lucky enough to live above their workplace? I have no intention of staying with my mother. We'd drive each other crazy."

Robert swirled the Scotch in his glass. "Why did he have to come back now? I don't want to relive all the ugliness. This town is one big gossip mill."

His words hit her like a fist to the gut. "I'm sorry. I can't keep people from talking. My first priority is John. I can handle Nick. You understand that, don't you?"

Robert stared into his drink. "I just don't want to add fuel to a fire that's nearly burnt out. Hopefully, he's left town already, but if he hasn't I'd like to keep this as quiet as possible."

"Do you really think you can keep Nick a secret?" Clea said, her voice rising with anxiety. "John's paternity aside, you were part of that summer ten years ago. Danny was your brother."

"And he was murdered by the father of your child." Robert set his drink down on the coffee table with enough force to spill some of the Scotch onto the smooth oak. "I've tried to put all that behind me. I know you have too. I'm not about to let a loser like Nick Lombard come back to this town and pull all those terrible memories to the surface."

"How're you going to stop him?" Clea asked. "Nick's paid for his crimes. He's a free man."

"He killed my brother." Robert frowned, his mouth tight.

"In self-defense," Clea reminded him gently.

"So he says," Robert shot back, turning a dark scowl on her. "No gun was ever found to back up Nick's story. And do you really think it was a coincidence that the lakeside robberies stopped when

Nick was arrested?"

"I don't know what to think." Clea replayed that night over in her mind as she had done so many times before. All the evidence had been stacked against Nick, yet she'd believed him when he'd claimed Danny's death had been an accident, that he'd knocked Danny to the ground in an attempt to loosen the gun from his hands, a gun that had been pointed at Nick's younger brother, Billy. Danny's head had struck a rock, the blow killing him. Nick had been trying to save his brother's life and instead he'd taken Danny's. When the police investigated, no gun had been found. Clea could understand Robert's hatred, his bitterness. He'd lost his only brother. She'd lost her son's father. That night had changed all of their lives forever.

"Let's elope," Clea suggested, desperate for a solution they could all live with.

Robert shook his head. "How can we elope? My parents' party is this weekend. The wedding is next month. The invitations have gone out. Three hundred guests are coming to us - here, in Port Bliss."

Clea took Robert's hand, threading her fingers with his. "It would be romantic to elope. We could come back and have the reception here, later in the summer."

"No." Robert pulled his hand away and stood. He paced over to the window, then back. "I want to press forward with our plans. I've waited ten years for you to be ready to marry me. I want the entire world to witness our marriage. We'll find a way to keep Nick Lombard out of our lives."

"Maybe he won't bother us. So far he hasn't made any trouble. His mother just died." Clea held her hand out to Robert. "Come here. Sit down. I don't like to see you upset."

"No one tells Nick Lombard what to do," Robert said, ignoring her invitation. "Trouble follows the man like a bad stink. It always has, and it always will. Don't worry about Nick. I'll take care of him. I've already started the paperwork for a No Contact Order."

Clea's stomach clenched. A No Contact Order seemed brutal and uncalled for. Nick hadn't asked for anything yet. Did she want to anger him? "I'm not sure I want to do that."

"It's for the best, Clea. You don't want Nick to think he can become involved in John's life do you?"

"No, I don't." She had no intention of letting Nick near her son. He didn't deserve to know John. On the flip side, she hated to anger him with a No Contact Order. "He may have left town already and we're worrying for nothing."

"Maybe, but I'm going to push the No Contact Order through tomorrow anyway, just to be safe." Robert sighed. "I don't want to talk about Nick. Come here." He pulled Clea up from the sofa and into his arms, hugging her. "I should be going."

"All right." Clea returned his embrace, wanting the strength he could give her. She understood his anger and pain, wished she could make things better for him.

Robert pressed a kiss to her temple. "Call me if you need anything, anything at all."

"I will." She tilted her head back and he kissed her.

Clea wound her arms around his neck, wanting him to make her forget Nick, forget the past. She wanted her body to sizzle with the kind of desire she knew she should feel. Robert's arms came around her, holding her closer, and he deepened the kiss.

She tried to lose herself to his kiss, but the passion, the hunger, just weren't there. She pressed her body more fully against his, willing a spark to erupt inside her. She wanted to be on fire for Robert. He deserved her love. John adored him. Robert was the right man for her.

"Maybe I will stay," Robert said, responding to her the way she wished her own body would react to his. "You make me crazy, Clea. When I'm with you I want to take risks, let go of everything and just feel." He ran his hands down her back to cup her butt, pulling her intimately against him.

Clea closed her eyes, hoping, praying for desire to fill her like it always had with Nick. Nick. His name sent a shiver straight through her.

"No. Go," she said, breaking the kiss. Suddenly, she didn't want Robert to stay. Her emotions felt pulverized, like they'd been put into a blender and whipped on high speed. She needed to think, to be alone. "I'll be fine. I'll see you tomorrow."

For a moment Robert couldn't seem to focus, his eyes clouded with passion. Then he sighed, running a critical hand over his hair to make sure he didn't have a strand out of place. "I'm just a phone call away."

Clea walked him to the door. Before he left, she gave him a final kiss. When he was gone, she shut the door and locked it, but she knew from personal experience that a lock wouldn't keep Nick out if he wanted to get in.

Going to the window, she looked across the street to the Port Bliss Tavern, to the room above it. Was Nick there, staying at his mother's place? Her eyes sought the location of his childhood bedroom. The room was dark. She'd been inside the apartment once. The place had been a mess. She'd never seen so many dirty dishes or empty liquor bottles. Maude wasn't much of a housekeeper. She remembered feeling sorry for Nick and Billy. She also remembered Nick telling her he didn't want her pity. He'd been so angry. When she'd tried to soothe his anger, he'd kissed her. Clea brought her fingers to her lips. A flutter of desire began to beat low in her belly. A desire she couldn't raise a moment ago with Robert.

She spun away from the window, her hand against her stomach. Nick Lombard had finally come home. She'd seen the questions in his eyes at the funeral, heard the frustration in his voice. Did he blame her for everything? More importantly, was she to blame? She didn't know, but deep down she knew that Nick wasn't finished with her yet.

And that thought scared her to death.

CHAPTER TWO

Nick pushed the apartment door open.

The smell of booze, stale cigarette smoke, and cheap perfume rushed to greet him, reminding him of everything he'd tried to forget in the ten years he'd been away. Disgust rolled through his belly and for a second he considered jumping back into his car and leaving town that night.

Steeling himself for the unpleasant memories to come, he left the door open, went to the window, and unlatched a lock made rusty by the salt air. When the frame refused to give, he struck the wood with the butt of his palm. The window creaked open, and fresh sea air moved into the room. Nick took a massive breath into his lungs - air so pure he could smell the saltwater and seaweed that hugged the beach of the canal. God, he'd missed that smell.

The gray water of Hood Canal lapped at the shore behind the row of business across the street. Oyster shells littered the beach, some bright white, others a dull gray. How many hours had he spent on that beach, skipping rocks, hunting for oysters, making out with girls? Until Clea. He looked across the street at The Coffee House. He'd never figured Clea for the type of woman to stay in this one-block town. The town of Port Bliss existed for the tourists, the rich, the people who lived seven miles up the mountain on Lake Bliss year-round, or in the summer. The locals here worked thirty minutes away at the factory in nearby Bradley, or like his mother, held low paying jobs in town.

The apartment above The Coffee House had to be about the

same size as the one he stood in now. Billy told him Clea lived there. Why would she live in town when her mother owned one of the largest homes on the lake? He'd been inside the Rose house on Lake Bliss. In his eyes, the place had been a palace, fit for a princess. The perfect setting for Clea. The house had been filled with plush carpets, white furniture, with a dramatic lakefront view. Living on the lake meant you had money, lots of it. And while Clea's family might not have as much money as some, her father was a doctor, a pillar of the community. What the Rose family had lacked in wealth, they'd made up for in respectability.

A movement in The Coffee House caught his attention. On his way over, he'd seen Clea working behind the counter. Billy had told him Clea co-owned the shop with Mitzi, her best friend from high school. That was another thing that didn't fit. Clea had wanted to be a photographer. The pictures she'd done in high school had won awards, earning her a scholarship to The Seattle Art Institute. Why hadn't she used her talent? A million questions ran through his mind. He wanted to ask Clea what had happened to her dreams, but knew he had no right.

"The place is a mess."

Nick turned at the sound of his brother's voice.

Billy came inside and set a box of cleaning supplies down on the kitchen table. That done, he went back to the door and pulled it shut.

"Leave the door open." Nick came away from the window, his emotions as mixed as his memories. "The place needs to air out."

"It smells the same as always," Billy said with a shrug, but he opened the door. "You can't air out thirty years of bad living. Why don't you stay with me? It's worked out okay the past couple of nights, right?"

"Thanks for the offer, but I don't want to crowd you." He didn't want to stay anywhere else, not while Clea lived across the street.

While he'd been in prison he'd done nothing but think about Clea and John and how he'd win them back, but reality had intruded the minute he'd been set free. A terrible fear had begun to grow in him, a fear laced with doubts and regrets. Instead of coming home, he'd taken a job in Bradley, giving himself time to breathe, to figure out his next move. Three months had slipped by since his release, three months where he'd almost managed to convince himself that John and Clea were better off without him; but now, after seeing her, he couldn't walk away. Standing close to her and inhaling her sweet scent had brought back memories he'd thought long buried.

He'd forgotten how beautiful she was, all that long blonde hair, and those soft green eyes. He'd seen those eyes burn with desire for him, but yesterday, he'd seen them bright with fear. And when she'd run from him, he'd been unable to let her go without a confrontation. She'd been afraid, and that saddened him. More than anything he wanted to talk to her, but knew he needed to give her a few days to get used to the idea he'd come home; then he'd move forward with his plan to meet with her.

He didn't want his son to think he didn't give a damn. It's what Nick thought about his own father and it hurt, a deep down hurt that never went away. Prison had given him time to think, to form a plan, but reality was a million times harder. Could he win Clea and John back? The thought terrified him more than being caught alone in prison with no weapon, his back unprotected.

"I'm glad you're here, Nick," Billy said, his words dragging Nick back to the present. Billy lifted a can of cleanser from the box of supplies. "I've missed you. Things will be better now that you're home."

"I hope so, Billy. I keep asking myself if I'm doing the right thing by staying." Nick glanced around the apartment. "I do know one thing; if I'm going to live here, the apartment needs to smell better than this." He moved into the kitchen. Dirty dishes and empty food containers littered the counters, filled the sink. "I see Mom's housekeeping skills stayed the same after I left."

Billy smiled. "A clean house was never a priority for Maude Lombard." He went to the supplies and pulled out a box of garbage bags. "I say we bag everything up and put it in the dumpster out back."

"Sounds good." Nick wandered through the living room. Several years' worth of framed school photos of himself and Billy were placed helter-skelter on the end table. Maude's large, cut-glass ashtray was filled with butts, in easy reach of the couch.

It surprised him that his mother had not only purchased the school photos, but had kept them displayed. She'd never had much time for her sons. Her social life had always come first. The thought left a sour taste in his mouth. His fingers closed over a picture of himself standing next to his car - a photo Clea had taken. The '69 Mustang looked as it had the day he'd bought it. Faded paint, bad tires, a small dent in the left fender. The photo didn't match the car he'd come home to. Fully restored by Billy while Nick was in prison, the Mustang was in cherry condition, from the restored 302 under the hood to the six-coat paint job on the exterior.

"Some change, huh?" Billy pointed at the picture.

"Yeah." Nick set the photograph back on the table. "I'm going to pay you back every last penny you put into that car."

"No way." Billy shook his head. "It's my gift to you. I owe you brother, and this is my way of repaying you. Besides, I got most of the stuff for free or at cost. I have connections at the garage." He winked, the gesture reminding Nick of how fun loving Billy could be.

"It's too much, Billy."

"You started the restoration; I finished it for you." Billy's grin softened into a sad smile. "I want you to take the car, no strings attached. Please, for me."

"For now," Nick said, but he still intended to pay Billy back every cent. He understood his brother's need to make things right between them, but he didn't want Billy to feel like he owed him. He didn't. Wanting to change the subject, he said, "Let's take a look at our old room."

Together they entered the room they used to share. The room smelled musty, old. Dust motes swam in the beam of light shining in-between the broken slats of the blinds. Their two beds were still there, the mattresses bare and depressing. Filthy orange and brown shag carpet covered the floor. The colors in the rug had always reminded Nick of a calico cat.

"It's the same." Billy smiled at Nick. "We had some good times in here, remember?"

Nick smiled back. "We did." But the bad times had far outweighed the good. Back at the doorway, he turned to look at the room, pitiful, barren, and dirty. They'd had nothing. He'd been so angry. He spun away, not wanting Billy to see his disgust for the childhood they'd shared.

He turned to Billy. "Pass me one of those plastic bags."

Each faded dishtowel, chipped plate, and moldy food container reminded Nick of his ugly childhood. As he added more trash to the bag, he felt like a traitor to his mother's memory. He tried not to think about her as they bagged up her life, but thoughts of Maude intruded. He remembered Christmases with no presents, his mother so drunk she couldn't stand up. He remembered days with no food in the fridge, nights with no heat. The memories hammered at him, opening wounds he thought long ago scabbed over.

Together the brothers worked to rid the apartment of the life of Maude Lombard. For hours they removed garbage, hauled out the cigarette smoke infused furniture, cleaned the rugs, and washed the walls.

And the place still wasn't livable.

But it was cleaner.

They didn't go into Maude's room, and they didn't talk about why. Instead, they simply closed the door on their mother's life.

"I think if you paint the walls, it might help with the smell," Billy said as he surveyed the work they'd done.

"Maybe." Nick's stomach rumbled. The noon hour had long since passed. "What do you say we take a break and get something to eat?"

"Sounds good." Billy tied off the garbage bag he held. "I'll take this down on the way."

They left the apartment together and were on their way down the stairs when a man approached them.

"Nick Lombard?" The man gave Nick an odd, knowing smile.

"Who wants to know?" Nick asked, instantly wary. The man looked harmless enough in his polo shirt, tan pants, and suede jacket. He stood on the sidewalk at the bottom of the stairs, holding an envelope out to Nick.

"If you are Nick Lombard this is for you."

Nick reached the sidewalk. Cold February air stung his cheeks.

The man thrust a big yellow envelope into Nick's hand.

"Have a nice day," the man said, his smile widening.

As far as Nick knew, Maude didn't have a will. Whatever awaited him in the envelope was sure to be bad news. For a moment he considered chucking it in the dumpster with the rest of the garbage.

"Who do you think it's from?" Billy asked.

"No clue."

"You have to open it, Nick. It might have something to do with

John."

Against his better judgment, Nick tore the envelope open and pulled out two pages of folded paper. Quickly, he scanned the print. "Shit."

"What's it say?" Billy asked, trying to read over Nick's shoulder."

"It's a No Contact Order. I'm not to go within one hundred feet of Clea or my son."

"Jesus, she's playing hard ball," Billy said, a note of sympathy in his voice.

Nick nodded, too angry to speak. Was Clea across the street in The Coffee House, watching him, waiting? A sharp ache started in his gut. Clea hadn't even tried to talk to him; instead she'd taken steps to keep him away. Part of him could understand why, but a bigger part of him seethed with anger and he wanted to rise to the challenge she'd put before him. "I think I might have to take a rain check on lunch, Billy."

"Whoa," Billy said. "I know that look. You're not thinking of going over there, are you?"

"If Clea wants to play hardball, I'll play." Nick started forward, but had to stop and wait for traffic on the street to clear.

Billy grabbed his arm. "Don't be stupid. Think about it. If you go over there, she'll have your ass thrown back in jail. Is that what you want? Do you want to lose your son before you even get the chance to know him?"

"No." Nick glanced away, fighting to ignore the tightening in his chest.

Billy squeezed his arm. "Clea's getting to you, just like she always has. Damn her. Think about things before you do something you'll regret."

He'd always been quick to act on his temper, and his temper had always gotten him in trouble. Billy made sense. Maybe he should have listened to him ten years ago. If he had, he wouldn't have gone to prison. He'd know his son, be a part of his life. "You're right."

"I know I'm right. Let's go and get some lunch. You need to think strategy, and I'm going to help you. If you want the chance to know your son, you need to play by the rules."

"I don't want to mess up his life. I don't want to play games, Billy, not when it comes to John." Something sad pricked his heart as he said the words. Did his son want to know him? That question had kept him awake nights when he'd been locked up. Was John better off without a father? Nick didn't know the first thing about being a parent and would probably do a lousy job, but more than anything he wanted the chance to try, which was more than his own father ever did.

Billy let go of his arm. "Maybe you need to tell Clea you don't want to make trouble so she can relax." He grinned. "In the meantime, the first thing you need to do is forget about that No Contact Order. Get your life back together and get an attorney."

Nick frowned. "I can't afford an attorney, and I don't want to take any kind of legal action against Clea. What happened between us wasn't her fault."

"Let me help you, Nick," Billy said, his tone insistent. "I know somebody. A guy I roomed with in college. He's a lawyer. We've stayed in touch. It's my fault you don't know your son. I want to help *you* this time."

"No, thanks. I can make it on my own. I don't need or want an attorney."

"Maybe." Billy gestured to Nick's car. The Boss was parked at the curb. Billy walked over to the Mustang and ran a hand over the glossy yellow paint. "You're back now. Give up the job in Bradley. Do what you love. Go to the garage and ask Mr. Mullin for your old job back. You're the best, Nick. Cars are your passion."

Billy made sense. Nick had only just begun to explore old car restoration when he'd gone to prison. He'd loved the work, loved taking an old car and restoring it to its original state. While in prison he'd taken classes, earning his Automotive Service Excellence certification, with follow up courses in suspension, steering, and engine repair. The thought of working at the garage unleashed a raw excitement. Working for Mr. Mullin would bring him one step closer to his goal - owning a first class car restoration business.

"Do you really think Mullin would hire me?" Nick asked, warming to the idea.

Billy grinned. "Hell, I know he would. Not only does the old man love you like a son, you're the best mechanic around."

Nick looked at his brother, really looked at him. Billy wasn't a scared sixteen-year-old kid anymore. He was a man. He no longer needed protecting.

"Come on," Nick said, catching Billy's enthusiasm for the future. "Let's get some lunch. Besides, it's damned cold out here." Turning his back on The Coffee House, Nick started toward the café. He'd work on securing a job first, then he'd worry about Clea. Clea Rose had money, respectability, and social standing in the community. If he wanted to win her, he had to play by her rules, have something to offer her. He couldn't afford to make stupid mistakes, not this time.

* * *

"It's a great party, Clea."

Clea smiled at her best friend, Mitzi. "Robert's mom has done a wonderful job, as usual." They stood in the living room of the Bloomfield's house. Other guests milled around them, glasses of sparkling champagne in their hands.

Mitzi smiled. "I'm going to miss you when you're gone, kiddo."

"I'll miss you too, Mitzi." Clea embraced her best friend and business partner. The tall brunette gave Clea a peck on her cheek.

"It won't be the same here without you," Mitzi said. "I don't know how I'm going to get along without you at The Coffee House."

"I'm not selling my interest," Clea reminded her. "You can reach me by phone whenever you need to. We'll still be partners. I'll just be in New York, that's all."

A waiter passed with a tray of champagne and Mitzi snagged two fresh glasses, handing one crystal flute to Clea. "Here's to you getting everything your heart desires. You deserve it." She clinked her glass with Clea's.

"Thank you, sweetie," Clea said, her throat thick with emotion.

Mitzi sipped her champagne. "I've always adored this house."

The lakeside home of Senator Bloomfield and his wife, Ellen, was the largest and most spectacular on Lake Bliss. In the late 1800s, the house had been a "gentlemen's retreat" housing ladies of ill repute. Robert's family had owned the house for over thirty years. They'd renovated the house, turning it into a showplace.

Robert lived alone in the house year-round, but his parents still spent their summers with him. The senator and his wife were in residence now for the fast approaching wedding. The party tonight had a dual purpose, celebrating the Bloomfields' return to the lake and Clea winning the Graceland Mitchell Internship for the Arts.

She had to admit that Robert's parents had done a fabulous job with the party. A jazz quartet played, filling the air with seductive music. The entire room sparkled with small white lights, as did the trees surrounding the pool outside. Earlier Robert had told her he wanted her to feel enchanted, like a princess. She frowned. Being called a princess always made her think of Nick.

"Why the frown?" Mitzi smiled gently. "You're thinking about Nick, right?"

"You know me so well." Clea sighed. "I can't get him out of my mind. I know he's still in town, and I can't help but wonder why. It's like I'm afraid to exhale, to relax, because the moment I do all hell will break loose."

"I'll bet Nick's furious about the No Contact Order. I would be if I were him," Mitzi said matter-of-factly. "What are you going to do? Nick was your first love. Do you still want to marry Robert?"

"Of course I do," Clea said, her voice harsher than she intended. "You know things are finally going my way. I have so much to look forward to - the wedding, the move to New York, and the internship. For once, my personal life and my career are both on track. Nick isn't going to change anything. I've worked too long and too hard. All of my dreams are coming true." But Nick clouded her happiness. The year she'd spent with him seemed like a lifetime ago. She didn't want to relive those days, but as long as he stayed in town, she couldn't let the past die.

Suddenly, Clea wanted to be alone, away from the press of the party guests, away from the probing questions that stirred up emotions she didn't want to remember. "Excuse me, Mitzi. I need to use the ladies room."

She stepped around her friend and headed down the hall, but spotted her mother's neighbor, Mrs. Harrison. Not wanting to talk with the older woman, she did a U-turn and went back into the party, stopping in front of the window. Behind her the guests laughed. The smell of roasting meat filled the air. Outside, the lights twinkled and beckoned. She wanted to enjoy tonight, but her heart just wasn't in the party. All day long she'd been tormented by thoughts of Nick.

For a moment today, she'd thought he might come into The Coffee House. She'd seen him on the sidewalk in front of the tavern. She'd watched as he'd been served the No Contact Order. He'd looked over, had even started to cross the street, but Billy had stopped him. And as much as she didn't want to admit it, she'd been disappointed. A part of her wanted to talk to Nick, but a bigger part of her told her she'd done the right thing.

She couldn't trust him. He'd made her promises the night he'd taken her virginity, empty promises of love and commitment. He'd lied to her, shattering her faith in men, in love, and in living happily ever after. She didn't need the kind of crazy, consuming emotion she felt for Nick. She couldn't handle it, and she wouldn't put her son through that kind of heartache.

Clea's insides churned, making her stomach burn. She needed to clear her head, get some fresh air. Taking her coat from the closet, she slipped out the back door. Overhead the stars winked at her. Cold air bit at her nose and exposed fingers, but the urge to be alone overpowered her need for heat.

Between Clea and the water stood a large patio with a swimming pool in the center, followed by a half-acre of lawn. She made her way around the pool, coming to a stop when she spotted Senator Bloomfield. He sat on a concrete bench, and when he saw her, he stood. Always impeccably dressed, he wore a black suit, white shirt, and black tie; distinguished described him perfectly. His blond hair held streaks of gray at the temples, giving him even more character.

"Hello, Senator." She walked toward him.

"Clea, what are you doing out here in the cold?"

His speech sounded a little slurred, and Clea noticed the drink in his hand. "I might ask the same of you."

"I needed a breath of fresh air." He took a sip of his drink. "I hope you're enjoying the party."

"Of course I am. It's lovely. Thank you so much for hosting."

"You're most welcome." He looked out toward the lake. For a minute, neither of them spoke. When he faced her again, he gave her a small smile. "I'm afraid it's colder out here than I thought. I'm heading back inside."

"I think I'll go on down to the lake." The senator seemed a bit sad, but she wasn't sure why. "I'll see you in awhile."

With a wave of her hand, Clea left the patio. When she reached the dock she walked out to the end, taking a seat on the bench. The lake surrounded her on three sides, making her feel like she sat on an island, isolated and alone. She inhaled, taking fresh air into her lungs, wanting to clear her head.

Silence filled her, the night void of the sounds of summer: the croak of a frog, the whir of crickets, the call of a lone duck. Instead, a layer of glittering frost coated the dock, bringing with it a numbing cold. She closed her eyes. In the distance, she could hear the low purr of an electric motor.

There was a boat out there. Clea opened her eyes, scanning the dark lake. She could see the boat, a soft green light at its bow. It wasn't uncommon for people to row or take evening cruises on the water, no matter the season.

She'd done it with Nick, more than once. The lake had been a favorite make-out spot for them.

Clea crossed her arms over her chest and rubbed her arms with her hands. They'd had a strange relationship from the beginning. She'd moved to Lake Bliss the summer before her senior year. Robert had lost no time in asking her out. They became boyfriend and girlfriend that first summer. In the fall Robert left to go back to the city. Clea started school in Bradley, and she'd met Nick.

Right away, Nick had pursued her. Her "lake" friends had warned her about Nick, telling Clea he was the town bad boy. There had been a line of class distinction drawn between them from the beginning, a line they never should have crossed. Nick had seduced her with words, kisses, and promises, pushing all thoughts of the summer she'd spent with Robert from her mind.

Clea watched the boat approach. When it was even with the dock, it stopped; Clea wondered if the occupants were just curious party watchers. Her hands tightened on her arms.

Nick had liked to "borrow" a boat and cruise the lake, looking at the lit up houses from the outside. He'd always been on the outside looking in.

Nick.

Slowly, Clea rose from the bench. The hairs stood up on the back of her neck. She could feel him, out there, watching her with those intense eyes of his.

A slow heat started in the pit of her belly. She couldn't even see him, but she knew he was there. Lord help her, he still had a hold over her, the same raw power that had gotten her into trouble.

Clea backed up, her shoes slipping on the icy dock. She had to get away from him, get away from what he made her feel. She had to think with her head and ignore the rush of raw desire pulsing through her. Turning, she ran back to the house, back to the man she was going to marry and the security he offered her.

* * *

Monday afternoon, Clea pushed open the door to the Port Bliss Café and went straight to the counter, taking a seat on a vacant red-leather barstool. The smell of meatloaf filled the air. Her stomach rumbled in response as she placed her camera bag on the counter. She'd hoped she'd have time to take a couple of pictures before returning to work. The cloudy day provided the perfect lighting for beach shots.

"Hi, Betty," Clea said, greeting the waitress. "Robert's meeting me for lunch. We'll take two vegie sandwiches, on dark, with Swiss cheese." Betty Schuster had worked at the café for longer than Clea had been alive. For years she'd worn the same faded pink uniform, her tired platinum hair tortured into a tidy French twist.

"Any chips with those?" Betty took a pencil from its resting place behind her right ear.

"No, just the sandwiches, but how about a couple of colas?"

"Okay," Betty said with a wink. "Coming right up."

She left the counter and went into the kitchen. Clea swiveled on the stool to look and see who else was in the café. It was still early and most of the booths were empty, except for one near the back. From this angle she couldn't see who occupied it, but she could see a pair of legs encased in denim. The contrast of the denim legs against the red vinyl intrigued her. She removed her camera from the bag, and took the shot, the neat click of the shutter satisfying.

Smiling, Clea returned her camera to the bag, wondering what was keeping Robert. Not seeing any sign of him, her thoughts went back to Saturday night, to the boat on the lake. Had it been Nick watching her, or had it been her imagination? She'd been unable to get Nick out of her mind all night. She had to tell John about Nick's return soon, before someone else did, but finding the words was harder than she'd imagined.

Every time she looked at her son the words wouldn't come. John knew about Nick, about why he'd gone to prison, yet they never spoke of Nick. John had no idea Nick was out of prison. How did she tell him? What if Nick hurt John? Lately, John had become withdrawn, angry. He was having trouble in school and she wasn't sure why. Would meeting Nick make things worse? She didn't know.

Bottom line, she feared John's reaction to Nick.

Betty came out of the kitchen and set the sandwiches in front of her. "Here you go, honey. Enjoy."

"Thanks, Betty." She smiled at the waitress, taking a napkin from the chrome holder on the bar. "I can't imagine what's keeping Robert. He was right behind me. I'm starved." Picking up half the sandwich, she took a bite.

"Hey, Nick," Betty said.

Clea swiveled around, her mouth full of bread. Nick stood behind her, his check in his hand. She glanced down at his denim-clad legs. He'd been in the booth.

"I'll take that." Betty held her hand out for his check.

Clea tried to chew, to swallow, but the sandwich lodged in her throat.

"Hello, Clea," Nick said, his tone dry. "Who's violating the No Contact Order, you or me?"

Clea swallowed. She didn't know what to say to him.

"Here's your change, Nick." Betty dropped the coins into Nick's palm. "Have a good afternoon." To Clea she said, "I'll just go and get your drinks."

The waitress disappeared back into the kitchen, leaving them alone.

"See you around, Clea." Nick walked away. Just before he opened the door, he said, "No, I guess I won't be seeing you around, otherwise I might find myself back in jail."

"Nick, wait," she said, her voice returning.

He raised one dark brow. "For what? For the sheriff to come and arrest me for being within one hundred feet of you? Maybe you should give me a copy of your schedule so I can be sure to avoid you."

Clea's stomach clenched. Anger had punctuated his words. "Robert and I thought it best that we all know where we stand."

"Boomer?" Nick laughed. "Is he still panting after you?"

Anger flared in her chest. "He's my fiancé, Nick."

The muscle in Nick's jaw tensed. "You're going to marry Boomer? Shit. Why didn't Billy tell me?" He shook his head, and his disgust washed over her. "Boomer's not the right man for you. He doesn't make you feel anything, Princess. We both know that."

A surge of anger pushed Clea off the stool and she took a step toward him. He was getting to her, just as he had in high school. She knew she should rise above this teenage baiting, but she couldn't. She wanted to fight back, wanted him to feel the same hurt he'd made her feel ten years ago. "You don't know anything about me, Nick. You never did."

He came toward her, closing the gap between them. "I know what makes you tick, Clea, and it isn't Boomer Bloomfield. You didn't even give me a chance to explain. It didn't have to be this way. You're still a coward."

"I'm a coward?" she said, her voice heavy with sarcasm. "You've been out of prison for three months. Where have you been? Why didn't you come back sooner, say good-bye to your mother, say hello to your son?" The smirk left his face. "Oh, that's right, I forgot, you don't want your son. From where I stand, I'd say you're the coward, Nick."

His hands closed over her arms. They glared at each other, and Clea had never felt more alive. Her blood sizzled in her veins. She tilted her head back to look into his eyes, eyes that snapped like two blue flames.

"I've never been afraid to take what I want, Clea," Nick said, his tone low and dangerous. "You know that."

His words knocked the breath from her lungs. His mouth lowered to hers.

Behind them the door opened, the tinkling of the bell breaking them apart like guilty children caught with their hands in the cookie jar. Robert strode into the restaurant, an angry scowl on his face. Behind him stood Sheriff Kincade.

"I couldn't believe my eyes when I saw you through the window, Lombard," Robert said. "I knew you were stupid, but I never dreamed you'd risk going back to jail. Arrest him, Sheriff. He's in violation of a court order."

"No," Clea protested, a strange déjà vu coming over her. The scene before her played out like it had years before. The same feeling of helplessness rolled through her, and she knew Nick would hate her for this.

The sheriff stepped around Robert, heading straight for Nick. "Nick Lombard," Sheriff Kincade said. "You are under arrest."

CHAPTER THREE

"Who are you trying to call, Mom?" John asked, glancing up from the video game he played. He sat on the sofa, the controller in his hands.

"An old friend." Clea pressed the phone to her ear. With each unanswered ring, her anxiety grew. "How's the game? Are you winning?"

He nodded, his attention returning to the television screen. Like most nine-year-olds, John had a fondness for video games. Clea doled out his video game playing time like treats to be savored; she disliked the games, preferring John play outside in the fresh air.

On the tenth ring Clea pressed the end button and set the phone on the coffee table. Her thoughts returned to Nick. The minute the sheriff had put the cuffs on Nick, she'd known it was a mistake. This whole mess was her fault. She'd never wanted him to go back to jail. He hadn't sought her out today. He hadn't done anything but return to town to attend his mother's funeral. She knew it, and the heat of her shame could set the entire town ablaze.

Clea glanced out the window, fighting to get her guilt under control. Nick's arrest today had pleased Robert. No one had missed the superior look in his eyes as the sheriff had handcuffed Nick. Robert's attitude made her want to fight for Nick.

She and Robert had argued after Nick was put into the sheriff's car. She'd stuck up for Nick, telling the Sheriff that Nick had been at the café first, but Robert said only the end result mattered - Nick was going back to jail where he belonged. Clea had stormed back over to The Coffee House. Robert hadn't followed, and for that she'd been grateful.

Back at The Coffee House, Clea immediately had placed a call to Robert's secretary. His secretary had given Clea the instructions she needed to dissolve the No Contact Order. Clea had spoken to the prosecutor, and had left a message for Judge Payne, Port Bliss's judge. In order for her to explain why Nick shouldn't be in jail, the prosecutor told her she needed to appear at Nick's hearing. The hearing was scheduled for tomorrow morning. Judge Payne was a dear family friend; Clea knew he would listen to her. She'd been trying to call him every few minutes, but so far, no answer.

"Oh!" John said, shaking the hand-held controller. His brow creased, his eyes focused on the TV screen. She had to tell him about his father, but how could she do that now, when she'd just sent Nick back to jail? John would never understand.

Sighing, Clea went over and sat on the sofa next to her son. He snuggled against her side, still playing the game. Together they had survived. Nick had no idea what he'd missed. He was the loser in all of this. Love for her son filled her. She ran her fingers through his silky hair. John meant everything to her.

"Mom." He groaned at the gesture.

"Sorry." She couldn't help but smile. More than ever he needed a male influence in his life, someone he could count on. John needed Robert. The two had bonded since they'd come back to Port Bliss; John looked up to Robert as a father figure. She liked watching the two of them together. Robert possessed integrity and honesty, two traits she wanted John to possess. Nick could offer John only a scandalous past. The phone rang and Clea snatched up the receiver. "Hello."

"Clea, it's Judge Payne. I understand you want to speak with me about Nick Lombard."

"Yes." Clea glanced at John. "Can we meet privately?"

"I'm at the jail now," he told her.

"I'll be right over," she said.

"See you in a minute." The line went dead. Clea dialed Mitzi.

"Mitzi," she said, when her friend answered. "Can you come over and watch John for a little while? I have something important to do."

* * *

Nick paced back and forth in the tiny cell. It hadn't taken him long to land back in jail. This cell bore little resemblance to the one he'd lived in for close to ten years. This one didn't have a toilet or sink. It was a simple room with beige flooring, beige walls, and a double metal bunk bed with a mattress so hard and thin he thought it might be made of plywood.

A slow anger still burned in his gut when he thought of Clea's betrayal at the café. He didn't belong in this cell, and they both knew it, yet she'd kept quiet, her lips clamped shut. Did she hate him that much? Could he blame her if she did? The instincts he'd sharpened in prison had urged him to fight back today, to put his hands around Boomer's neck and choke the life from him, but he'd held back. Keeping his hatred in check had taken every ounce of control he'd possessed. Thoughts of his son had kept him from making one more mistake.

Unable to sit still in the confining cell, he'd spent the better part of the afternoon pacing, thinking about the words he'd exchanged with Clea at the café. He'd been about to kiss her when Boomer had intruded. He replayed the scene between the two of them. He still had no idea how they'd wound up that close together.

They'd been arguing, hadn't they? He never should have looked into those emerald eyes of hers. The minute he had, he'd been lost. He'd never been able to explain his attraction to her. It was almost like a sickness he couldn't shake, an obsession he couldn't ignore.

The woman set him on fire.

Nick sat down on the edge of the bunk and ran his fingers through his hair. How had Clea wound up with Boomer? There was no way in hell he would let Boomer Bloomfield raise his son.

He had no idea what to do next. He'd tried calling Billy, but hadn't been able to reach him. Billy had mumbled something that morning about going out of town, but Nick had no idea where he might be and he was scheduled to go before the judge in the morning.

The only thing that had gone right since he'd hit town had been talking with Mr. Mullin today. Mullin had welcomed him back, giving him a job. Getting a job at the garage brought Nick one step closer to putting his own plans into action. He'd already asked Mr. Mullin about renting one of the bays from him. One bay would be enough to get his business started. He'd given a lot of thought to how he'd advertise, and he itched to put his plans for a website into motion. For a few minutes today things had finally been going

Nick's way. Now, everything he wanted was in jeopardy.

The rattling of keys caught Nick's attention. He went to the cell door, his fingers curling around the cold bars. Footsteps echoed down the hall. Soon the sheriff appeared. He stopped at Nick's cell, opening the door.

"You're free to go," he said.

His heart jerked in his chest. "I'm free?"

The sheriff nodded. "Follow me."

Sheriff Kincade had run this town for at least twenty years. Nick remembered him as a fair man, even when the cards had been stacked against Nick. Time had taken some of the sharpness from the sheriff's features, his brows were bushier, his mid-section a little softer. Streaks of gray colored his blond hair now, but his face still gave nothing away. He hadn't wanted to arrest Nick today, but the No Contact Order had been clear. Nick didn't know what to think about this sudden freedom, but he wasn't going to ask any questions.

He left the cell, heading for the front of the building where the sheriff had his office.

"I'm going to need your signature on some documents," Sheriff Kincade said from behind him.

Nick nodded. At the counter, the sheriff had him sign a paper that listed the personal items they'd taken from him: his watch, his wallet, his jacket. Nick looked around the office, expecting to see Billy. "She's gone." The sheriff glanced toward the door.

"Who's gone?" Nick signed his name to the form the sheriff slid toward him.

"Clea. She left right after she told Judge Payne what really happened today. She's taking steps to have the No Contact Order withdrawn, said the whole thing was a mistake. Judge Payne has waived the hearing and signed your release."

Nick eyed the sheriff with suspicion. Was it a trick? "Are you telling me that Clea Rose was here? That she's withdrawing the No Contact Order?"

"Yes, sir." The Sheriff put Nick's paperwork in a manila file folder and laid it on his desk. "You're free to go."

"Am I free to come within one hundred feet of Clea or her son?" Nick asked, wanting to make sure he understood what was happening.

"You might not want to do that until she makes it official," the sheriff told him, his bushy brows drawing together. "But remember this, Nick. There are a lot of folks in this town that don't like you and don't want you here. They will look for any excuse to lock you back up. Keep your nose clean, boy. I don't want to have to bring you in again. Next time you might not be so lucky."

"Thanks for the advice, Sheriff," Nick said on his way to the door. He remembered another time when the sheriff had tried to help him, to urge Nick to tell the truth, but Nick hadn't listened. Had Sheriff Kincade been on his side ten years ago? Did it matter? Nick couldn't change the past. He had no idea why Clea had dropped The No Contact Order, but he intended to find out. There had definitely been some tension between her and Boomer at the café. Maybe things weren't as good between them as Clea claimed.

With each step Nick took his heart sped up in anticipation of his freedom and a second chance here in Port Bliss. Outside, he took in a hit of clean air. Clean air was something he couldn't take for granted. He'd always loved the outdoors, but prison life had put him off on fresh air. Life in the prison yard was rough and dangerous. He'd learned to do without the fresh air in order to survive. Now, he savored each breath, each stretch of his leg muscles during his walk down the street to his temporary home.

At the tavern, he took the steps two at a time and let himself into the dank apartment. The stench of cigarette smoke still permeated the air, so he made a beeline for the window and opened it, letting the frosty air into the already cold room.

The curtains to Clea's place were open and he could see her talking to someone, another woman - Mitzi? It had to be, all that black hair. She didn't look like she'd changed much since high school. Mitzi and Clea had stuck together like crazy glue.

Mitzi left his view and a child ran up to Clea.

Nick's heart stopped beating. His son. Johnathan Rose. A tightness spread through Nick's chest and the fresh air froze in his lungs. *His son.* Damn, he couldn't breathe. John looked so much bigger than he'd imagined. He wasn't a baby any more, but a boy with dark hair like his. Did he have Clea's green eyes, or his blue ones? Did he smile easily? Did he laugh? Did he wonder about his father? How much did the kid know?

Nick leaned closer to the window, trying to get a better view, but he was too far away. Frustration ate at him. It wasn't fair. He'd been robbed of the chance to know his son, now Clea was about to marry the man responsible for putting him in prison. He couldn't let that happen. He needed to level with Clea. For the past ten years he'd done nothing but think of his regrets and heartache. He'd been too stupid to realize what he was throwing away when he'd pushed Clea from his life. Instead, he'd felt he'd done the noble thing by letting her go.

If he'd told her truth - that he wanted her and their baby more than anything else in the world - could they have made it through the ten-year separation? He didn't know. He'd only known that he'd had nothing to offer them.

Tonight Clea had changed her mind about the No Contact Order. Why? If she'd been worried enough to have the papers drawn up in the first place, why have them revoked? It didn't make sense, unless she'd had a change of heart. A tiny flutter of hope beat in his chest, hope he had no right to feel but couldn't ignore. He needed to talk to Clea. It was time to clear the air between them.

* * *

The minute Mitzi left, Clea changed into her most comfortable pair of flannel pajamas, the ones with the cowboys all over them. After slipping her feet into her bunny slippers, she checked on John. The sound of his deep, even breathing put a smile on her lips. It sure hadn't taken him long to fall asleep. She knew sleep wouldn't claim her as easily. It had been a long, emotionally charged day.

And tomorrow would be even longer once Robert and her mother discovered that she'd had the No Contact Order removed. She prayed she'd done the right thing. Would Nick seek her out and demand to know why she'd helped him? The thought made her pulse race, but with dread or excitement? She didn't know.

Clea dropped down on the sofa and picked up her cup of peppermint tea, taking a sip. Mitzi had made it for her, telling Clea the tea would calm her nerves. So far it wasn't working. She sought out the photos that lined her mantel; photos she'd taken of John as a newborn, a toddler, and on his first day of school. Her stomach ached. God, she had to tell him about Nick. Nick was right. She was a coward.

A knock sounded at the door. Clea jumped. Her body tensed. She wasn't expecting anybody. Surely her mother and Robert couldn't have learned of Nick's release already? Pulling herself together, she walked to the door and looked out the peephole. Nick. Her heart sped up. The sheriff must have told him she'd dropped the No Contact Order.

He knocked again, louder this time. She stole a glance at John's door. The last thing she needed was for him to wake up. Making her decision, she unlatched the dead bolt and pulled the door open.

Nick's stare moved from her face, to her pajamas, to her bunny-clad feet before meeting her eyes again. "I saw John's light go out. Is he asleep? Can I come in?"

"He's asleep, but you can't come in," she said, wishing she'd grabbed her robe. Even fully clothed, she felt naked. He had a way of looking at her that left her feeling like he could see into her soul.

"I just want to talk," he said.

He didn't seem angry and a little of her fear subsided, but there was no way she'd let him in. She couldn't risk John seeing him.

"I'll come out," she said. "Just let me grab my coat." Clea took her pink sweatshirt jacket from the coat rack and shrugged into it, zipping it up to her neck as she stepped outside onto the enclosed landing. A dim porch light burned overhead, bathing Nick in faded yellow light.

"It's cold out here." Nick cupped his hands over his mouth and blew on them to warm his fingers.

Clea thought it seemed stupid to discuss the weather when they had so much of importance to talk about. She closed the door behind her, but didn't shut it all the way in case John woke. "What do you want, Nick?"

He ran a hand through his hair. "I want my life back. I want to know my son."

"Why now?" Clea pressed her hand against her stomach to quiet the nerves jumping there. "You've been out of prison for three months."

"I should have come back right away. I made a mistake," Nick said, frowning. "It's hard being on the outside. Harder than I imagined. I couldn't come right back. I had to adjust, to figure things out. This world is completely different from the world I knew ten years ago. I know you can't possibly understand what I'm talking about. Transitioning is tough."

The wounded look in his eyes seared her soul. What had he endured in prison? She'd lain awake nights, imagining the atrocities he must have lived through. How had he survived?

"It's too late now," she said, unable to keep the bitterness from her voice. "I have a different life. I had to move forward. I'm getting married."

"I've missed ten years, Princess," Nick said. "Give me a chance to catch up. That's all I'm asking."

"No." Clea backed away from him. "I can't."

He stepped toward her. "I want the chance to know John, but I want what's best for him. Does he know I'm here?"

"Not yet," she admitted. "He knows you're his father, but you're an abstract father, one he knows about, yet doesn't know at all." She wanted to add how mixed-up she felt, too, but bit back the words. Nick closed his eyes for a moment, and she could see the pain on his face, feel it. "I didn't tell him you were released from prison. I didn't want him to get his hopes up. I'm not sure what he feels for you."

"I'm sorry for all of this, and even sorry for what I'm about to say." He glanced away from her, then back. "I can't let you marry Boomer."

Any sympathy she felt for Nick dissolved in a poof, anger taking its place. Without thinking, she slapped him.

Nick's head jerked to the side. Their eyes locked together in battle.

"Is that what this visit is about?" Her voice rose to meet her temper. Nothing had changed. Nick still had no interest in his son, but he had every interest in controlling her. Her first instincts had been right. Her guilt over the No Contact Order had turned her into a fool. She should have left him in the jail.

"I guess I deserved that."

"I've waited to do that for ten years." Her hand stung, but she didn't care. It felt good. "John isn't an inconvenience, or a mistake. He's a boy. He's your son whether you like it or not. If you don't want to be a part of his life, that's fine with me; in fact, it's what I want. Leave us alone. Get out of Port Bliss." She stepped forward and rammed her index finger into his chest. "Don't ever tell me who I can and can't marry. It's none of your business."

His hand closed firmly around hers, holding her fingers prisoner against his chest. His heart beat under her palm.

"It is my business when the guy is Boomer Bloomfield." Nick rubbed his chin with his free hand. "You're right. I've made a mess out of things. I never wanted it to be this way between us. I'm not saying things right." Confusion filled his eyes.

Clea jerked her hand free, refusing to give him one ounce of compassion. "Well, it's too late. Things are messy between us, Nick."

"Why'd you drop the No Contact Order, Clea? I can understand why you served me with the papers, but I can't understand why you dropped the charges."

He watched her intently. Suddenly uncomfortable, she looked away from him. "It seemed like the right thing to do. I never wanted to do it in the first place, but you scared me. You've been away a long time. I didn't know what to think. My instincts tell me to protect John. I don't want to see him hurt."

"I'd never hurt him," Nick said softly. "And I'm sorry I hurt you."

For ten years she'd waited for his apology, but it didn't ease the ache in her heart the way she'd hoped. Old hurts throbbed within her and a single apology couldn't make them disappear. "Are you sorry, Nick?" She couldn't keep the bitterness from her voice.

"You'll never know how much."

Clea looked into his eyes, eyes filled with pain. In all the years they'd been apart she'd never imagined that he regretted his words to her in the jail ten years ago. Did he?

"Don't marry him, Clea." He reached for her hand.

Clea stepped back, avoiding his touch. "Of course I'm going to marry Robert. What is it with you, Nick? You don't want us, but you don't want Robert to have us either? You just can't stand to see me happy."

"That's not true," he said quietly. "I've seen you happy, remember?"

Clea flashed back to the year she'd spent with him. She'd been blissfully happy and so in love. "Stop it. I won't let you do it to me again."

"Do what?"

"I don't want to remember. I can't." She wanted to run from him, but her feet wouldn't budge. He had some kind of hold over her she couldn't break. A part of her wanted to give in to him, to his smooth words, but she knew better. She needed to remember the lies he'd told her before. The memory of those lies helped her to break free. "Please go."

"I don't want to fight with you. That's the last thing I want to do," he said sincerely. "I'll leave, but before I go tell me about my son."

Her emotions warred. She wanted to tell him everything, every precious detail he'd missed, every detail she'd longed to share with her child's father. She wanted to tell him to go to hell. He didn't deserve any answers.

"What's he like?" Nick asked. "I'm just asking. Give me something I can hold onto, Princess."

The anguish in his voice tore at her, broke down her shell of defense. If only for this moment, she wanted him to understand what he'd missed. "He's wonderful," she said. "He's a nice boy. He's always made good grades, until this last report card. Recently, something's changed in him. He's angry and sad, and I don't know how to help him. Robert seems to be the only one he'll respond to anymore."

His jaw tightened. "Son of a bitch. Is there any way that John could have learned about my release?"

"I didn't tell him," Clea said. She suspected John was upset about the move to New York, but she didn't want to tell Nick about the upcoming move, not yet. "I suppose he could have found out, but I'm sure he would have come to me with questions."

"I hope you're right."

Was it her imagination; or was his voice a little hoarse with emotion? "Do you want visitation rights?" She paused, unsure of what she wanted his answer to be.

"Would you give them to me if I asked?"

"No. I don't know." She pressed her fingers to her temples. Robert would kill her if she allowed Nick anywhere near John. "I'm not sure what to tell John now. If you're here to stay, I have to tell him something."

Nick walked to the top of the stairs and stared down at the street below. "I know you don't think I have any right to John, and maybe I don't. God knows I don't know anything about being a father, but I don't want John to think that I didn't want him. I did want him Clea, and I still do."

Clea's thoughts spun at the implication of his words. "It's not that simple. You can't just change your mind. He doesn't know you. He thinks of Robert as his father. They love each other."

"Boomer is not John's father." Nick whirled to face her. "Boomer didn't make love to you that night. I did."

Clea wanted to close her eyes against the memory of Nick touching her, kissing her. Ten years later she could still remember the way he tasted, the way his skin felt under her fingers. She forced the images from her mind and met his stare head on, but the hunger she saw in his eyes made her turn away. "Are you staying in Port Bliss?" she asked.

"Yes. I took my old job back at the garage."

Clea exhaled, not realizing she'd been holding her breath. "If you want to get to know John, it has to be on my terms. I'm warning you, it's not going to be easy. John's already going through a lot of changes."

"Life is never easy."

She faced him again. "I suppose not."

A long moment of silence passed between them and Clea used the time to study Nick. Hair as black as a raven's wing brushed the collar of his winter jacket, not his leather jacket, but a forest green Eddie Bauer type coat, a more grown-up type jacket. She could still remember what the silken strands of his hair felt like in her hands. His blue eyes appeared dark, masking his thoughts from her. Unable to help herself, she observed his mouth. His lips were strong, not too full, with a masculine curve to his upper lip.

Clea leaned toward him, wanting his kiss, but caught herself, her insides clenching to an almost physical ache. She'd never been as attracted to anyone. There was something about him that turned up the heat on every emotion she possessed, be it anger or desire or fear. Could she share her child with him while keeping her own conflicting emotions under control? He didn't play by the rules; he never had. Would he now? Could she trust him with John's tender heart? The thought terrified her more than anything ever had. This wasn't just about her and Nick. John's feelings had to come first.

"It's cold," she said, breaking the silence. "I'm going inside. I need time to think. John has school tomorrow. I'll tell him about you when he gets home."

He took a step toward her. The clean scent of his soap teased her nose. She tried to back away, but came up against the doorjamb.

"Remember, Clea," he whispered, his breath warm on her forehead. "Remember that summer. I know it didn't end the way either of us wanted it to. I was too young and stupid to know what really mattered. I'm older now, and for the first time in a long time I know what I want. This time, I'm going to fight for John, and for you. I want both of you."

Clea's heart raced. Her thoughts scattered. Nick turned away and started down the stairs. Clea fumbled for the knob, pushing the door open. Once inside she leaned her back against the wood. Nick Lombard was dangerous. He wasn't the kind of man a woman married. He didn't have a penny to his name. He had a criminal record. He could offer her nothing but a physical attraction that left her reeling. She couldn't allow Nick to sway her from the course she'd set for her life. She'd trusted him once with disastrous results.

Robert was the best choice for her, the only choice. Her career, her future, awaited her in New York. She wouldn't give up her dreams for Nick, not this time. It was up to her to make sure Nick understood that. She didn't want him to fight for them. It was too late.

* * *

Nick let himself into his apartment and walked straight to the fridge. Reaching inside, he extracted a beer, twisted the cap off, and took a long swig.

He'd gone to Clea's place ready to tell her every reason she shouldn't marry Boomer, and instead had wound up remembering every reason he wanted her himself. Tonight he'd been honest with her. If only he'd been as honest ten years ago things might be different now.

He took another swallow of his beer.

He'd committed to Clea and his son. The thought scared the hell out of him. He didn't know the first thing about commitment, and he knew even less about children. Yet, he'd never been one to back away from a challenge. Winning Clea back would be the biggest challenge he'd ever faced. She didn't trust him, and with good reason. He'd lied to her ten years ago. He could offer her nothing - yet. He'd been in prison for manslaughter. She was engaged to a man who could offer her everything, a man the world thought was "respectable."

The thought burned a hole in his gut.

If he wanted to stop the wedding he needed to set his own plans into motion. Tomorrow morning he'd start his job. He'd work hard, because he had something to work hard for. The time had come for him to provide for his family, and he wanted to rise to the challenge. He wanted to be someone Clea could depend on. If he could win her trust, the rest would follow.

It wouldn't be easy.

But the reward would be his family.

CHAPTER FOUR

"There's someone here to see you, Nick," Mr. Mullin said.

"Yeah, who?" Nick asked. From his position under the '56 Chevy all he could see of his boss were his greasy boots. Right now he didn't need the interruption. He'd just cleaned and installed a new fuel tank, and wasn't quite finished with the job. He didn't want to come out from under the old beauty unless he had a good reason.

"It's me, Nick." Clea's voice crawled under the car with him and he forgot all about the '56. "I need to speak with you, if you have a minute."

He turned his head to the left. It was her all right. The expensive black boots and jeans were a dead giveaway. Somehow she managed to stay true to herself, to the simple style of clothing he knew she liked, even with a mother like Vivian Rose.

Using his hands, he wheeled himself out from under the car. Grease covered him from his head to his boots, and he wished she'd given him some warning that she might come by. He didn't want her to think less of him because he got his hands dirty to make a living. Not everyone could be a senator's son. His mother always said it took all kinds of people to make a world, and for once he agreed with her.

Clea stood to the side of the car, staring down at him. She'd pulled her honey-colored hair back in a ponytail. Straight hair, not the curly hair she'd had in high school. The look made her appear more serious and in control of her life, but was she? What would it take to make her control slip? The black turtleneck she wore clung to her curves and looked sexy as hell tucked into her tight jeans. Still flat on his back, he wanted nothing more than to pull her down on top of him, grease and all.

"I'm sorry to bother you at work," she said, her brow wrinkling as if she searched for the right words to say.

"It's okay." He sat up. Glancing at his boss, he asked, "Okay if I knock off for ten?"

"Yeah, sure," Mr. Mullin said, with a knowing shake of his head. Nick swore he saw the old man smile as he went back into his office.

Nick came to his feet. He nodded toward the utility sink. "I'm going to wash some of this grease off. Don't go anywhere."

He kept one eye on her as he used the sink, scrubbing most of the grease away. As he dried his hands, Clea paced. She was nervous about something, and that made him nervous. Had she told John about him? Judging from her body language, she didn't have good news to share. He tried not to let disappointment seduce him. "Let's go outside," he said when he joined her. "I could use a little fresh air after being under a car all morning."

"All right."

He opened the door for her and she walked through. The scent of watermelon teased his nose as she passed him, the fragrance transporting him back to the year they'd been together. She'd always worn those shiny, flavored lip-glosses in the brightly colored tubes. Did she still?

In front of the garage sat an old park bench where some of the guys took a smoke on their breaks. "Do you want to sit?"

She sank onto the bench, a sigh leaving her lips.

"Whatever it is, it can't be that bad," he said.

"What?" she asked as if she hadn't heard him.

"Something's bothering you. What?"

"You were telling me the truth about working at Mullin's," she said.

"Yes. I started this morning. I meant everything I said last night."

She looked everywhere but at him. Across the street the bell tinkled on the kite shop door. Elizabeth Spencer drove by in her old Lincoln Continental.

"Did you come here to check up on me, or is this visit about

John?" he asked. "Did you tell him about me?" Cold dread swirled in his gut. He could take just about anything, but now that he'd made the decision to stay in Port Bliss he didn't want to lose the chance to know his son.

"No. I haven't told him yet." She took a deep breath. "It's about what you said last night, about wanting to fight for me."

He grinned with relief. She wouldn't be here, worried, if she felt nothing for him. His determination to win her back doubled. "I haven't changed my mind."

"You can't be serious." She pressed her fingers to her temples. "I'm engaged."

"But you're not married yet." He reached over and took her hand in his. She pulled away. "Give me a chance, Princess, the chance I never got ten years ago."

She came to her feet. "No. I can't do that again, not with you."

"Why not?" He stood. She glanced away from him toward the street. "Look at me, Clea."

"No."

That one word told him what he needed to know. Her feelings for Boomer weren't solid, and that gave Nick the opening he needed. "He's not the right man for you." He longed to tell her about the Boomer he knew, the Boomer with a mean streak and a ruthless nature, but he knew Clea wasn't ready to hear the truth. "Boomer will stifle you. He'll try to turn you into someone you're not. I'd never do that."

That brought her focus to him, her eyes flashing with anger. "Do you really think you're the right man for me, Nick? We don't have anything in common except a physical attraction that produced John. Well, I'm stronger now, and wiser. I'm not the same girl you knew before."

"Oh, I have a pretty good idea what you're like."

Her hand balled into a fist and he thought she might slap him again, but she didn't. He wished he could take his words back, crass words she didn't deserve, but the apology lodged in his throat.

"It's taken me a long time to find the right man," she said, the words brittle and sharp. "You have to respect my commitment to him."

She asked the impossible. He could never accept Boomer Bloomfield, but he knew he would never earn Clea's respect by belittling Boomer.

"I'm sorry I left," he said, "but it couldn't be helped. I didn't want to go to prison." He reached for her, his fingers curling around hers. "I'm sorry I wasn't there for you when John was born. You'll never know how much I regret that. But I'm here now. I'm not eighteen anymore."

She raised her chin a little higher and pulled her hand free. "Let me go, Nick." Her eyes and words filled with a plea that hurt his heart. "Don't make it hard for me."

"If it's hard for you, then maybe you're marrying the wrong man."

She shook her head.

"I've been wondering something since I came back," he said. "Why is it that you haven't married Boomer before now? If you love him so much, if he's the man for you, then why the ten-year wait?"

Clea turned away and he knew he'd struck a nerve. "The timing just wasn't right. We were both in college. Robert went back east."

It was a lame excuse and they both knew it. "Give me a chance, Clea." He put every ounce of what he felt for her in those words, walking around her to see her face. Something flared in her eyes. Anger? Passion? He didn't know, but he wanted to find out. He closed the distance between them; and reached out to touch her cheek. Her skin felt like the softest rose petal under his work-roughened fingers. While in prison he'd felt starved for human contact. Touching Clea made every nerve ending in his body come alive. The urge to pull her to him and kiss her until neither one of them could think drove him. He brought his other hand up to cradle her face in his hands.

"I want you to remember how it was between us ten years ago," he said, the words low and for her ears alone. Her eyes darkened to a smoky green, and the lust in his gut tightened. "Remember the fire between us, the almost desperate hunger we felt for each other? Those feeling aren't dead, Princess. Like me, they've just been locked up. It's time to set them free."

"Ten years ago you lied to me," she said, her voice small.

"I know. I'm sorry." He rubbed his thumb against her jaw and she sucked in a breath.

"I can't do this again, Nick," she whispered without taking her eyes from his. She knocked his hands away and stepped back. "I knew this would happen. That's why I came here. To warn you off, to make sure you understood I'm not interested."

He grinned. "Oh, you're interested, all right. What you're feeling is desire, baby. And between us we have enough to set this town on fire."

Clea covered her mouth with her hands. A strangled sound came from her. "I've won a photography internship in New York. The Graceland Mitchell Internship. I'll be working with Graceland Mitchell herself. Her work is phenomenal. It's the chance of a lifetime for me. I'm moving next month, Nick."

Nick felt like he'd been gut-punched. She couldn't go. He wouldn't let her. "Clea..."

She held her hand up to stop his words. "The move will be a fresh start for John, Robert, and me. All my dreams are finally coming true. I want to put the past behind me. I don't have room for you in my life."

She turned, running away from him just like she had ten years ago. Nick sat on the bench, a numbness spreading through him.

In the past few days he'd made some tough decisions concerning Clea and John. He hadn't even stopped to consider that Clea might have dreams of her own. She hadn't given up her photography like he'd thought. Her revelation today threw all his plans into chaos. He couldn't follow her to New York. Under the conditions of his parole, he couldn't leave the state. Could he ask to relocate? There would be terms he must meet. Did he want to follow her to New York? Yes. He would follow Clea anywhere if she wanted him. Before he worried about moving out of state he had a bigger problem. Clea had to want him in her life.

She made him crazy, but he knew without a doubt they belonged together. He'd been a fool to think he could just blow into town and fix the past. Everyone here had moved on with their lives. In so many ways, he was stuck at age eighteen. The time had come for him to catch up, time to show Clea he could take care of her and John, time to show her how much she meant to him.

"Come on, Nick," Mr. Mullin called from the doorway of the garage. "Break's over. The '56 isn't going to put itself back together."

Nick rose, wishing he could see into the future. He didn't know if he were doing the right thing, but he did know he wanted the chance to live the life he had been robbed of.

* * *

After her encounter with Nick at the garage, Clea went back to The Coffee House, but her mind wasn't on her work. In the space of a few days Nick had managed to take her life and twist it into something she no longer recognized.

With the threat of snow in the forecast, business was slow today. She'd only made two coffee drinks since noon, and that left her time to think as she and Mitzi restocked the shelves.

She couldn't forget the way Nick's hands had felt on her face, her neck. The smell of grease still filled her head. She knew she should find the odor offensive, but it was part of Nick, always had been. The scent made her weak in the knees. He'd made it clear that he wanted her, but she could resist the physical pull she felt for him. She was older and wiser. Sweet-talking a seventeen-year-old girl into bed had been his specialty in high school, but he'd find her a lot harder to seduce now. Sex didn't make a relationship. There were many more important things to consider - stability, honesty, respectability. And sadly, Nick lacked in most of those departments.

Clea glanced at the clock on the wall. John would be home soon. She planned to tell him about Nick right after he had his after school snack.

What if he didn't take Nick's return well? Worse, what if he wanted to go live with Nick? John wasn't crazy about moving to New York. What if he saw Nick as a way to stay in Port Bliss? Would Nick's return accelerate the anger issues John was having?

The bell on the door tinkled. Robert came into the shop. As always he looked more put together than she did, a fact she'd come to accept. Wearing a navy suit, and an eye-catching red tie and white shirt, he projected just the right image; successful, powerful, in control.

"Hello, darling," Robert said, his tone brisk. "Good afternoon, Mitzi."

"Hi, Robert." Mitzi came to her feet. She tucked a dark strand of hair behind her ear. "Can I get you a coffee?"

"Not just now." He frowned. "Clea, I'd like to speak to you alone."

"All right." She knew what was coming. Robert had learned about her dropping the No Contact Order. "We can use the office."

Robert followed her to the back of the shop, to the office.

Once inside, she shut the door. Robert's mouth had a puckered look, as if he'd sucked on a lemon. Steeling herself for the worst, she took a seat in the desk chair.

"Why didn't you tell me you spoke with Judge Payne, Clea?" Robert asked, the words sad and filled with hurt.

Clea sighed. "Nick didn't deserve to be thrown in jail. He hadn't done anything wrong. No matter how upset I am, I just couldn't do that to him. It wasn't fair."

Robert glanced away, and she knew he was trying to hide his distress from her, increasing her guilt over setting Nick free. She wished her loyalty lay solely with Robert, but something about Nick compelled her to rally to his defense. She didn't want to hurt Robert, but they would never agree when it came to Nick.

"I think I know what's best for you and for John," Robert said, the words controlled. He walked away from her, then turned to face her. "You don't know Nick like I do."

"I think I know him pretty well," Clea said, a touch of defiance in her tone.

"I don't mean carnal knowledge, Clea."

The words were brutal, unlike Robert, and they pierced her like tiny barbs. "Excuse me?" She understood his jealousy, but not his need to hurt her. "I don't mean carnal knowledge either. I have had one or two conversations with Nick that didn't involve sex. I don't think he's a threat to John. Putting a No Contact Order on Nick will just make him angry and difficult to deal with. I don't need that, and neither does John. Things are hard enough with the upcoming move. I need your support, not your accusations, Robert."

He came toward her, a hard gleam in his eyes. "I know what's best."

"You don't." She stood. "I know what's best for John. I'm his mother."

Robert's cheeks reddened. "Yet another slap to my face for not being his father."

"Oh, Robert." Her heart grew heavy. They'd had this discussion many times. "This isn't a contest. I don't want to fight about Nick. I need your help. I have to tell John about him. I have no idea how he will react to his father being in town. John loves you. He needs you."

"I'm sorry," Robert said, his tone contrite. "Nick makes me

jealous. I know it's stupid, but I can't seem to help it. I love you. I love John." He pulled Clea into his arms. "I'm afraid I'm going to lose you."

She stepped into Robert's embrace, needing the comfort he could give her. The musky scent of Robert's aftershave chased the smell of grease from her mind. It would be easy to let Robert take over, let him make the decisions, but she couldn't, not when it came to John.

"I'm sorry," she murmured against his jacket, her cheek brushing the fine fabric. "I don't want to fight."

"Neither do I." He kissed the top of her head. "Every time I think of Nick putting his hands on you it makes me insane."

Clea tipped her head back to better see him. "That was a long time ago. We were teenagers."

"I know." Robert pressed a kiss to her lips. "Forgive me. What can I do to help?"

"I'm going to tell John when he gets home," Clea said. "There are things only Nick can explain to John, things I think John needs to hear from his father. You can't bad-mouth Nick, Robert. John looks up to you, takes his cues from you. He picks up on your anger."

Robert glanced away. "In almost every respect I am John's father. Do you know what you're asking?"

"John will have two fathers," Clea said, not wanting to hurt him. "He is a lucky little boy. You know John adores you."

"This is hard for me." Robert searched her eyes. "Is it wrong for me to want you all to myself? It's all I've ever wanted."

"No. It's not wrong." Clea smiled. "It's a lovely sentiment, but unfortunately, life can get in the way. Help me make this transition in John's life easy. We have to help him nurture his friendship with Nick, even if we aren't crazy about the idea."

Robert made a sound of disgust. "Letting Nick into John's life isn't right. The man killed my brother. Do you really want a killer around your son?"

"Nick never meant to kill Danny. He's paid for what happened in more ways than one."

"And what about the lakeside robberies?" Robert asked. "Nick's a thief and a murderer."

"Stop it, Robert. We've been over this. I'm not going to discuss it again. Please, can't we concentrate on the present, on John?"

"I'm sorry." Robert gathered her close again. "I'll help you. I'll do whatever you want. You know that. I love you, Clea."

He kissed her, and Clea responded, or tried to, but her heart wasn't in the kiss, or in making Robert feel better. Instead, her mind wandered to John.

"I love you," Robert whispered against her lips, kissing her cheek, her neck.

Suddenly, he drew back.

"What?" Clea asked. He stared at something. She brought her hand up to touch her neck.

"You have grease on the side of your neck; and on your shirt. How did you get so dirty?"

"I don't know," Clea lied, remembering the grease on Nick's clothes, his hands.

"It's going to ruin your shirt," Robert said. "You should run upstairs and change." He smiled. "I could join you."

"I think you just want to part me from my clothes," she teased, glad to think of something other than Nick. "I'm off work in a few minutes. I'll change then."

The office door whipped open, and John's best friend, Toby, raced in. He skidded to a stop in front of Clea. Mitzi came in behind him, her brow creased with worry.

"What's wrong?" Clea's stomach knotted and she knew Toby's presence had something to do with John.

"There's a fight," Toby said out of breath, his cheeks pink from running. "At the bus stop. John's bleeding."

* * *

"Want to tell me what happened?" Clea passed John a fresh tissue. She'd been relieved to find John in one piece, but that relief had faded quickly when she'd seen his distress. "Throw that one in the garbage." She pointed to the can next to the desk.

John did as she asked, holding the clean tissue to his nose.

Clea exchanged a worried glance with Robert. Thankfully, he remained silent, letting her do the talking.

"Well, it's obvious someone socked you in the nose. He must have had a reason."

"I hit him first."

"Johnathan Rose! You know better than that." His lower lip trembled. In a softer tone, Clea said, "Did this have something to do with your father?" She saw the same defiance in her son's eyes she'd seen in Nick's so many times before. Even the way John slumped in the chair reminded her of Nick. They were so alike it scared her.

John shrugged.

She smoothed the hair from his forehead.

"Is my dad here?" he asked, the words loaded with hope, hope that broke Clea's heart.

"Yes. You know Nick's mother died. He came home for her funeral."

Robert stalked to the window, his distaste for the subject they discussed obvious, but she didn't have time to soothe him, too.

John's lower lip puffed out again. She had no idea what he thought about the news, but she did know he was hurting inside.

"Brandon Green said my dad was back, but I didn't believe him," John said. "He called my dad a jailbird. I hit him."

"Then he hit you back?" Clea prompted.

"In the nose."

"I'm sorry, honey." Clea put an arm around his shoulders. "It seems you and I have a lot to discuss."

"Is Dad going to come and see me?" He looked up at Clea with blue eyes an exact mirror of Nick's.

"Do you want him to?" Clea asked.

John shrugged.

"Nick is staying on in Port Bliss. He wants to get to know you. You are all he can talk about." She could see the conflicting emotions on John's face, and it pained her to think John was afraid both that Nick wouldn't want him and that he would. "How's your nose?"

"I think it's okay now." He dropped the tissue into the garbage can.

Clea inspected his nose, and seeing no further bleeding she said, "It looks good."

"Do I have to see my dad?" John asked.

Robert spun around. "Of course you don't."

Clea's heart sank. She shot Robert a look of disapproval before returning her attention to John. "I'd like you to meet your father, but when you're ready. He understands this is hard for you. It's hard for Nick, too. He doesn't want to upset your life."

John didn't reply, but he seemed to consider her words.

"Do you have any questions?"

His lips were clamped shut, another trait he'd inherited from Nick.

"Well, I can tell you what I know," she offered. "Your father works at Mr. Mullin's garage. He is very good with cars, but you know that. You've seen his brother driving The Boss around town."

"He works at Mullin's?" Robert came away from the window and headed for the office door. "I'll be back later. I have something to do." Before Clea could ask what, he left, and she gave a silent prayer he wasn't going to confront Nick.

"Is my dad driving that car now?" John asked, pulling her thoughts back to him. "I saw it parked across the street."

Clea smiled internally. She'd hoped that talking about cars would get John's attention. He loved cars as much as Nick. "Yes. I think he's staying at his mother's apartment."

"Oh." John slumped back in the chair.

Did he wonder why Nick hadn't come to see him? So many doubts plagued her, making her question every move she'd made since Nick's return. "Let's get you cleaned up, and have some dinner. We can talk more about your father then."

He didn't reply.

Somehow she had to repair the damage between Nick and John. She had no idea how to unite them, but for John's sake, she would have to try. John came first, now and always.

* * *

At seven o'clock Nick finally made it home. He'd left work just after three-thirty. After that he'd driven over to Bradley to pack up his things and tie up loose ends. Bone tired and filthy, he stripped off his clothes. Before he could jump in the shower, a knock sounded at the door.

"Hang on," Nick called, going back into the bedroom to pull on his pants. He wasn't expecting anyone, but a small kernel of hope erupted in him at the thought that it might be Clea coming to talk. He opened the door.

Boomer Bloomfield.

His hope shattered. "I was wondering when you'd show up."

Boomer looked Nick over from top to bottom. They'd never seen eye to eye, literally, with Boomer a good three inches shorter than Nick. Boomer didn't bother to hide his hatred. His eyes grew hard. His hands were knotted into fists at his sides. Boomer was one big ball of anger and frustration and tension, just like he had been as a teenager. Nick didn't know why, but he had the sudden urge to laugh.

"Get out of town, Lombard," Boomer said. "You're not wanted here."

"What is this, an old Western?" Nick asked, amused by the statement. "Are you going to ask me to draw my pistol next?"

Boomer's face went red. "Don't you think you've upset Clea enough?"

Nick didn't reply. He didn't owe Boomer any kind of explanation and they both knew it.

Boomer took a step toward him. Would Boomer hit him? Probably not. The man was too smart. He'd always thought of Boomer as an iceman, a man who didn't show anyone but a select few, what he was really like. His talent for keeping his cool, for playing the victim, had landed Nick in jail for a crime that should have been labeled self-defense. More than anything he wanted Boomer to crack. He wanted Clea to see for herself what kind of man Boomer Bloomfield really was.

"You aren't going to come between me and Clea again," Boomer said. "She belongs to me now. She always has. If you have any respect for her or for John you will get out of their lives. Don't drag them down with you."

Nick didn't comment, but inside his blood boiled. He held his anger in check, a skill he'd perfected in prison.

"Did you hear me, Lombard?"

Boomer's eyes had a wild look Nick remembered from high school.

"What's between Clea and me has nothing to do with you." Nick kept his tone calm and even, despite the turmoil churning within him.

"It has everything to do with me," Boomer shouted. "Stay away from her or…"

"Or what? You'll send someone after me? Just like you sent your brother after me? Why don't you just be a man and do the job yourself this time?"

Boomer's fist went flying, hitting Nick square in the nose. He stumbled back and felt the warm gush of blood. Anger rushed up to meet the frustration he felt, but he didn't hit back. He wasn't about to blow it, but he did gain some satisfaction from knowing

Boomer could be provoked; that he wasn't made of ice after all.

"Stay away from her, or you'll be sorry." Boomer spun away, the heels of his expensive shoes clicking as he ran down the stairs to the street.

Nick closed the door. Going directly to the bathroom, he turned on the shower and climbed inside, letting the warm spray calm him down and wash the blood away. Boomer had issued his warning, just as he had ten years ago. Only this time Nick would beat the rich prick at his own game. He'd control his temper, and he'd win. He was smarter than Boomer in every way.

Every way.

CHAPTER FIVE

Clea set the double mocha with extra whip down on the counter. "Here you go, DeAnn. Be careful, it's hot."

"Thanks, honey." DeAnn passed her a five-dollar bill. "God it smells great in here. I'll take the aroma of fresh brewed coffee over permanent solution any day."

Clea smiled as she made change. For a moment she'd considered calling Mitzi out of the office to make DeAnn's drink. The last thing Clea felt like doing was chatting with DeAnn, the town busybody. The beautician was sure to ask her about Nick, and while she didn't want to talk about her relationship with him, hiding from the townspeople wouldn't make her problems go away. She needed to be strong for John and part of that entailed fielding curious questions.

"So," DeAnn said, tapping one red lacquered nail against her coffee cup, "have you seen much of Nick since he's been back?"

Clea closed the cash register, bracing herself for the questions and comments to follow. "I've seen him around."

"Really?" DeAnn said, one perfectly waxed brow raised. "He's just as delicious as he ever was."

"I guess."

"He's the father of your child." DeAnn dipped a finger into the whipped cream, and bringing it to her mouth she sucked the rich topping from her finger. "You have a bond with him that can't be broken, even by Boomer Bloomfield."

Clea turned away, busying herself with making a vanilla latte for a man at the end of the bar.

"I was Maude's best friend," DeAnn reminded her. "I think deep down she regretted how things ended between you and Nick. She'd want you to be together. Maude loved John."

Clea glanced up, spilling hot milk onto her hand. "Ouch." She pressed a wet towel to the burn. "How do you know Maude loved John? She never gave him the time of day."

"Maybe that's what she wanted you to think." DeAnn sipped her coffee.

"What do you mean, DeAnn?" Clea asked, her attention totally focused on the beautician.

"Nothing. I just think she had a soft spot for him. He was her grandson." DeAnn smiled. "I remember when you and Nick were teenagers. Passion like that doesn't fade. Make sure you know what you're doing, Clea. Don't throw away your happiness because you think you're doing the right thing. Follow your heart this time around."

Clea frowned. "Thanks for the advice, but I'm a big girl. I know what I'm doing."

DeAnn smiled smugly, the smile of a woman who'd taken a turn or two at love. "What a gorgeous picture of John." She pointed to the photograph Clea had hung behind the coffee bar that morning.

The Coffee House walls held dozens of Clea's photos, everything from landscapes to her more creative hand-altered designs. To her delight, Clea had made several sales over the past few years.

"Yes. I like this one." Clea turned to look at the picture of John on the beach. He squatted at the edge of the canal. Around him, as far as the eye could see, were discarded oyster shells. Beside him stood the white plastic five-gallon bucket that had been his constant companion on the beach since he'd become big enough to tote it around. The bucket had housed everything from small crabs, to shells, to driftwood.

The day she'd seen him on the beach the light had been fantastic, the day cloudy but bright, the water a steel gray against a cold January sky. She'd been afraid she'd be unable to catch the different shades, the textures of the shells and sand and water. But to her surprise she'd been pleased with the finished work. She'd captured John perfectly, from his dark hair to the untied tennis shoes on his feet. She didn't usually display photos of her son, but in this particular shot, with his head bowed, his face was hidden from view. Even after she'd framed the picture, she'd debated showing it, not sure she really wanted to sell this one.

The shop bell rang, and John came through the door, followed by Robert. Since Clea worked until three-thirty, Robert had offered to meet the bus, hoping to avoid a repeat of the fight yesterday afternoon.

"Hi, guys," Clea said. The smile John usually had ready for her was absent.

"Hello," Robert greeted, shrugging his shoulders as if to tell her he had no idea of John's mental state.

John came to the bar and climbed up on a stool. His tousled hair made him look younger than his nine years. They hadn't really talked since last night. He'd been so angry and closed off. She'd given him some private time to digest the news of Nick's return.

"How was school?" She watched his face, looking for a sign of how he felt.

He shrugged. "Fine."

"Do you want some cocoa?" she offered, hoping to soften him up. She couldn't stand to see John upset. His closed look upped her anxiety.

"Okay."

Another one word answer. Disappointed, Clea turned away to fix the cocoa. "Robert what can I get you?"

"Cocoa sounds good to me."

"Coming right up." Every bad feeling she had about Robert since Nick's return to town melted away as she made the cocoa. He'd promised to be there for John, and he was. She could always count on Robert to live up to his word. He was John's life preserver, something solid John could hang onto during this difficult period.

"John and I are going to go and play some basketball before dinner. Toby's going to meet us at the court. Is that all right with you?" Robert stirred an extra spoonful of sugar into his cocoa before taking a sip.

"Of course. I'm off in a few minutes anyway. I've got a nice salmon upstairs. Will you join us for dinner?" She glanced at John. "Toby, too. If he wants to come."

John shrugged again.

Robert gave her a smile of understanding. He knew how much John's indifference bothered her.

"I'd love to come to dinner. Thank you." Robert tugged John's arm. "Come on, buddy. Let's take our cocoa with us. Toby's probably waiting."

Together they left the shop. Quickly, Clea tidied up her workspace. If she hurried, she could get a walk in before Robert and the boys returned. Getting some fresh air might help to clear her head.

She glanced over at DeAnn. The beautician smiled at her, no doubt eager to pick up the conversation where they'd left off. Well, she wasn't going to give DeAnn that chance.

"Mitzi?" Clea called.

"Yes?"

"I'm leaving."

"Gosh, is it that time already?" Mitzi came out of the office. "You okay?" She glanced at DeAnn.

"I'm fine. I need some air." Clea shrugged her coat on. "If Robert and John are looking for me, tell them I'll be right back."

"Will do." She walked Clea to the door. "Have a nice walk."

"Thanks." She smiled at her friend.

Clea left the shop and ran upstairs to get her camera. She intended to follow the line of the canal on her walk. She'd seen some blue herons earlier that morning, and hoped to see them again somewhere along the shore.

Back on the street, the brisk air stung her cheeks. She walked, her pace fast, putting one mile, then another between her, the town, and her problems. Thoughts of Nick danced through her head, mixing with images of John. Unsettled, she continued to walk, finding no solutions to her problems. Confusion swirled around her, propelling her forward, causing her to lose track of time and distance. She spotted the herons close to Oyster Point. Taking her Hasselblad from the case, she focused the camera, taking several shots.

The wind whipped up, and the sky darkened overhead. Not wanting to get caught in the rain with her camera, she turned around, but didn't get more than a quarter of a mile before the rain started. Cold, frozen rain, the kind of rain that could turn to snow. Clea held her camera bag under her coat, trying to keep it dry.

Behind her she heard the sound of an approaching truck. She

quickened her step. The truck slowed as it neared her. Clea checked to see if she knew the driver. Instantly she recognized the tow truck from Mullin's Garage, but the driver wasn't old man Mullin; it was Nick.

He pulled alongside her. She kept walking. She didn't want to get in the truck with him. She didn't want to be alone with him. Her feelings for him were too sensitive. She glanced over at the truck. Nick leaned across the seat to roll down the window.

"Need a lift?" he asked.

"No, thanks." Freezing rain ran down her face to soak the collar of her coat.

"Don't be stubborn, Clea," he said. "Get in. It's at least a mile back to town and you're already soaked. If you stay out in this weather you'll get sick. Is that what you want?"

Clea glanced up at the sky. The rain wouldn't be letting up soon. She didn't want to expose her camera to the rain if she didn't have to. "All right." Against her better judgment, she climbed up into the truck. The heat inside the cab warmed her chilled skin. An old Aerosmith song played on the radio, reminding her of the year she'd spent with Nick. An instant longing for him shot through her, and she wondered if the song had the same effect on him.

"What are you doing way out here?" Nick asked, as he put the truck into gear and they started forward.

"I shot some photos of two blue herons." She pulled her camera bag out from under her coat.

Nick glanced at the camera. "Ah. I see." He drove in silence. Clea stared straight ahead. She didn't want to look at him. His presence filled the truck, making her stomach do crazy flip-flops. She scooted closer to the door.

"How's John?" he asked, breaking the silence that stretched between them like a frayed rope.

"He found out about you at school before I had a chance to tell him. I've tried to explain. He's upset."

"I'm sorry," he said. "How can I help?"

She turned to look at him. "Would you have come home sooner if you had known John was waiting for you?" The past twenty-four hours caught up with her. All the pain she felt for John rose to the surface. She needed an outlet for her feelings of frustration.

"You said he didn't know about my release. Did he know?"

"I don’t think so," Clea said. "Just answer the question."

"I'd like to say yes, but I don't know. Meeting him terrifies me." Nick sighed. "I'm afraid of my own son, of what he thinks of me, of how he'll react to me."

Surprise shot through her. She'd never considered that Nick might be afraid of John. She'd never considered Nick's feelings at all. "John got into a fight."

Nick pulled the truck over to the side of the road and shut the engine off. "Was he hurt?"

"He got punched in the nose, but he threw the first punch."

"Jesus." Nick frowned. "I'm sorry, Princess."

"Don't call me that." She whipped her head around. "I'm not your princess. I'm the mother of a nine-year-old boy who aches inside. Do you know how he feels? Some kids at school called you a jailbird."

Nick's hands curled around the steering wheel, his anger obvious. That anger crept across the seat of the truck, pressing Clea more tightly against the door.

"Do you want me to leave town?" He glanced over at her, his eyes filled with pain, and that pain did something to Clea.

She wanted to say yes, but she held her tongue.

"Do you?" he asked again.

"I don't know." The prick of hot tears stung her eyes, but she wasn't sure if the tears were for John or for her. "It's not about you and me anymore," she said sadly. "It's about John. I think it would be worse if you left."

"What do you want me to do?"

"I don't know."

"Clea." He brushed a tear from her cheek, his touch tender. "If I could change things I would."

Clea sniffed, searching her coat pocket for a tissue. She wanted to believe his words, but didn't know if she could trust him, especially when it came to John.

Rain pounded the top of the truck, filling the silence between them.

She blew her nose.

Nick started the truck. The windshield wipers danced across the window. Snow mixed with the rain now. Up at Lake Bliss snow would be falling.

Nick pulled away from the side of the road. They made the drive to The Coffee House in silence. When they arrived, Nick pulled over to the curb.

"Thanks for the ride." Clea reached for the door handle.

Nick touched her arm. "I'm here if you need me. Just say the word. I'll do whatever you want."

"Really?" she asked, surprised.

"I'd do anything for you and John." Leaning over, he kissed her cheek.

His words sent unwanted excitement across her already cold skin, jolting her into action. Clea opened the door and jumped from the truck, needing to get away from him and the turbulent feelings he aroused in her. She watched as he drove away in the sleet.

When she couldn't see the truck any longer, she turned toward the shop and looked up. The curtain moved, as if it had just been dropped into place. Had Robert been watching? Had he seen Nick kiss her? She hoped not. An argument with Robert was the last thing she needed.

Bracing herself for the confrontation to come, she started up the stairs to her apartment.

* * *

Nick wanted to get drunk.

He walked through the door of the Point Bliss Tavern and headed for the bar. Every nerve in his body throbbed. He wanted that feeling to go away.

"Give me a whiskey, straight up," he said to the bartender. He'd hoped that Billy would be home, but he'd gotten his answering machine when he'd called. He'd left a message asking his brother to meet him at the tavern. Tonight, he needed a friendly face.

The bar smelled exactly the same, like stale cigarette smoke and cheap beer. Neon signs covered the west wall, selling every kind of beer imaginable.

He'd been in the bar dozens of times, but always as a kid. He'd come in the back door, hiding behind the bar, needing something from Maude, usually food, but sometimes he'd needed help with Billy, like the time Billy had broken his arm and wouldn't stop crying. That time, he'd walked right through the front door and gone straight to Maude. She hadn't been able to ignore him. Her boss had given her the rest of the night off to take Billy to the hospital. Nick grimaced at the memory. Maude had bitched the entire time they'd waited at the hospital about the night's pay and tips she was losing. His stomach turned at the memory.

The bartender poured the whiskey, then slid the glass across the lacquered surface of the bar toward him. Nick downed the amber liquid, welcoming the burn as the liquor made its way down his throat to warm his belly. "Hit me again."

The bartender obliged. Nick knocked the drink back. "Once more."

"Okay." The bartender poured a third drink, setting it in front of Nick. "Aren't you Maude's kid?"

"Yeah." He never should have come here. The place reeked of Maude and bad memories.

"I'm sorry about your mother," the bartender offered.

Before he could reply someone behind him said, "Nick?"

Nick turned. A short, balding man who looked to be in his late sixties took the stool next to him, a can of Budweiser in his hand. He looked familiar, but Nick couldn't place him. "Do I know you?"

"I'm Bernie. I was a friend of your mother's."

"Ah. One of Mom's male friends." Nick took a swig of his whiskey. He'd seen Bernie at the funeral. The old man had been crying.

"It was more than that." Bernie fondled his can of Bud as if it were his best girl. "I loved her."

"How touching." He didn't want to hear any more.

"It broke her heart that you didn't come before she died. She knew you were out of prison. She hung on, hoping every day that you would show up. But when you didn't come, she just let go."

Bernie's words twisted his insides. He couldn't imagine Maude pining for him. If she had, she would have visited him in prison. "I don't need this." Nick threw a twenty on the bar.

"Don't go." Bernie's gnarled hand closed over Nick's arm. "I'm sorry. I didn't tell you those things to make you feel guilty. Maude was the first one to admit she was a lousy mother. Sometimes a broken heart will do that to a woman."

Nick stared at Bernie's fingers, and the older man let go of his arm. "You don't know shit about my mother."

"I know quite a bit." Bernie smiled sadly. "There are things I want to tell you about Maude."

"Yeah, well I don't want to hear them." Nick slid off the stool.

"She loved you," Bernie said. "She loved you and your brother. She just loved your father more."

At the mention of his father, Nick sat back down. He knew almost nothing about his father, other than he'd left Maude for another woman when Billy was a baby. His mother never talked about Hank Lombard other than to say he used her, then abandoned all of them.

"What do you know about my father?" Nick asked, his tone low.

"Nothing," Bernie stammered. "I don't know anything, except that Maude loved him."

Bernie's eyes were a bit too bright, his skin too pale. Did he know something more about their father, or was he merely a pathetic old drunk?

"Hey, Nick." Billy joined them, grinning. "I got your message." He took his jacket off, and shaking the moisture from it, tossed the coat on a vacant barstool. "Have you two met?"

Nick turned away, trying to get his anger under control. He never talked about his father with anyone, not even Billy. Yet this old man acted like he might know something more about Hank Lombard, but what? If Billy hadn't interrupted, would Bernie have spilled his guts?

"I was just telling Nick how much Maude loved the two of you." Bernie took a sip of beer.

"You don't say?" Billy exchanged a curious glance with Nick. "You okay?"

"Yeah." Billy could read him so well. He sensed something wasn't right.

"Come on." Billy clapped Nick on the shoulder. "Grab your drink and let's get a booth. You can catch me up on your life." To the bartender, Billy said, "Bring me a cola." Then, "Excuse us, Bernie."

"Yeah, sure," Bernie muttered.

Nick picked up his whiskey and followed his brother to a booth at the back of the bar, eager for a little privacy to test the information Bernie had provided.

"How well do you know Bernie?" Nick asked as he slid across the cracked black vinyl seat. Someone put a couple of quarters in the jukebox and the Patsy Cline song *Crazy* filled the air.

"Pretty well. He and Mom were…"

"Friends?" He didn't need details.

Billy grinned. "Something like that."

The bartender brought Billy's drink, setting it on the table.

Nick waited for the man to leave before continuing. "Bernie told me Mom used to talk about our father, about how much she loved him. Do you know anything about that?"

Billy shook his head. "No. Bernie's probably just drunk."

"He's never mentioned anything to you about Hank before?"

"I swear, Nick. You know Mom never talked about our father. Why the sudden interest?"

"I got the impression Bernie knew something." He shrugged. "I guess I'll just have to go and ask him." He watched his brother, looking for a sign that he didn't want Nick to pursue the matter.

Billy gave him a lopsided grin. "You're too sensitive, man. Forget him. Drink up. Let's celebrate your return to town and your new job. Cheers." He clinked his cola to Nick's glass. "Here's to you getting everything you deserve."

Everything he deserved.

Nick thought of Clea. She was the reason he'd come to the bar. He'd wanted to forget her. He'd wanted to forget the tears he'd wiped from her cheeks that afternoon. Instead, he'd walked into something more, something he wanted to pursue. He looked for Bernie, but the man had vanished.

Funny, he had no taste for whiskey now.

* * *

Clea could feel a chill in the air and it wasn't due to the cold temperature outside. All through dinner Robert had barely spoken to her, giving all his attention to John and Toby, who was spending the night with John. She knew Robert had seen her with Nick, but she couldn't smooth things over until they were alone.

"Good night, boys." She pulled the blanket up to John's chin, before making a check on Toby who lay on the floor inside a sleeping bag.

"My dad said he might take us to the fort tomorrow," Toby told her.

The fort was a favorite camping spot for the boys. About an hour's walk from town, John and Toby looked forward to their visits there.

"It's cold tonight," Clea said. "There might even be snow up at Grandma's. I think the walk to the fort will have to wait for another time."

"Can we go up to Grandma's tomorrow if there is snow?" John

asked, his eyes wide with winter wonder. "We could go sledding on her big hill. Toby could come, too."

"Yeah," Toby said with enthusiasm, his idea of going to the fort forgotten.

"We'll see." Clea smiled at the boys. The excitement in John's voice pleased her, gave her hope that he was feeling better about Nick.

"Good night, boys," Robert said from the doorway. "Sleep tight. I'll see you tomorrow."

"Good night," John returned.

"Good night," Toby echoed.

Clea longed to kiss John's cheek, but didn't want to embarrass him in front of Toby. She smiled as she followed Robert to the living room. "Thanks for all your help with John today. It meant a lot to him, and to me." She could hear the boys talking and laughing in the bedroom. The sound lightened her spirit.

Robert sank down onto the sofa. "I saw you with Nick."

"I know." She could hear the disappointment in his voice. She'd hoped to avoid this conversation. Hurting Robert was the last thing she wanted to do.

He stared at her - hard. "Why were you with him? This is just like that summer all over again. Every time my back was turned you two would be together."

"We didn't go behind your back, not then and not now. Nick and I were a couple that summer," Clea reminded him. "I was out shooting pictures today when the rain started. Nick passed me on the road and gave me a lift. I wouldn't have accepted the ride, but I didn't want the Hasselblad to get wet. You know how much that camera means to me." The Hasselblad had been a graduation gift from her father. The camera had great sentimental meaning, as well as value.

"It was just a ride. That's all?" Robert tilted his head slightly, as if he waited for her to admit everything.

"We talked."

"About?"

"John. I told him about the fight John got into. Nick's worried about John, too."

"If Nick really cared about John he never would have come back," Robert said.

"John needs Nick."

"John's a child," Robert said. "He doesn't know what he needs. Do you really think he'd be surprised if Nick ran out on him? I can help him forget. He loves me."

"I don't want him to forget," Clea said, desperate for Robert to understand. "A child doesn't forget his father, no matter who his father is. John needs to meet Nick. If he doesn't he'll always have questions and unresolved issues. It could affect his whole life."

"I disagree." Robert shook his head. "John is happy with the way things are. Nick has never been a father to him. Trust me, being a sperm donor isn't enough. It takes much more to be a good father."

Clea sighed. "I know that Robert. But I think John would like the chance to know Nick."

"He hasn't indicated that to me." Robert frowned.

Clea shifted on the couch, drawing her legs under her. "Did you talk about Nick today?" Picking up a brightly patterned throw pillow, she hugged it to her, needing something solid to hold onto.

"Not really." Robert let his head drop back against the sofa. For a moment he closed his eyes, and Clea could see the lines of fatigue on his face. Nick's return to town hadn't been easy on Robert either. "John asked me if I knew Nick."

"What did you say?" Her stomach clenched. "You didn't say anything negative did you?"

He rolled his head to the side, opening his eyes. "Of course not. I would never hurt John's feelings. He means everything to me."

"I know." She touched Robert's arm. Letting go of the pillow, she slid over closer to him. "Sorry."

"What're you going to do, Clea? Nick's going to spoil everything between us." A wild look filled Robert's eyes, a desperation she hadn't seen in him since high school when he realized he'd lost her to Nick. Nick threatened Robert in a way no one else did. Was it just her connection to Nick that scared Robert or was there something more, something she didn't know about that night ten years ago?

"I don't know what I'm going to do." She shrugged. "I'm going to take my cues from John."

"I hope you won't be sorry." Robert's mouth moved into a tight line.

"So do I."

"Why don't the two of you come up to my place tomorrow? It's

Saturday. You could spend the night at your mother's. It's snowing up at the lake. We could all go sledding."

Leaving town and heading up to the lake sounded heavenly. "I wish I could, but I can't. Saturday is our busy day at The Coffee House. You know that. Mitzi depends on me. Besides, I have so much packing left to do before the move."

"I'm sure Mitzi wouldn't mind." Robert threaded his fingers with Clea's. "She knows how much stress you've been under, first with the wedding and the upcoming move, and now from Nick."

"Not on a Saturday." Clea squeezed Robert's fingers. "We are too busy."

"Then let me take John. Toby, too, if he wants to tag along." He pulled Clea closer, into the circle of his arm. The wool of his sweater tickled her nose.

"I'll ask John in the morning. I'm sure he'll jump at the chance to spend time with you." She smiled. "Thank you, Robert. I don't know what I'd do without you."

Robert kissed the top of her head. "You'll never have to find out, Clea. I'm going to see to that."

CHAPTER SIX

Nick shook the snow from his coat then hung it on a hook near the booth. He'd been looking forward to dinner at the café all day. His stomach rumbled with hunger.

"Hey, ya, Nick," Lucy said, dropping a menu on the table. "Coffee?"

"I'd love some." He tugged his gloves off. "It's damn cold out there."

"The weatherman was sure wrong this time. The snow hasn't let up all day. I've never seen anything like it. This is as close to an all-out blizzard as we've ever had." Lucy poured the coffee. "I'll bet you've been busy over at the garage with all the fender benders."

"Yep." Nick wrapped his hands around the warm mug, hoping to chase the chill away from his fingers. "I've had the tow truck out all day."

Lucy smiled. "Do you know what you want? Pizza's the special tonight."

At the mention of pizza his stomach growled. "Sounds good. How about one with everything on it?"

"Coming right up." Lucy winked at him, then headed toward the kitchen.

Due to the snow the café was pretty deserted. Only one other booth was occupied, and he didn't recognize the young couple. Their two small children colored on paper placemats while they waited for their food. Reaching over, the mother stroked her son's hair. The boy lifted his face, giving her a smile. Nick's insides seized up like an engine run dry of oil. What did it feel like to receive a smile like that from your son? He couldn't begin to imagine, but he longed to find out.

Unable to take his eyes off the young family, he took a sip of his coffee. He'd seen the lights on at Clea's. What were she and John doing tonight? Did they have a fire burning? Were they playing games or watching television? What did normal families do in the evening?

As a boy, his nights had been filled with looking after Billy, making him something to eat, watching the old black and white TV before going to bed. And later, as a teenager, he'd spent the evenings out, looking for trouble and finding it.

He grimaced at the memories.

The bell at the door tinkled. Clea came into the café, closing the door behind her. She paused to stomp the snow from her boots, then made a beeline for the counter.

Something inside him softened as he looked at her, pulled him toward her. Nick came out of the booth. She turned.

"Nick."

He half expected a hardness to fill her eyes, but instead he detected happiness in her tone. The knowledge pleased him.

Her cheeks glowed pink from the cold. Snowflakes clung to her hair, which was already starting to curl from the dampness. He longed to reach out and wrap one of those golden curls around his fingers.

"Hi. Where's John?" he asked.

"With Robert." She frowned, her back straightening, almost as if she dared him to challenge her. "They're snowed-in at his place. I'm supposed to be there with them, but by the time we closed The Coffee House the snow was too deep on the road to the lake."

Nick took a deep breath, hoping to quiet his temper. He didn't want his son alone with Boomer, yet as long as Clea and Robert were engaged it was inevitable. Even though the thought of Boomer and John alone bothered Nick, he didn't want Clea to know it, didn't want to argue with her. Not tonight. Thinking about her plans to leave town already had him in knots.

Lucy came out of the kitchen. "Hey, Clea. Did you come for pizza?"

"I sure did." Clea smiled at the waitress, some of the tension leaving her shoulders. "I'll take one with everything to go."

"I just ordered one with everything," Nick said, not wanting her to leave. With both Robert and John gone it left the door wide open for him. Time alone with Clea was just what he needed. "Join me for dinner."

Clea glanced around the café, and he knew she wondered if anyone would tattle to Robert.

"I can't eat an entire pizza," he coaxed.

Clea raised one blonde brow. "I seem to remember that you can." She smiled, enhancing her beauty, making him ache for the easy conversation they'd once shared.

"Not anymore." He grinned back. It felt good to banter with her, making him remember how they used to laugh. "Join me. I promise I'll behave. I could use the company." He pointed to the booth.

"Oh, all right. I'll probably regret this." To Lucy she said, "Cancel my pizza. I'm joining Nick. Would you bring me a soda, please?"

Lucy nodded and smiled. "Coming right up, honey." The waitress sailed back into the kitchen.

Nick led her to the booth. "Let me take your coat."

"Thanks." She pulled the black jacket off and he took it from her, his fingers brushing against hers.

The contact sent tiny sparks through him, making him want to touch more than her hands. "Your hands are cold." He hung her coat up next to his, longing for the freedom to take her icy fingers in his warm ones.

"It's cold outside." She slid into the seat opposite him. "I'm surprised you're not busy towing cars out of ditches."

"I hope people will stay in tonight. I spent the day hauling cars out of the snow. Mullin has my cell number in case I'm needed."

Lucy brought Clea's drink and set the glass on the table.

"Thank you," Clea said to the waitress. She picked up her straw and removed the paper before inserting it into the soda.

Nick watched as she sucked on the straw. She had the most beautiful mouth. He'd always thought so, but it was more than that. She had an inner beauty that had charmed him from the beginning, and it was that part of her he wanted to reconnect with most. She'd been so open with him, so honest when they'd been kids. She'd disarmed him in a way no one ever had before or since.

"You're staring at me." Clea pushed her drink away.

"I can't help it." Nick took a sip of his coffee, savoring the fresh brew. "For ten years I stared at your photo. Seeing you in the flesh is a sight to behold."

"You had my photo with you?" she asked, surprise lacing her tone. "I don't remember giving you a photo."

"Remember when we had our pictures taken at the photo booth at that discount store?" Nick looked into her eyes, eyes the color of summer grass. He wanted to drown in the crystal green depths, but he had to move slowly. He'd spooked her with his photo confession. Her body had tensed. Worry shadowed her features.

"I remember," she said. "I just can't believe you kept them."

"Did you keep yours?" He willed her to say yes. They'd split the photos that day.

"No."

The single word caused a sharp disappointment to knife through him. Had she cut up the pictures when he'd sent her away? He couldn't blame her if she had. She hadn't sent him one photo of John. And the money he'd sent Clea while in prison had been returned to him unopened. The lack of contact between them told him more than words ever could. He had so much to make up to her he didn't even know where to begin, but having dinner with her seemed a good place to start.

The pizza arrived and the next minutes were spent eating.

"God, this is good." He took a monster bite.

"I know." Clea wrapped some wayward mozzarella around her finger then popped it into her mouth. "John and I look forward to pizza night all week." She licked her fingers. "We're regulars."

"I've missed this." A wistful note crept into his voice and Clea brought her eyes to his.

"Missed what?"

"All of this." He glanced around. "Pizza, the smell of fresh air, the freedom to do what I want to do, when I want to do it. Freedom is endless here. It's more than coming and going as you please. In prison, your choices are limited and regulated. Here, on the outside, anything is possible. Anything."

She stopped eating. The way she looked at him, as if she couldn't bear what he'd been through, cut to his soul.

"Was it awful in prison?" she asked.

He swallowed his pizza, not sure how much he wanted to tell her. The reality of prison life was brutal. "Yes, but I got used to it."

"I don't think I could." She took another bite of pizza. "What did you do all day?"

He wanted to say, *Think of you. Think of our son.* But that was only half-true. Fighting to stay alive and in one piece exhausted every minute when he wasn't in his cell. Instead he said, "I kept busy. I earned my Associates of Arts degree in Business through an online program. I also earned my certifications for collision repair and refinishing, brakes, suspension and steering, and engine repair. That's why Mr. Mullin was so interested in hiring me back."

"That's amazing." Her eyebrows shot up, her pizza forgotten. "I'm impressed."

"Don't be." He shrugged. "It filled the hours."

"If you have your AA and so many certifications why are you working at Mullin's?" she asked. "I'm sure there are higher paying, more specialized jobs out there."

"It's where I want to be right now." He looked at her and her eyes darkened. "What I'd like to do is open my own classic car restoration shop. I've drafted a business plan. A solid restoration business can be run from anywhere, even Port Bliss, thanks to the Internet. Parts can be located, bought and sold with a keystroke. It's exciting. There's big money to be made in classic car restoration."

"Wow." Clea smiled. "You managed to go on with your life even though you were locked up. You should be proud, Nick."

The pride in her words embarrassed him. He'd been in prison. There was nothing to be proud of. Wanting to change the subject, he said, "Let's talk about something else." He finished off his pizza.

Clea leaned back. "It looks like we are both finally getting what we want."

"What do you want, Clea?" he asked, almost afraid to hear her answer.

She twirled the straw in her drink. A myriad of emotions crossed her face. He could see her hesitation to tell him anything, but also her need to tell him everything.

"Tell me." He wanted to know, to understand her.

Clea let go of her straw. "I want to make a living from my photography. I'm so close, Nick. I told you about the internship I've won. Winning the internship guarantees me a show in the Mitchell Art Museum. Doors will open for me. I'll be on my way to getting everything I want."

"Everything?" The knot in his gut tightened. He didn't want her to leave, not when he couldn't follow, not when things were unresolved between them.

"Everything. It will be a fresh start for me and for John."

"What about Boomer?" Nick asked. A terrible hollowness burned in his chest at the thought of losing Clea and his son. "Where does he fit in?"

She shook her head. "What do you mean? You know where he fits in."

"Is he part of your dream?"

"Of course he is," Clea replied, her tone defensive. "He's going with us. He's got a good job waiting for him with a prestigious law firm in New York. He's going to help take care of John while I do my internship."

Nick sat up straighter. Suddenly everything seemed clearer. A tiny ray of hope shone on his despair. "Is Boomer your babysitter, Clea? Is that why you're marrying him?"

"No!" Her cheeks reddened. "I can't believe you would suggest such a thing. No, wait. I can believe it. You haven't changed at all, Nick." She waded up her napkin and tossed it on the table.

"That's why you didn't say yes to him before," Nick said, ignoring her words, needing to dull the ache inside him. He didn't want to lose her, but had no idea how to keep her. Anger drove him, and he wanted to strike back. "You didn't need him like you do now. I'm right."

"You're crazy!" Clea pulled some money from her pocket. "I have to go."

"Keep your money. It's my treat." He'd upset her. He needed more time with her, time to find answers.

"No." She held the money out to him. "I don't want to take anything from you, Nick."

Her words cut him to the core, making him remember the returned envelopes of money. Refusing to take her cash, he picked up the check, went to the counter and paid.

Clea joined him. The anger had left her eyes, leaving behind a sadness he didn't want to acknowledge. "I didn't want to fight with you, Nick." She passed him, heading for the door.

"Wait a second." He didn't want to fight either. "I'll walk you home."

"No, thank you," she said coolly. "Believe it or not, Nick, I can make my own way home. I've been doing it for years. I'm good at being alone."

She brushed past him, leaving him to stare at her back.

Bullshit. No one was good at being alone. He'd been alone for ten years. He'd hated the isolation, the wanting, the needing that went unfulfilled. He'd bet his freedom that Clea hated being alone as much as he did, and he intended to prove it.

* * *

A cold blast of air hit Clea in the face when she stepped outside. The smell of frozen seaweed mixed with the fresh scent of snow. She welcomed the sting of the snow against her cheeks, hoping the flakes would help cool her temper. Inside her body glowed red-hot with anger at Nick and she didn't think any amount of frosty air could cool her down.

"Clea, wait," Nick called from behind her.

She walked faster. Under the snow a layer of ice had formed, making the sidewalk slippery. Clea lost her footing, but Nick's hand closed around her elbow, keeping her upright.

She tried to yank her arm free, but he held fast. "Let me go, Nick."

He didn't. "I never should have said those things."

She pressed her lips together. She didn't reply; she couldn't, because deep down she knew there might be a grain of truth in what he'd said. A part of her was afraid of being alone, on her own, with John. She'd always had support both financially and emotionally from her family. Had that swayed her decision to marry Robert? Until Nick had spoken the words tonight, she'd never considered the possibility. She loved Robert. He'd asked her to marry him many times, but she'd never said yes until now. Had she said yes out of fear?

"Just let me go, Nick." Her voice cracked.

"I don't want to."

His voice held a caressing tone that brought a deep need for him to life inside her, a need she'd buried long ago. Clea concentrated on the snow-covered sidewalk, on keeping her footing. Nick saw things in her she didn't want people to see. He challenged her to face the truth, even when she didn't want to. That's where he was so different from Robert. Nick wanted her to see the truth. Robert wanted what looked best, what kept up appearances.

"Clea, look at me." When she didn't, he placed two fingers under her chin, guiding her head up. "If I said things that upset you, I apologize. Let me walk you home."

Giving in seemed the quickest way to be free of him and all he made her feel. "All right."

They didn't get more than a few steps when there was a loud crack followed by a flash of sparks up near the street corner. In unison, all around them, the lights went out. Sparkling snow covered everything, giving the town a luster, a natural light. Behind them, on the other side of the street up on the hill, Clea could hear children laughing, playing, probably sledding.

"A limb must have broken under the weight of the snow, falling on the power lines," Nick said. "Let's get inside."

They walked toward The Coffee House, their boots crunching in the snow. Beside them, the street stretched, an empty ribbon of white. On the other side of the street a couple of people came out of the tavern. Someone threw a snowball.

Nick climbed the stairs to her apartment with her. The enclosed stairway didn't have the benefit of the glow of the snow. An intimate darkness pressed in on Clea as she fumbled in her pocket for the keys. She'd never realized it before, but without the overhead light the landing outside her apartment was dark, giving her more privacy with Nick than she wanted.

She didn't need to see Nick to feel his presence. In the dark all her senses tuned in on him. She could hear the soft sound of his breathing, smell the spicy male scent of him, feel the warmth of his hand on her arm, right through the sleeve of her jacket.

Locating her keys, she said, "Thanks for the pizza and the escort home."

"Let me come in." Nick's voice wrapped around her in the darkness. "I don't feel right leaving you and letting you go into a dark apartment."

"I told you, I'm a big girl, Nick." A current of longing ran through her, making her want more from him than just talk. *It's a physical attraction*, she reminded herself, the keys jingling in her nervous fingers.

"I insist."

Nick's hand closed over hers in the darkness, and he took the keys from her. Stepping around her, he inserted the key, then opened the door.

When they were inside, he asked, "Where do you keep a flashlight?"

Clea opened a drawer near her kitchen sink and switched the flashlight on. She kept two hurricane lamps for power outages, and she took them from the shelf, lighting them both.

Soft amber light filled the room, making Nick's eyes glow with desire, passion, or regret? Uncomfortable, Clea glanced away.

"It's going to get cold in here," Nick said. "Do you want me to light the fireplace?"

"Sure. It's gas. You need to open the front and ignite the pilot by hand."

Nick started the gas burner. The fire jumped to life, bringing more light with it. "The fan won't blow, but it's some heat anyway."

"I'll be okay. Don't feel like you have to stay." She rubbed her hands together to ward off the chill.

"I'd like to stay for a while," Nick said. "My place is just as dark, but I don't have candles, a fire, or even a flashlight."

"Are you trying to make me feel sorry for you?" Clea shook her head, a smile on her lips. "I know you too well for that. Nice try."

"Come on, Clea," he said, his tone low and smooth. He held his hands out to her in a gesture of surrender. "Take pity on me."

Her stomach curled. That deep voice of his had always been her undoing. "All right, but I can loan you some candles if you want to go home."

Nick ran the beam of his flashlight around the living room, touching the light on the leather sofa, the brightly patterned rugs, the photos on the walls. He straightened, shining the beam of light on the mantel, on the photos of John. He didn't speak, just moved the beam of light from one photo to the next.

"He was a beautiful baby," she said.

"Did you take these?" He still had his back to her, but he reached out, tracing the line of John's cheek in the photo, the gesture as intimate as if he touched John in the flesh.

"Yes." She had the sudden urge to comfort Nick, to tell him everything would be all right, but she held back, afraid to let go, afraid to feel too much.

Nick turned. "I've missed so many years."

"I know."

He walked to the sofa and sat down, but he couldn't take his eyes off the pictures. "How is it possible to love someone you've never even met?"

His words touched her heart. "He's a part of you. There's bound to be a connection."

She went to her hall closet and removed a couple of extra blankets. She tossed one to Nick. "You'll need this. This apartment is old and drafty, and with no heat it's going to cool down fast."

He caught the blanket. "Thanks." Nick leaned back, his long legs sprawled out in front of him. His head lay against the back of the sofa, and he turned to look at her. "Tell me what I missed while I was gone. What ever happened to Tyler Montgomery? When did the old library burn down? Anything. Just talk to me."

"All right." These subjects were safe. Clea spent the next hour talking about old classmates, births, deaths, and whatever else she thought he'd be interested in. He listened to every word, an intent look on his face. Clea couldn't imagine what prison must have been like for him, couldn't imagine how hungry he must be for news, or what it must be like for him to learn that life had gone on without him.

"Tell me what you did the last ten years," he said when she finished.

"I've been raising my son. I was a stubborn teenager, and I didn't do things the easy way." She tried to keep the bitterness from her voice, but failed.

"What do you mean?" Nick asked, his eyes narrowing. "What happened after I left?"

"After John was born I left, too. I couldn't stay here." She picked at the edge of the blanket on her lap. John's first years were hard for her. She didn't like talking about them.

"Billy told me you went to Seattle."

"My parents wanted me to go to The Seattle Art Institute, to resume a normal life, only my life wasn't normal. I had a baby and no husband. My father was all right. Oh, he wasn't happy about the pregnancy, but he lived with it, and he made sure I had good medical care. But you know my mother. She couldn't let it go. In her eyes I was a tramp, letting a boy from town touch me, shame me, disgrace my family. She was humiliated, and I'm sure she prayed every day I would just disappear."

"How did you make it?"

Clea thought of the money he'd sent, money that she'd been too proud to accept. "I had some money from the trust fund my grandmother left to me." She pulled the blanket up to her neck, using it as a shield, hiding herself from his view. "I lost the scholarship to The Seattle Art Institute when I didn't enter the program right after high school, but lucky me, my parents picked up the tab. I used my trust fund to pay for a small apartment, and my parents helped me hire a nanny. Her name was Mrs. Applebee. She was an absolute doll, a second grandmother to John. Every spare minute I had went into my photography." Photography had been her salvation then. Every emotion she had, be it fear or love, had gone into those early photos. It still pained her to view them. For that reason she kept them hidden in a closet.

"I had a booth at a street fair in the summers where I displayed my work," she continued, pushing her unhappy memories aside. "I even sold a few. Then my father got sick. That's when I came back to Port Bliss. He died three years ago."

"I'm sorry." Nick reached over and took her hand in his.

"After I'd been home for a while, Mitzi and I came up with the idea for The Coffee House. I sunk the rest of my inheritance into The Coffee House. It's been a great place for me to show my work."

He brought her hand to his lips and kissed it.

Clea closed her eyes. She knew she should pull her hand away, but she couldn't because if she did she might lose the fragile connection she felt to Nick, and she didn't want to do that. For so many years she'd hated him and loved him at the same time. The conflicting emotions tore at her until she just wanted peace, and right now, she had peace, if only for a few minutes.

"In some ways John and I grew up together," she said. "I know I had it easy. I had a trust fund. I had parents who supported me, even if it was from a distance. But at that time I would have traded the money and my education for a life with you and John," she said, very conscious of Nick's fingers brushing hers, so conscious she could barely breathe.

Nick kissed her fingers, her hand.

Butterflies took flight in Clea's stomach. Nick turned her hand over and kissed the pulse point at her wrist. She wondered if he could feel how fast her heart beat. A swirling desire built inside her and she knew she had to stop him, or she wouldn't want to stop him at all. "I can't do this, Nick."

His lips grazed her wrist.

"Don't make me remember." Finding strength she didn't know she had, she tugged her hand free. "I don't want to remember what it was like between us. I can't go back."

"I can't forget." He reached for her, his fingers trailing over her cheek. "I can't forget a single thing, not how you smell, how you feel, how you taste. Thinking about you got me through the last ten years."

"No. You're lying." Clea stood. Her knees threatened to buckle. "You didn't want me. You didn't want John. I can't forget that. You told me things. You preyed on my physical attraction to you. Our time is past. I need to get on with my life. You need to get on with yours."

Nick came to his feet. "That's where you're wrong, Princess. Our time is not past. I wanted you both so much my insides cried for you."

"No." She backed away from him, from what he made her feel. "Sometimes I think that going to prison gave you an easy way out. You didn't have to feel too much, or take on too much responsibility. You told me if I slept with you, we'd be together forever. You lied, Nick."

He reached for her, his hands closing gently around her arms, his touch tender.

"I remember that day, when I came to see you," she said, all the old hurt coming to the surface. "You told me to go, that you didn't want us, that we were a mistake."

"I wanted you to get on with your life." His eyes burned into hers. "I was no good. Everything I touched turned black. I didn't want to bring you down with me."

"No." She pushed against his chest. "You nearly destroyed me. Do you understand that? You can't play with people's emotions. How do you expect me to believe anything you say?"

"I always wanted John."

His eyes held a sadness that made her question everything she'd come to believe over the past ten years. "I don't want to hear any more." Clea tried to twist away, but he pulled her closer, gathered her to him until her breasts pressed against his chest. The contact sent a jolt of electricity through her, jumpstarting the whirlwind of intense emotions only he could make her feel.

"But as much as I wanted John," he said, his breath warm on her face, "I wanted you even more. Let me convince you. Tell me it's not too late."

"I can't." She wanted to believe him, but past experience wouldn't let her. Deep down, she didn't trust him, yet that didn't stop her from wanting him with every breath she took.

Nick's hands came up to cup her face, and ever so slowly he guided her face to his. Clea's eyes slid shut. His lips brushed against hers, his tongue coaxing her lips apart.

Clea moaned. Her will to resist him crumbled into tiny grains of sand taken away in the wind. She remembered this, all of it, his taste, the way he kissed, the way he touched her. Right now she wanted to trust him, even though her mind told her not to. Wanting to forget everything but the way she felt, she reached for him, her hands curling in the flannel of his shirt.

Nick's hands moved from her face, to her shoulders, to her back. He molded her to him, and she fit against him like they were made for each other.

Every nerve in her body came alive for him, for his touch. The kiss grew hotter, more carnal. Without breaking the kiss, Nick lowered her to the sofa, his body following her down until he lay full on top of her.

Clea's fingers slid into his hair, hair that felt like silk against her skin. This time, Nick moaned, the sound sending a rush of pleasure through her. His lips moved to caress her jaw, her neck, while his hands found their way under her sweater. Her skin caught fire where he touched her.

The lights came on.

The refrigerator hummed as it restarted.

The microwave beeped.

Reality came rushing back. "What am I doing? This is wrong." She shoved at Nick. "Let me up."

He lifted his head to stare down at her. Passion still burned in his eyes. "I want you, Clea. I don't want to stop."

She didn't want to stop either. "I'm engaged," she said, blurting out the one thing she hoped would affect them like a dousing with ice water.

Nick groaned, but moved so she could get out from under him and sit up. "You're not married yet. Break your engagement."

"I can't. I don't want to," she said, meaning it. She loved Robert, what she felt for him was real and solid. What she felt for Nick was physical, not something she could build a life on.

"Do you love him?" Nick pushed his fingers through his hair. The hunger in his eyes made her want him even more.

"Yes. He's everything I want in a man. He doesn't deserve to be cheated on." Guilt assailed her. "Please go."

"How can you love him and kiss me like that?"

Clea glanced away. "I don't know."

Nick stood. "You better think long and hard about that, Princess." He grabbed his coat. A minute later the door closed behind him.

Clea curled up into a ball. She didn't want to think about her reaction to Nick. Her body ached for him. She wanted him, despite everything he'd put her through. Did she still love him, or was she merely feeling a lust more powerful than her will to refuse?

She wasn't ready to throw Robert away for a moment of stolen passion. Robert had to come first this time, no matter how attracted she was to Nick.

This time she was sticking to the choices she'd made. She'd stay away from Nick from this point on. She had to.

CHAPTER SEVEN

The sound of the snowplow pulled Clea from a fitful sleep the following morning. Jumping out of bed, she dressed quickly, then ran out to her car. She intended to follow the plow up the mountain. After last night Port Bliss wasn't big enough for both her and Nick. She needed to get away from him before she lost sight of the things that were truly important to her, John, Robert, and her internship.

She couldn't see the plow when she turned her car up the road to Lake Bliss. Snow continued to fall, the flakes thick and heavy already covering the road in winter white where the plow had just cleared the pavement.

The Honda's wheels spun over the icy road, the back end sliding as she rounded the first bend. Clea's hands tightened on the steering wheel. The road held a film of ice making driving worse than she'd expected. Seven miles of curves stood between her and Robert's house. She considered turning the car around and heading home, but the thought of another confrontation with Nick kept her foot to the gas pedal. She didn't want to be alone with him again, not when his kisses stole her will and made her forget all about her fiancé.

Last night she'd wanted to give in to Nick, even though she'd known it was wrong. When Nick hadn't returned after his release from prison, she'd wanted to be anywhere but Port Bliss. For ten years she'd harbored hope. While she'd never acknowledged that feeling, she realized now that it had been there, simmering just below the surface. She didn't want to have that kind of all-consuming passion again. It hurt too much.

Clea gave the car some gas and sped forward. The studded tires spun, but she kept going. Snow hit her windshield as fast as her wipers could clear it away. For the first couple of miles trees bracketed the road, the forest growing thicker as she climbed the mountain. Covered with snow the firs looked as pretty as a picture on a Christmas card, but Clea didn't take the time to enjoy the sight. The car fishtailed as she rounded a curve. Her breath left her lungs in a whoosh when she noticed she had just missed the ravine that served as a drainage ditch on her right.

But she didn't stop; she couldn't. If she did, she might never get going again. Studded tires were fine on snow, but did her little good on the ice. She figured herself to be about three miles up. The forest to her right gave way to a solid rock wall. To her left the road dropped off into a deep gully. There were no guardrails. She couldn't afford to make a mistake under these conditions.

Two more miles and she'd reach the Lake Bliss Grocery, a tiny store where the locals could pick up a paper or a quart of milk. Once there, she'd abandon her car and ask Mr. McGinley, the store's owner, to take her to Robert's on his snowmobile.

Clea held on to that thought as she eyed the hairpin curve just ahead. She let off the gas, then slowly accelerated as she went into the curve. Her backend slid a little, but as she righted the wheels, a vehicle came around the curve toward her in her lane.

She turned the steering wheel sharply, and her right two tires slid into the ditch. The on-coming vehicle sideswiped her car, latching onto it. The sound of ripping metal filled the air. Her car came up against the rock wall, and for a split second she thought she might be squished between the large utility vehicle and the rock. The SUV dragged her backward along the rock, jolting to a stop. Her head snapped forward striking something solid.

A numbing pain shot through her head.

She tried to focus, but it felt as if she looked through a long, dark tunnel. Her field of vision narrowed as everything faded to black.

* * *

Nick frowned as he drove up to the accident. Why didn't people just stay put? The snow hadn't let up at all, yet people continued to drive in conditions that weren't even fit for the snowplow.

He brought the truck to a stop, opened the door, and jumped out. His boots sank into several inches of fresh snow. The snowplow waited nearby to clear the road back to town, its yellow caution light circling round and round. An aid car blocked his view of the vehicles involved in the accident, but he could tell there were at least two cars.

"Hey, Nick," Sheriff Kincade said, giving Nick a nod.

"Anybody seriously injured?" Nick rounded the aid car. A burgundy Ford Expedition had slid off the road, taking another vehicle with it. Small and red, the second car lay crushed between the Expedition and the rock wall that lined this section of the drive up the mountain.

A red car. Clea had a red car. His heart sped up and he took a step forward. The sheriff grabbed his arm.

"Hold on, Nick," the sheriff said, and for once Nick could read the expression in Sheriff Kincade's eyes. Something was wrong, terribly wrong.

"Let me go." A wave of nausea hit him, nearly bringing him to his knees. It couldn't be Clea.

"Why don't you just wait here with me until they get her out? You'll only be in the way."

The sheriff's words confirmed the worst, twisting the fear buried deep in the pit of his stomach. Nick pulled his arm free.

"Is she alive?" he asked, the words a tortured rasp. He couldn't bear it if he lost her now. A deep ache filled his chest.

"She's alive and talking, but she's got a nasty bump on her head. She refused to let me call her mother or Robert. I'm hoping to talk some sense into her once they get her free."

Nick's heart began to beat again. Clea was alive and talking. "What happened?"

"Both vehicles were going slow," Sheriff Kincade said. "The folks in the Expedition lost control going around the curve. They forced Clea off the road and dragged her car a ways before they both came to a stop. The damage looks worse than it is. The folks in the Expedition are all right, just shaken up."

The little red car looked crumpled, smashed, the windshield shattered. The firefighters worked to free Clea. The sound of twisting metal filled the air, then Clea's car door broke free. The EMTs worked on her and Nick thought he heard her moan. He held onto that sound, praying she'd be all right.

A stretcher appeared and they moved Clea onto it. Nick got his first look at her. A large white bandage covered her forehead. A brace circled her neck. Her arm lay in a splint. Snow fell on her, on all of them as they took her to the aid car. Nick followed, a sick wrenching in his gut.

"I'm riding down with her," he said as the EMTs loaded her into the vehicle.

"Sorry," the young EMT said. "It's against the rules. You'll need to follow in your own car."

"Where are you taking her?" Nick asked. Her skin held an ashen color that scared the hell out of him. Her lips were pale. He willed her to open her eyes.

"To the hospital in Bradley," the EMT said.

The sheriff came up beside them. "Let her go, Nick. You're needed here. Come on."

"Wait." Nick stepped up into the aid car. "Clea?"

"Nick." Her voice sounded weak, but she opened her eyes. "It looks worse than it is. I'm fine. I just bumped my head."

"I'll be at the hospital as soon as I can. I promise." He squeezed her hand. "Hang in there, Princess. These guys will take good care of you. Don't worry about anything." Leaning down, he kissed her cheek.

"I'm glad you're here," she murmured.

"All right," the EMT said, placing a hand on Nick's shoulder. "We need to go."

Nick nodded. He let go of Clea's hand, then jumped from the aid car. The doors closed. The plow started and together the vehicles drove away.

Clea's words echoed through his head, "I'm glad you're here." He didn't care if she'd said them in delirium. The words had come from somewhere and he wasn't about to let her take them back.

* * *

"I'm fine, Doctor, really," Clea said. She'd been in the emergency room for hours. She'd suffered a bump on her forehead the size of a hardboiled egg. The grogginess had left, leaving behind a headache, but not much else. Her wrist hurt, but wasn't broken. Her legs worked fine, but most of her muscles were sore. "Let me go home."

"It's best if you stay, Miss Rose." Dr. Martin peered at Clea over the top of his glasses. Well past middle age and graying, Dr. Martin had a kind but firm bedside manner. He made it easy for Clea to trust him. "Unless you'll allow me to call your family?"

"No. I don't want to worry them, or risk their safety by having them come out in the snow. I'm sure Mitzi is in town. Let me try her number again." She'd hoped Nick would show up to take her home, but he hadn't kept his promise to her. She still couldn't trust him, and that hurt more than she wanted to admit.

"You need to be awakened every two hours. You have a concussion." Dr. Martin pursed his lips. "You've been unable to reach your friend and confirm that she can care for you. You said you tried her cell phone and there was no answer. I really can't release you without confirmation of a caregiver."

"I'll take care of her."

Clea and the doctor both turned at the sound of Nick's voice. He stood in the open doorway. His boots still held snow. A dark knit cap covered his head. The fleece lined Carhartt jacket he wore looked soaked clean through. He'd been out in the weather, most likely working at removing her car from the ditch. Lines of fatigue, or worry, creased his forehead, and she wondered if he'd been worried about her.

"I came as soon as I could." Nick walked toward her, pulling his gloves off. "I had a couple of cars I had to tow down the mountain before I could get away."

"Nick." He'd kept his promise.

"You scared the hell out of me."

The tenderness in his voice touched her. "I'm fine." She offered him a smile.

"She's not fine," the doctor said with a frown. "She wants to leave. Her injuries were minor, but she needs someone who can watch over her. She has a concussion and she needs to be awakened every two hours."

"I'm your man," Nick said to the doctor. "Just tell me what to do and I'll do it."

"Is that all right with you, Miss Rose?" Dr. Martin raised one bushy brow.

She wanted to leave. She didn't want John to find out she was in the hospital. Since she was unable to reach Mitzi, Nick was her only choice.

"Miss Rose?" the doctor prompted.

Her need to be home outweighed her fear of being alone with

Nick. "Yes, it's all right with me." Her eyes met Nick's and she saw triumph, or was it relief?

"Well, then, I'll prepare the paperwork." Dr. Martin wrote another note on her chart, then left the room.

"You don't have to do this," Clea said, not knowing what else to say.

"I want to." Nick pulled a metal chair up beside the bed and sat down.

"You can find Mitzi once we're back in town. She's probably staying at my place anyway."

He pulled the cap from his head, releasing his wild, uncombed hair. "You don't need Mitzi. I'm here."

Clea resisted the urge to reach over and smooth his wayward hair. She glanced away from him. "I don't want John to find out I've been in the hospital. It would scare him. He's been through so much lately. I don't want to add another worry to his shoulders. Promise me you won't call my mother or Robert."

"Clea," Nick said, taking her hand. "Shut up. I can take care of you. Let me."

The husky tempo of his voice caused her heart to skip a beat. For a moment, Clea lost herself in the clear blue of his eyes. A sweet ache started inside her. It would feel so good to just let go and let him take care of her, but could she?

A nurse came into the room, a clipboard in her hand. "Here's the paperwork."

She jerked her head toward the nurse. The motion made her head pound. "Thank you."

"Sign here," the nurse said, "and here." When she finished, she handed a sheet of instructions to Nick, going over them, telling Nick what signs to look for and how to care for her. Nick nodded as he listened.

Clea swung her legs over the side of the bed. She was going home to spend the night with Nick Lombard. If her mother found out, she'd kill her.

* * *

"Wake up, Clea."

Clea fought for sleep. The gray fuzziness of oblivion called to her, cradled her, held her in its comforting arms. A delicious warmth cocooned her body. She rolled over and snuggled more deeply into her pillow.

"Clea, wake up."

Something brushed across her face. Clea's eyes snapped open. Nick leaned over her, his hand on her head.

"Are you awake?" he asked, so close she could feel his warm breath on her skin.

"Yes." Her mouth felt dry. She tried to move, but the pounding in her head intensified.

"How do you feel?" His fingers brushed the hair back from her brow, his touch tender, careful to avoid the bandage on her forehead.

"I felt better before you woke me." She grimaced. "My head hurts. I'm thirsty."

Nick got up, returning a minute later with a glass of water. He sat down on the edge of the bed. "Drink this."

Clea sat up, one hand on her throbbing head. Nick held the glass to her lips and she drank. The water tasted sweet and cool against her parched tongue.

"Are you nauseated or dizzy?" he asked.

"No." She gave him a weak smile. "You make a great nurse, Nick. Maybe you should consider changing professions."

"Yeah, right." He grimaced.

"What time is it?"

"Four a.m."

"Every time I go to sleep you wake me. I'm going to be a walking zombie tomorrow, or should I say this morning, when I open the shop."

"You are not opening the shop. Mitzi can open. You need to rest, doctor's orders."

"I don't think she's in town. She's probably stuck somewhere."

"This town can survive without coffee for one day, Clea." Nick set the glass of water on her nightstand. "You need to rest. You said yourself that your head is pounding."

Clea winced as she settled back against the pillow. "Maybe you're right." Hair rumpled, lines of fatigue around his eyes, Nick looked as tired as she felt. "Thank you for staying with me, and for making me call Robert and my mother. I know I was stretching the truth a bit, telling them I was in a little fender-bender, but at least they won't be shocked when they see the bandage on my forehead. I'm glad they took my advice and stayed put last night."

"You gave me quite a scare." He reached for her hand, and

threading his fingers with hers, brought her hand to his mouth and kissed it.

"I scared myself." The horror of seeing the SUV bearing down on her came to the surface, making her stomach do a sickening flip-flop.

"Why would you drive in this storm?" He shifted on the bed. Clea scooted over to give him more room. "You grew up here. You know how dangerous that road can be. It turns into an ice rink. All it takes is one wrong move."

"And I could have been killed," Clea finished for him. She shut her eyes against the image of her twisted car. "I know that. Don't you think I feel like an idiot?"

"Did I drive you from town?" Nick asked, his voice low. "Did you leave because of what happened between us the other night?"

"No," she lied. She didn't want him to think he had any power over her.

He sighed. "I don't want to drive you away."

"You didn't." Soft light from the hall spilled into the room, bathing Nick in shadows. A dark stubble coated his jaw. His eyes drooped a little, and she knew he hadn't gotten any sleep at all. He'd done everything right since returning to town, and she'd done everything wrong. She'd been less than honest with him, trying to protect herself from getting hurt again.

"Maybe I did want to get away from you," she said, watching his face for a reaction to her words.

He ran a hand over his whiskers. "When I saw you at Maude's funeral, I didn't know what to think. I sure as hell never expected you to be there. It was a shock." He stroked her hair, his touch gentle. "Maybe if you hadn't been there, if I hadn't seen you, I might have left right after the funeral, but that's not the way it happened. You were there. I did see you. After that I started to imagine the possibilities if I stayed."

"I'm glad you stayed," she said, the words leaving her mouth before she could stop them. "I'm glad for John. For better or worse, you're part of his life now. That won't ever change, even after we move to New York."

"I want to meet him. It's time."

"Okay," she agreed. "I'll set something up."

Nick nodded. "Thank you."

"John's a little boy," she said, wanting him to understand their son. "Robert is the only father figure in his life, and this change won't be easy for him. I have to trust you with my son. Don't hurt him, Nick." She longed to add, *Don't hurt me*, but she bit back the words.

"I won't." He touched her arm, giving it a light squeeze. "I promise."

Clea's head throbbed. She never thought she'd be having this conversation at four in the morning with a head injury. She needed to sleep. She didn't want to think anymore.

"Go back to sleep," Nick said.

"Go and sleep on the sofa, please." It unnerved her that he sat in the chair, watching her. To shield herself from his intense scrutiny she snuggled more deeply under the covers. "I'll be fine."

"Not a chance. I'm staying right here where I can keep an eye on you."

"Then at least stretch out on the bed. I trust you," she murmured, her eyelids growing heavy. "You won't try to take advantage of an injured woman."

Clea let her eyes close. She listened as Nick pulled his boots off. The bed moved, and she could feel his weight as he stretched out beside her. He didn't get under the covers and she didn't invite him. She'd given him a blanket earlier, and although she didn't check, she felt sure he used it now to cover himself up. She'd never been in bed with him before. Not even when they'd conceived John; they'd done that in the Boss. It felt a little unsettling to share so intimate a space with him.

"I'll wake you in two hours," Nick said, his voice close to her ear.

"Um hum," she replied, too tired to form coherent words.

"Sweet dreams, Princess."

* * *

Nick came awake slowly. A pleasant sweet scent teased him. He inhaled. His nose touched something soft, silky, and he knew without looking he touched Clea's hair. His eyes flew open. Sometime after he'd woken her at six-thirty he'd become intertwined with her. She had rolled over, into his arms, her head on his chest. Even though blankets separated them from the chest down, he could feel enough of her, the bare skin of her arms, the satin of her hair, to become fully aroused while he slept.

He glanced at the watch on his wrist. Eight forty-five. It was time to wake her again, but he hesitated. For a moment he wanted to pretend. It felt damn good to have her in his arms. She felt softer than he remembered. He buried his nose in her hair and just breathed. He could stay like this forever.

The click of the front door brought him fully awake.

Voices followed.

"Wake up." A jolt of reality ripped through him. He gave Clea a gentle shake. "Someone's here. Wake up."

"What?" she mumbled, snuggling more fully against him.

"Mom," John called. Footsteps brought him closer.

"We're home," Robert echoed from the other room.

"John?" Clea tried to move, but her hair was caught beneath Nick's arm. She opened her eyes and they instantly widened when she realized the situation they were in. "Nick? Oh no."

"Clea?" Vivian Rose called.

The bedroom door flew open. Three pairs of astonished eyes pinned them where they were.

"My God, your head." Vivian rushed forward. "You didn't tell us you'd been hurt in the accident."

"John." Clea untangled herself from Nick and sat up. "This isn't what it looks like. I can explain."

"What the hell is he doing here!" Robert cried, before launching himself at Nick.

CHAPTER EIGHT

Robert charged the bed. "You son of a bitch!"

"Robert, stop," Clea cried.

Beside her, Nick threw the blanket off, meeting Robert halfway. "Calm down, Boomer. This isn't the time or the place for you to lose your temper."

"Why are you near her, you filthy loser?" Robert's hands hit Nick in the chest, shoving him. "Get the hell out of here."

To Clea's relief, Nick didn't push back, but there was an anger in his eyes that she prayed he'd hold in check.

John ran to her. "Mom, your head is hurt." He glared at Nick. "What did you do to my mom?"

"Everyone, please calm down," Clea said, knowing she needed to turn things around fast. "You're upsetting John." Her head pounded. Daylight streamed in through her bedroom window, making her eyes hurt. How on earth had she gotten so tangled up with Nick? She remembered falling asleep, but he'd been next to her, not intertwined with her.

"What exactly is going on here?" Robert demanded. He looked wildly around the room. "Someone tell me what's going on!"

Clea held a hand up to silence him. "Please." She reached for her son and pulled him down on the bed next to her. "I'm all right. I told you on the phone that I had a car accident yesterday. Nick's been taking care of me."

Nick no longer looked at Robert. At that moment he had eyes only for John. A myriad of emotions flashed across Nick's face, awe, hope, fear. She couldn't begin to imagine what it must be like for him to see his son in the flesh. She ached for both Nick and John. Two people who should know each other, but were strangers.

"John." Clea took a deep breath. "This is your father, Nick Lombard." She touched John's hair, but he jerked his head away, his wary eyes still on Nick.

She didn't want them to meet this way, under stressful circumstances, with her mother and Robert watching. What was between Nick and John was personal and emotional, not for onlookers.

"Hello, John," Nick said, a barely suppressed longing in his voice. He reached out, then pulled his hand back, as if he wanted desperately to touch his son, but didn't dare.

John kept his eyes downcast, but his silence said more than words could have.

There was so much Clea wanted to say, but not in front of Robert and her mother. She exchanged a glance with Nick and the naked hope in his eyes shook her.

"John," Clea said carefully. "Nick is here because I needed someone to take care of me last night. I got a bump on my head. A concussion."

"What!" Robert exclaimed, the anger in his eyes turning to concern. He sat on the edge of the bed. "Why didn't you tell us you were seriously hurt? I would have come at once."

"How badly were you injured?" Vivian said at the same time.

"I'm fine." Clea forced a smile of reassurance she didn't feel. "I foolishly thought I could make it up the mountain in the snow. I wanted to be with all of you. A car came around the hairpin corner in my lane and forced me off the road. I hit my head. I have a bump under this bandage, and some bruises, but I'm okay. My car, however, needs a little more work." Nick's eyes were on John. It was almost as if he couldn't look away, like he was trying to memorize every inch of John's face and body.

"Robert," Clea said, bringing Robert's attention to her. "I didn't want you to come in the snow. I couldn't have lived with myself if you'd had an accident, too. Nick towed my car, then he came to the hospital and drove me home. The doctor insisted he stay with me to wake me every two hours because of my head injury. It's been an exhausting night."

"So you're going to be okay?" John asked.

"Yes, honey," Clea confirmed, giving him a genuine smile. "I'm tired, but fine."

"Dear Lord." Vivian's hand went to her throat. "You could have been killed. Was it Dr. Martin who saw you at the hospital?"

"Yes. He was wonderful."

"I know him personally," Vivian said, the ring of pride in her words. "I'm going call and talk to him myself."

"Darling, I'm so glad you're all right." Robert patted her leg through the blankets. "You never should have tried to come up to the lake. Thank God your injuries were not more serious." He turned to Nick. "Please leave. I'll take care of Clea now."

"I'll leave when Clea asks me to," Nick replied, his tone hard.

Robert came off the bed, his stance rigid. "Get out."

Tension as thick as old glue stretched between Robert and Nick. They stood on either side of the bed, Clea and John in the middle. Clea didn't want John in the center of their male feud. She would already have to do damage control over the words Robert had shouted at Nick earlier, calling him a loser.

"Robert, Mother," she said. "If you'll excuse us for a minute, I'd like to talk to John and Nick alone."

"Really, Clea," Vivian replied. "I don't think that's a good idea."

"I have to agree," Robert said.

"I'm not asking your permission," Clea told them.

"Fine." Robert walked to Clea's mother, taking her arm. "Let's go and put some coffee on, Vivian. I think we could all use a cup. And while the coffee brews you can check in with Clea's doctor."

Her mother gave Clea a frown of disapproval.

Robert led Vivian from the room.

"John," Clea said when Robert and Vivian were out of earshot. "I know this is difficult for you. I wanted to introduce you to your father in private."

John kept his eyes on Clea and his misery seeped into her, unleashing long suppressed anguish.

"I loved Nick very much when you were born." She paused for a minute to absorb the words she'd just spoken; surprised to find she'd spoken the truth. She had loved Nick then, with every fiber of her being. Her throat tightened with emotion and she didn't dare look at Nick or she might fall apart. "I know this isn't easy for you. It's not easy for Nick either."

Nick took a step toward them. "John, I'm sorry I wasn't here to watch you grow up." He came around the bed to where John sat, but he didn't sit down. He merely stood close - close enough that John could touch him if he wanted to. "But I want you to know I thought about you every single day."

John lifted his head to look at Nick.

"I know you think of Robert as your father, and that's okay. But I hope we can be friends."

When John didn't reply, Nick shifted to Clea. "I'll go now. Call me if you need me." Nick sat on the chair near the bed and pulled his boots on.

"Thank you." Clea's heart overflowed with emotion. Nick's words to John had touched her, made her believe he could be a good father to his son. He'd shown a softer side with John, a more open side. Nick had to be hurt and humiliated, yet he'd hidden his disappointment from John, and instead had worked to build a bridge between them.

She held her hand out to Nick. "Thank you for taking care of me last night."

He took her hand, giving her fingers a reassuring squeeze. "You're welcome."

Clea could see the torment in his eyes, the yearning he had for his son, and something more - a spark of hope.

Nick let go of her fingers and went to the door. He paused. "Good bye, John. I hope I'll see you soon." He slipped out into the hall. A minute later she heard the apartment door shut.

"John?" He'd been so quiet. With a gentle touch, Clea turned his face toward her so she could look into his eyes. Instead of seeing the beginnings of love in the blue depths, she saw an emptiness that chilled her soul. "Are you okay?"

John bolted from the bed, his eyes bright with the shine of unshed tears. "I don't want him here. He's going to ruin everything. He's a stupid loser. I hate him."

Clea stretched her fingers toward him, but he spun away, running from the room. A second later his bedroom door slammed. She winced. Tears stung her eyes. Her head pounded. Had John poured his hopes for a father into his relationship with Robert? Did he love Robert that much, or was he afraid to love Nick?

Robert appeared in the doorway. "I knew this would happen. Nick is trouble. Look what he's done to John."

"Nick hasn't done anything to John. Your words upset John. What were you thinking going after Nick that way with John watching?" Clea tossed the covers back. "I need to go to him."

"Give him a few minutes to cool off," Robert said. "It had to be a shock to come home and find his mother in bed with his father."

"It wasn't like that, Robert."

"Seeing the two of you together makes me sick." Robert came toward her. "I can't take it, Clea. I should have been here last night."

"I honestly didn't want to worry you." She touched her head, hoping to stop the pounding. "Nothing happened between Nick and me."

"I couldn't bear to lose you to him again," he said, his voice cracking. "I can't, Clea. I'd go crazy." He came to her, sitting on the edge of the bed. Leaning forward, he kissed her bandage. "I love you so much."

"Oh, Robert." Clea sighed. "You're not going to lose me. I promise."

The hard lines around his mouth relaxed. "What can I do to help?"

She held her hand out to him, and he took it. "When it comes to John, I need you to put your feelings for Nick aside. You belittled Nick in front of John. I can't have that. John has enough to deal with right now without you making him feel like his father is a loser."

"You're right." Robert nodded. "I'm sorry. I didn't think. I just reacted."

Clea squeezed Robert's fingers. "We have to help John through this."

"I know." Robert sighed. "I'm trying, Clea, I am."

Clea gave him a soft smile. "We're all doing the best we can. Now, come with me. Let's go and cheer John up."

Robert returned her smile. "Sounds good."

He stood and helped Clea to her feet.

* * *

"This is it," Billy said.

Nick looked from his brother to the abandoned warehouse in front of them. Faded yellow paint peeled all over the building, revealing a depressing gray underneath. The upper windows were broken all the way around. A weathered For Sale sign was pasted to the door. The place looked like it had been abandoned years ago. Billy had dragged him out of bed at the ungodly hour of five a.m. on his day off to make the two-hour drive to Vancouver. "Just what are we looking at?"

"We," Billy said, clapping Nick on the back, "are looking at your future. Or should I say *our* future?"

"I'm still not following you," Nick said.

"Don't you get it?" Billy grinned. "It's the future home of the Lombard Brother's Auto Body and Classic Car Restoration Shop."

"You don't say?" Nick gave the building a second look. It did have potential. "Just how are we going to afford this place?"

"We'll get a loan," Billy said as if it were the simplest thing in the world to do. "We can do it. I have money saved. I own my trailer free and clear. Say the word, brother, and I'll get the paperwork started."

"I don't know." Nick stared at the building, enthusiasm building inside him. All his life he'd dreamed of owning his own shop, doing things his way. While in prison, he'd made plans and done research. He knew about what it would cost to set up shop. He had a good head for numbers. With enough money he could make it work, he just hadn't intended to start this big.

He'd planned to get the internet side of the business up and running first, and had already taken steps to make that happen. Over the next few days he was interviewing web designers. The rest of the money he'd saved, in prison, working as a production foreman for a fleece-wear assembly line, would go to purchasing a computer. They didn't need a fancy garage right away, especially now, since he'd rented the bay from Mr. Mullin. The shop could come later, when they had more money to invest.

"What do you say?" Billy tugged on Nick's arm. "Let's go inside. We can have the place for a song. The owner wants to unload it."

"Nothing comes that cheap." He followed Billy into the warehouse. In his experience everyone paid a price to get what they wanted. It happened in prison. It happened on the outside.

"The power is off." Billy led the way inside the dark building. The broken windows overhead let in enough light so they could see. Billy pointed to the right. "There are two offices. Over here we can put the lifts in." He swung around to the left. "The bay is huge. We can hold ten cars in here easy, maybe more."

"It's a great place," Nick said, catching Billy's fever. "How much?"

"Let me worry about that," Billy said.

"How much, Billy?"

"We can have the place for one fifty."

"One hundred and fifty thousand dollars?" Nick asked, his dream plummeting to the ground. "Jesus, Billy. We can't afford that."

"We'll get a loan," Billy said, the words coming out in a rush. He grinned. "We can make this work, Nick. Trust me."

"Who would loan us that kind of money?"

Billy sighed. He pushed his fingers through his spiky hair. "We have to try. Don't you want to get out of Port Bliss? I sure as hell do. I can't breathe in that town anymore."

"Why have you stayed?" Nick asked, wondering what the years had been like for Billy. It wasn't easy to live a lie every day; no one knew that better than he did.

"For Mom. She needed me."

The sadness in his words tore at Nick. "I'd like to leave Port Bliss someday, but it's John. He knows me now. I have to think of him."

"John can visit you here," Billy said. "You don't want to stay in Port Bliss after Clea leaves."

Nick turned away. He didn't want to discuss his feelings for Clea with his brother. He didn't want to tell Billy he hoped the wedding would never take place, or how much he hoped Clea would stay in Port Bliss. His dreams of a life with Clea were selfish because he knew deep down he would never keep her from following her dream. He didn't want to be the one who held her back.

"And besides," Billy said. "Look at what happened to The Boss last night. Do you really want to stay in a town where you aren't wanted?"

Nick frowned. He'd gone out to his car that morning to find the word *Jailbird* scratched into the shiny yellow paint. The Boss would need hours of sanding before the car could be restored to its trademark glossy yellow finish.

His first thought was that Boomer had written the word. He'd glanced over to find Boomer's car gone from the curb, but he'd discarded the thought. Boomer wouldn't resort to petty crime. Most likely it had been kids, maybe someone who knew John.

"Let's try to do this," Billy said, his tone calmer now. "You deserve this chance, Nick. I want to give it to you. I owe you, brother."

Nick turned. "You don't owe me anything, Billy. Not a damn thing. I owe you my life. If not for you, I'd be dead instead of Danny."

"I know, but you've given up so much for me. I should have gone to jail. I killed him."

"To save me. It was an accident. You were only trying to stop him."

Billy's jaw tensed. "I should have gone to jail, and the guilt has eaten at me every day since that night. I never should have listened to you. I never should have let you take the blame for what I did."

"What's done is done." Nick went to his brother, putting his hands on Billy's shoulders. "You were just a kid, a kid who got mixed up in my problems with the Bloomfield brothers. I'm sorry you felt you had to protect me. It should have been the other way around. It wasn't your fight. I could never let you pay for a crime that had nothing to do with you. Danny was after me that night. He was always after me. In fact, I'm sure it was Danny who tried to pin the lakeside robberies on me. Danny Bloomfield hated me. He managed to turn the whole damn town against me with his wild accusations. The fight between us was a long time coming."

Nick looked into his brother's eyes, eyes that held the shine of tears.

"Jesus, Nick." Billy's face crumpled. "I love you, man. I couldn't let him shoot you. I had to hit him. I just wanted him to put the gun down. I never meant to kill him."

"I know."

A well of long suppressed sadness overcame Nick, and he hauled Billy into his arms. They embraced each other, two brothers, trying to heal the deep hurt inside. When Nick finally pulled away, he felt better, lighter somehow, as if a burden had been eased.

They'd had so little time to get their story straight that night. Billy hadn't wanted Nick to take the blame, but Nick had insisted, and Billy had given in. Later, when no gun had been found to back up Nick's story, Billy had begged Nick to let him confess, but Nick had stood firm. He'd never expected such a tough sentence, six to ten years for manslaughter, for a crime that had been self-defense.

He'd been up for parole many times over the years, and each time Robert had been at his parole hearing, making sure he'd stayed put.

Until the last time. Robert had been absent. Nick had been granted parole. He'd often wondered why Robert hadn't come to the last hearing, but he sure as hell wasn't going to ask him.

"Everything's going to be all right, Billy," Nick said, wanting to give Billy something good to look forward to. "If you want to try to get the loan, I'm with you."

"Really?" Billy wiped his eyes on his shirtsleeve. "That's great, Nick. You won't be sorry. We can make this work. Together the Lombard brothers can do anything."

"A hundred and fifty thousand." Nick whistled. "It might as well be a million bucks."

* * *

Clea went to John's bedroom door and pushed it open. "Hey, honey."

John dropped the toy car he held into the case and shut the lid, turning the lock.

"Can I come in?" Clea asked. They'd spent the evening packing. John had given her the cold shoulder the entire time, speaking to her only when she required an answer. She wanted to clear the air between them before they went to bed. She wanted him to talk to her about Nick. She needed to know what John was feeling.

"I guess."

Clea smiled. She sat down on the edge of his bed. "I'd like to talk about Nick."

John pressed his lips together.

"He's not going to go away. We need to find a way to get along with him. He wants to get to know you."

"How do you know?" John asked, a defiant look in his eyes.

"I never told you this before, but he tried to stay in touch with you," Clea said. "I sent his letters back. I was angry with Nick, and a little afraid to let him into your life. I can see now how wrong I was to have kept the two of you apart. Nick's done nothing but think about you while he's been gone."

"While he was in prison," John said with disgust. He turned away from her. "He's a murderer. A loser. That's what Robert says."

Damn Robert. "No, honey. What happened was an accident. Nick protected his brother and someone got hurt. You know all this John. I'm not understanding your anger. Are you mad at Nick, or are you mad at me because we are moving to New York?"

She reached out to touch him. He moved away from her.

John kicked his box of cars, sending the case rattling across his bedroom floor. "Robert's going to be my dad."

The anguish in his voice broke her heart. "I know you like Robert. And I promise you he will always be in your life, but give Nick a chance. You don't know him, honey. You just know he's upsetting your life. He's upsetting my life too, but I'm glad he's back."

"Why?" John asked his tone belligerent.

"I'm happy for you." Clea smiled, surprised to find she meant the words. "I'm glad you are going to have the chance to know your father. He loves you very much. Won't you give him a chance?" She held her breath, waiting for his reply.

"Why should I? You're just going to make me move to New York anyway and I'll never see him again."

"No, John." His revelation startled her. Why hadn't she seen it sooner? John was afraid to lose Nick all over again. Even though he didn't know Nick, John's heart had taken as bad a beating as hers had. "Your father will always be in your life, no matter where we live. Please, won't you give him a chance? We don't have much time before the move."

"What would I have to do?" he asked, his voice sounding small.

She wanted to reach for him and hug him until he begged her to leave him alone. "We could start by spending some time with Nick. Why don't we have him over for dinner?"

John sat down on the bed.

Eyes just like Nick's stared up at her, and she could see John's fears and hopes in the blue depths. He was just like Nick, from his stubborn streak to the physical resemblance. If he agreed to see Nick would their lives change for the better, or for the worse? They'd both be taking a chance on a man who had a bad track record keeping promises.

"Let's give Nick a chance." Clea put her arm around John's shoulders, trying to instill a confidence in him she didn't feel herself. "I'll invite him to dinner and we'll see how it goes."

This time he didn't pull away.

Clea smiled, but instead of feeling relief, she felt as if she'd just taken a leap off a cliff without a parachute.

CHAPTER NINE

Clea checked on dinner again. Nervous habit. She paced the length of the kitchen, stealing a look at John. He sat on the couch, his dark hair neatly combed, wearing his Sunday best, tan slacks, blue shirt, and his "good" shoes. In fifteen minutes Nick would arrive. She pressed a hand to her stomach.

Tonight was a new beginning for them, especially for John. She prayed things would go smoothly. They had so little time left here in Port Bliss, only a handful of chances for Nick and John to build a foundation for a future. She wanted the threads in place before the move, giving John something solid to hold onto after they were gone.

She walked to the front window and looked over at Nick's apartment for the tenth time. Where there had been darkness minutes before, the light was on, then the light went out. A minute later, Nick appeared on the sidewalk and set out across the street.

He was coming. A dizzy relief flowed through her and she realized she'd been worried that he wouldn't show, that he'd break his promise to her and John.

A knock sounded on her door. She ran her hand over her hair to smooth it on her way to let Nick in. Once there, she paused. John had gotten off the couch and stood behind her.

"He's here," she said, praying she was doing the right thing for her son. "Are you ready? Are you okay?"

She knew how much he wanted to like Nick, knew how much he wanted Nick to like him, even if he claimed he didn't care about his father. Every little boy wanted his father's love and John was no different.

He nodded.

"All right," she said in a cheerful voice. She pulled the door open.

"Hi." Nick's glance lit briefly on Clea before bypassing her to settle on John.

John's face held no welcoming smile, but a wary glint shone in his eyes, letting Clea know he wasn't accepting Nick yet.

"Come in." She opened the door wider and Nick walk past her into the apartment. A new Nick. Gone were the jeans and the leather jacket. Instead, Nick wore black slacks and a black shirt with a collar. He'd dressed for the meeting with as much care as his son had.

"Hello, John." Nick dropped down to one knee in front of his son, and Clea noticed he held a present under one arm. "Thanks for inviting me to dinner. I've been looking forward to it all day."

"It was Mom's idea." John shrugged, his eyes going to her. He was proud, her son. He wasn't about to let Nick see how much this visit meant to him.

Nick stared at John, and Clea couldn't begin to imagine what he was feeling. Her own apprehension turned into pangs of sympathy for Nick and for John. This meeting was tough for both of them, yet a rush of completeness came over her, and for the first time she realized how much she had always wanted this meeting to take place, how much she wanted them to like each other. Nick completed John. John completed Nick. The realization struck Clea like a lightning bolt. She felt like their lives had been a puzzle, and the last piece had finally been fitted into place.

"I brought you something." Nick held the present out to John.

John looked at Clea, wanting her confirmation to take the gift.

"It's all right." She nodded and smiled. "Go ahead."

John hesitated, then took the gift from Nick. "Thank you," he said, the words stiff and formal.

Nick smiled. "You're welcome."

"Why don't you take the present over to the sofa and open it?" Clea suggested. To Nick she said, "Let me take your jacket."

John headed over to the sofa. Nick rose, but didn't take his eyes off his son. He shrugged out of his jacket. Clea took it from him and hung the coat up.

"Come on." She tugged on Nick's arm.

At her touch, his attention turned to her. "He's amazing. Is he okay?"

"Yes."

"How's your head?" His gestured to her bandage. "Are you feeling all right?"

"The headache comes and goes, but I'm okay. Follow me." Nick trailed her to the sofa and they sat down, one on each side of their son. John tore the wrapping off the box.

"It's a model car," Nick said, when the picture on the box was revealed.

"It's The Boss," she said with wonder, recognizing the Mustang.

"I thought we could build the model together," Nick said. "If you want to."

John studied the picture on the box. "I've seen your car. Mom told me how you and your brother fixed it up."

"She did?" Nick continued to stare at John.

"I've seen it parked at the curb in front of the tavern." John looked up at his father and Clea's heart caught. It was the first time John had made direct eye contact with Nick.

"I'd love to take you for a ride in The Boss any time you like." Nick exchanged a glance with her and she could see the gratitude in his eyes.

"Maybe. I like cars, too," John said, his voice a little less frosty now. "Mom says I get that from you."

"I hope so," Nick replied, his attention back on John.

The timer went off on the stove. "Excuse me," Clea said. "I need to see to dinner." She stood. Nick started to rise. "Don't get up. You two just get acquainted. I'll be right over here if you need me."

"Thanks."

The warmth in that one word curled Clea's toes. In a matter of minutes she had the grilled chicken on the table and they took their first meal together. Clea's nerves disappeared. Nick peppered John with questions, and the boy offered mostly one-word answers in return. John wouldn't give his heart easily, and Clea really didn't want him to, not until he was ready. She hadn't expected them to be instant friends. She just didn't want them to be enemies.

When the conversation lagged, she did her best to get it going again. When they finished eating Clea suggested that John show

Nick his room. Again, John gave a short, noncommittal reply, and the two of them left the table.

Clea cleaned the kitchen, listening to the sounds of her son with his father. Whether he knew it or not, Nick had given John a gift tonight, and it wasn't the model car, it was the gift of himself. He'd given John his true father.

* * *

Nick walked into his son's room, a room very different from the one he had shared with Billy. This room was clean, spacious, and cheerful. A quilted blue bedspread covered a bed shaped like a racecar. Colorful pictures lined the walls. A baseball bat coat rack held John's coats, and two hats.

Clea had done a fine job with John, providing for him, raising him. He envied the easy way she spoke to John. At times tonight, Nick's tongue had felt tied in knots. He couldn't remember the last time he'd felt this nervous, this afraid he would screw up. Parenting didn't come naturally for him, not like it did for Clea. Nick owed her more than he could ever repay. Seeing John's room made him want to take over, to be the one doing the providing for the people he loved. The room made him feel inadequate, like he'd failed as a father, and up to this point, he had. He had so much to make up to Clea and to John, and coming here tonight strengthened Nick's resolve to do just that.

"This is a nice room," Nick said. "You said you liked cars. Do you have a collection?"

"Yep." John dropped to his knees in front of a brown wooden chest. Opening the lid, he took out a large case. "Want to see it?"

"I'd love to." At last, common ground. Nick knew enough about cars to talk for hours. It was a safe subject they could share.

John crawled onto his bed, lugging the case with him. There were no chairs in the room.

"Okay if I sit on the bed?" Nick asked unsure of what to do.

"Sure." John unzipped the case. Row after row of small metal cars filled the case. The collection was impressive.

"You've got quite a collection." Nick removed a Mustang and held it out to John. "This one looks a little like The Boss."

"This one is better." John selected an exact replica of Nick's car. "See?"

"You're right. That's a '69 Boss. Even the colors are an exact match. You know your cars." Nick noticed a small, framed picture on the bedside table. He bent closer to get a better look. It was a photo of Clea and himself. Surprised, he picked it up. "Did your mom give you this?"

"Yes."

It was one of the pictures they'd had taken at the store when they were seventeen. Clea told him she hadn't kept those pictures. Nick smiled. Little liar. He vividly remembered the pictures being taken. They'd gone into the photo booth, wanting a memento of their day together. Five pictures for a buck. Four shots had been goofy, they'd been laughing and joking around, the fifth one, he'd been kissing Clea. He'd had that photo with him in prison. He knew every nuance of the picture by heart. It made him feel great to know that Clea had kept her photos, and even greater to know she'd shared the memory of the day they'd spent together with their son.

"It's the only picture Mom has of you, besides the big one." John squinted up at him. "Your hair was longer then."

"Yes, it was." He wondered what "big one" John talked about. Had Clea photographed him? He couldn't remember. She'd always had her camera with her in those days.

"It's still kinda long," John observed with a cock of his head.

"I guess I'm still a little wild." Nick grinned. "Does your mom have another picture of me?"

John nodded. "She doesn't like to look at it. It makes her sad." He leveled an accusing stare on Nick.

"I see." Clea had photographed him. The thought intrigued him, and he wanted to see the picture, but if he asked her would she show him?

"What was it like in jail?" John asked.

Nick's gut clenched, the question taking him by surprise. "Not very nice. I missed your mom, and I missed getting to know you."

"Were you scared there?" John dropped the car he held into the case, his attention focused on Nick now.

"Sometimes." He hadn't expected so many questions. It embarrassed him and he wished like hell that he could be the kind of father his son could be proud of. He glanced up to find Clea in the open doorway, her body leaning against the jam. She gave him a half smile of encouragement.

"What did you do all day?" John asked.

"Lots of things. I had a job working in a factory. I went to school. I read a lot. I studied a lot. Mostly I dreamed about the day I could leave." Nick made eye contact with John, trying to gauge the boy's reaction to his words, but John glanced away.

"I got hit in the nose," John said. He removed a '58 red Corvette from the case and ran the car over his bedspread.

"How come?" Nick asked, remembering he'd also been hit in the nose recently. Like father, like son? He hoped not in this case.

"A dumb kid told me you were out of prison. He called you a jailbird. I told him he was a liar and I hit him. Then he hit me in the nose."

Nick bit his tongue. He already knew this story, but hearing it from his son made the story so much worse. He wanted to swear. A protective anger surged through him. John had been hurt because of him. He didn't want John hurt. He was an innocent.

"I'm sorry, John." Never had he meant any words more. He didn't want his son to pay for his sins.

"It didn't hurt too much." John shrugged.

"It was my fault." Clea pushed away from the door and joined them on the bed, curling up near the headboard. She leaned back against the mound of pillows there. "I should have told John about you sooner."

This close together, Clea's seductive summer scent seeped through him, enticing him, making him remember her crazy watermelon-flavored lip-gloss. God, he'd loved to kiss that off her lips.

Clea sat at the head of the bed, Nick at the foot. Their eyes locked together over John's head. Is this what it felt like to be a family, to spend time together? An unfamiliar joy spread through him, and he knew he wanted more. He wanted Clea and John in his life every day, and not just for the next few weeks. He couldn't stop fighting for her and what they could have together.

The phone rang.

"Excuse me." Clea jumped from the bed.

He watched her walk to the door. Once in the next room, she said, "Hello." After that, she lowered her voice and he wondered if it were Boomer. The thought landed like a stone in his belly.

To get his attention off of Clea, Nick picked through John's case, examining the cars. There'd never been much money for toys when he'd been a kid, but at Christmases and on birthdays, the small cars made cheap gifts. He'd collected quite a few and he wondered if the cars were still in the apartment. His fingers closed around a custom orange T-Bird with a non-painted roof.

"I had one just like this," he said, holding the car out to John.

John snatched the car from Nick's fingers, put it in the case, and shut the lid.

Bewildered, Nick asked, "Did I say something wrong?"

John's lips clamped shut.

Something wasn't right here, but Nick wasn't sure what. John acted like he had something to hide.

"Why did you close the case, John?" Nick asked. "I liked looking at the cars."

"I can't tell you." John yanked the heavy case from the bed and it hit the floor with a thud. The lid popped open, the cars scattering across the carpet. John went down on his knees, frantically picking up the cars, shoving them back inside the case.

Nick joined him on the floor, wondering what he'd done.

"Don't," John said, when Nick tried to help. "You'll ruin everything."

"What do you mean?" Nick asked, more confused than ever.

John clamped his mouth shut.

Nick scanned the cars. Most were new, but some were old, probably picked up at garage sales. Then one caught his eye, a VW Beach Bomb. He'd had a car like this one, too. "Where did you get this?" Nick asked a terrible feeling of dread coursing through him.

"Don't know." John reached for the car, a wild look in his eyes.

Nick turned the car over, fearing what he knew would be there. Written in a child's hand the name *Nick L.* stared at him. For a moment he couldn't speak, couldn't think. How could John be in possession of his cars? Had his mother sold the collection? If so, why was John acting so strange?

"This belonged to me, didn't it?" Nick asked with a calm he didn't feel. "I'm glad you have it, but I'm wondering how you got it."

"I can't tell." John pursed his lips, as if trying to seal them.

Nick's stomach rebelled. What kind of secret was John keeping? Was Maude involved? "Why not?"

John ignored the question, picking up the last of the cars.

"I'll keep your secret," Nick said. "Did someone give you these cars?"

John nodded, but didn't look at him.

"Was it my mother? Did you know her?"

"It was a secret," John said, his voice a whisper. He lifted his eyes to Nick's.

Nick's fingers tightened around the car. Maude knew his son. How was it possible? Billy told him that Clea and John had no contact with the Lombards. Had Maude seen John on the side? Bile rose in the back of Nick's throat, threatening to choke him. He didn't want Maude anywhere near his son. What had she told him, said to him? Nick needed to know everything; he wanted to know nothing. Above all, he didn't want to scare John with the force of his anger. He had to be cautious, calm, and in control.

"Maude gave you my cars?" Nick asked.

"She gave me presents," John admitted. "She asked me if I knew who she was, and I said yes. Mom told me Mrs. Lombard was my grandma, only she wasn't like my other grandma. We didn't go over to her house or anything."

"I see."

"She said I looked just like you. One time she cried when she gave me a car."

She'd been drunk, no doubt. Nick glanced away, unable to squash the rush of emotion rolling through him. What the hell had Maude been thinking? Had she had a touch of remorse in her old age? Did she regret her neglect of her own children? Was she trying to right her wrongs by getting to know her grandson, by bribing him with gifts? It was sick and twisted. Or was it? How could he figure out John's relationship with Maude, when he couldn't even decide how he felt about her himself?

"Mrs. Lombard told me she was going to help you get out of jail," John said. "She promised me you'd be home soon. After that, I heard Robert tell Mom you were free. I knew Mrs. Lombard had kept her promise."

"You knew I was out of prison before your mother told you?" Nick asked.

John nodded.

Shit. Had John expected him sooner? And Maude, what a liar. She hadn't gotten him out of prison. She'd made false promises to win her grandson's gratitude and love. Most likely without Clea's knowledge.

"Does your mother know about your relationship with my mother?" Nick asked.

Before John could answer, Clea came into the room.

"Time for bed," she said. "You have school tomorrow."

Nick dropped the car into the case, a thousand questions burning inside him. John closed the lid, and Nick had his answer. Clea didn't know about the cars.

"I should be going," Nick said, rising. He needed to think, to sort out this information and he needed Clea's help to do it.

John put the case away in the trunk.

"Go and get ready for bed," Clea said to John. "Brush your teeth, then I'll tuck you in."

"Okay." John grabbed his pajamas and went into the bathroom, closing the door.

"Has he exhausted you yet?" Clea asked when they were back in the living room.

"No," he replied honestly. "He's great."

"He is, isn't he?"

"You're a wonderful mother, Clea." He didn't miss the light that leapt into her eyes.

"I've tried, Nick," she said with a smile. "It hasn't been easy."

"No, I'm sure it hasn't."

A silence stretched between them, a silence filled with regret. The bathroom door opened, and John reappeared. "Can I read for fifteen minutes?" He wore Spiderman pajamas, the shirt dotted with water from his teeth brushing. A rush of love seized Nick, and he longed for the right to tuck his son in, to kiss him goodnight.

"Sure, honey. Then it's lights out. Say good night to Nick."

"Good night," John said while still looking at Clea.

"Good night, John." Nick wished the boy would look at him, give him some sign that things had gone well tonight, but John turned and went into his room, closing the door.

"Have a seat." Clea sat on the sofa, curling her legs under her.

"For a minute." Nick sat beside her, feeling some relief that the hard part of the evening was over. He'd met John, and they'd survived.

Clea appeared to be considering him. "How do you think it went?" she asked.

Nick shrugged. "I'm not sure. I never expected to be frightened of my own son, but I am. I'm scared shitless. He's so important. What if I screw this up?"

"Give it some time," she said softly. "He'll come around. He wants to love you, Nick. I'm certain of that."

"Did you know that John and Maude were friends?" Nick asked.

Clea sat up a little straighter. "What do you mean?"

"I mean they talked. She gave him presents. I'm not sure, but I think he has my entire car collection."

"What!" Clea started to get up, but Nick caught her hand, pulling her gently back down on the sofa.

"Don't tell him you know," Nick said. "I'm not sure what was going on, but I think Maude wanted a connection with him."

"But she never said anything," Clea said, lines of worry on her forehead. "She lived across the street and never acknowledged us in any way."

"Obviously, you are wrong about that." Nick gave Clea a wry smile. "She told John she would get me out of prison, and according to John, she kept that promise." Nick could hardly keep the bitterness from his words. "He believed her. He liked her."

"Well," Clea said on a sigh. "It's not such a bad thing. She was his grandmother."

"You're not upset?" Nick said with a shake of his head.

"No, not really." Clea smiled. "I don't know why Maude wasn't a part of our lives. She just wasn't. I was gone for a long time, and when I came back, we just didn't speak. If she'd asked, I probably would have let her become a part of John's life, but the truth is, she didn't show any interest. It stung that she ignored us."

"It was probably for the best." He couldn't imagine his mother being a grandma. She didn't have any maternal instincts, any warmth, any softness for children. Or did she? If he stretched his memory he could remember a time or two when she'd enjoyed being with them, but those days had faded fast from his memory once her drinking had gotten out of control. Inside, had she really cared about them? Maude had shared something with John she'd never shared with her own children. It confused Nick, and made him wonder about the changes Maude had gone through the last ten years. Had she been different? Or had she been the same self-centered, addicted woman from his past?

"I think John expected me sooner," Nick said. "He overheard Boomer say I was out of prison. You said John's been angry and upset. Seems to me he's got a lot of reasons to be mad."

"Oh, no," Clea said. "Poor John."

"Mom, I'm ready," John called from the bedroom.

Clea rose. "That's my cue to tuck him in."

Nick stood. "I'll go. Thank you for dinner and for the chance."

"You're welcome."

"Where do we go from here, Clea?" he asked. "I don't know what comes next."

"Neither do I. I've never had to share custody before. This is all new to me."

"What happens when you leave?" Nick allowed himself one last long look at her face, the smooth line of her jaw, the creamy column of her neck. His body tightened. He didn't want to lose her.

"I don't know, Nick." Worry filled her eyes. "You could visit."

"Not for five years." He glanced away, trying to get his bitterness under control.

"What do you mean?" she asked.

"Mom," John called.

"Just a minute," Clea called back, her tone a little impatient. "I'm saying good-bye to Nick. I'll be right there." In a whisper, she said, "Why can't you visit New York?"

Nick wanted to drown in her eyes, in the pools of green. Unable to help himself, he reached out, winding a lock of her hair around his fingers. The strands felt like silk against his rough skin. "I can't leave the state for five years, Princess. I may be free, but I'm still a prisoner. If I apply to change the conditions of my parole, it has to be for a good reason. I have to have a job waiting, and a place to live."

"Oh, Nick."

Her tender tone touched him. Suddenly, he didn't want to think about the mess his life was in. Clea stepped toward him and laid her hand against his chest in a gesture of comfort, but Nick felt anything but comforted. Lips the color of ripe watermelon parted and he wondered if she'd taste like the fruit. Heat rose between them. Clea dropped her hand, taking a step back.

"John's upset about the move to New York," Clea said, and Nick knew she was trying to put some distance between them. "He doesn't want me to take him away. Maybe he was waiting for you. Now, you're here. If you can't visit, well, I'm not sure how I'm going to handle that."

Nick didn't know how to reply. He couldn't ask her to stay. She had everything to look forward to in New York. Hopelessness filled him.

"I've tried to reassure John that you will be in his life no matter where we live." She spoke quietly. "Is that right?"

"Yes." He wanted to reach for her, hold her, beg her not to go, but instead he said, "I don't want you to go, but I understand why you have to."

"Do you?"

"I understand dreams, Clea. Believe me, I wish our dreams were the same."

She smiled sadly. Was she remembering that at one time their dreams had been the same? They'd been happy that last summer, full of plans and hope for the future.

"Thanks for coming tonight," she said.

"Thanks for asking me."

Her lips parted, and he moved a little closer to her. It would be easy to kiss her. But as much as he wanted to kiss her, he wanted to earn her respect more. If he tried to kiss her he might scare her away, and he didn't want to do that. "I should go."

"All right."

Did he detect a little regret in her words? He hoped so. "Thanks for dinner. It's the best meal I've eaten in years." She'd given him a taste of what it felt like to be a family, and no matter what happened between them, he'd never forget tonight.

"You're welcome." She followed him to the door.

He took his jacket from the coat rack.

She smiled and those wet lips of hers beckoned to him.

He swore he could smell the watermelon. His insides seized up with lust. His hand closed over the doorknob. "Good night."

"Good night, Nick."

Outside, he took in a giant gulp of air. Cold air surrounded him, and he prayed for it to cool him down, because no one set him on fire like Clea Rose.

CHAPTER TEN

Clea stared at her reflection in the mirror inside Elizabeth Spencer's shop. The tiara on her head caught the overhead lights, sparkling in a thousand different directions. The crown was beautiful, she couldn't deny it, but it wasn't her. She'd never wanted to be a princess. She brought her fingers up to touch the white bandage on her forehead, thinking of Nick, of the tender care he'd given her. The irony of the situation struck her. She was trying on her bridal headpiece. She should be thinking of her groom, not her ex-boyfriend.

"I can't wait until that bandage comes off," Vivian said, her reflection joining Clea's in the mirror. "It's unsightly. The tiara, however, is stunning."

"It's beautiful, but I think I'm going to have to pass."

"Why?" Her mother reached up to touch the glittering jewels. "It's you. You can wear your hair pulled back in an elegant chignon. You have such a natural beauty."

"That's the key word, *natural*," Clea said. "The tiara doesn't feel natural to me. Why can't I just weave some flowers into my hair? Maybe some baby's breath. Something simple."

"That's common, Clea." Vivian's mouth turned down into a frown. "This is a society wedding. Flowers just aren't done, honey."

"It's my wedding." The minute Clea said the words something freed inside of her. "I want to do things my way."

"What's that supposed to mean?" Vivian asked. "What are you saying, Clea?"

"I'm saying this isn't me. Not the gown, not the gloves, and certainly not the tiara. Look at me, Mom. I like jeans. I like leather."

"Are you saying you want to be married in black leather?" her mother asked, her voice rising.

"No. I just want you to listen to me. Why can't you just listen to me for once?" Years of frustration spurred Clea on. She had so many things she wanted to say, to do. She'd kept silent for too long.

"Really, Clea!" Vivian glanced around the shop and Clea knew she was checking to see who might be overhearing her crazy daughter this time.

With a sigh, Clea pulled the tiara from her head. "I don't want to argue with you."

"Why must you always make everything difficult?" her mother whispered. "I know what's best."

"For you, maybe, but not for me." As long as she could remember Vivian had been giving her orders, making choices for her.

"Well for heaven's sake, what *do* you want?"

Her first impulse was to say, *I want Nick*. The realization froze Clea's vocal cords and made her heart skip a beat. Where had that thought come from?

"Well?" Vivian said, clearly losing patience. "You had plenty to say a few minutes ago. I asked you a question. What do you want?"

"I don't know." She pushed her fingers through her hair, smoothing it back into order.

"You don't know?" Vivian took the tiara from Clea's hand. "Well, then let me tell you what you want. You want to marry Robert Bloomfield. You want a stable, mature role model for your son. If there are any wayward thoughts running around in your head that involve Nick Lombard, I suggest you push them from your mind, Clea Rose. I won't stand by and let you throw your life away on a murderer, a man with no future. It just isn't done. Not in our family."

Clea met her mother's reflection in the mirror. Eyes as hard as chips of gray granite stared at her and Clea realized for the first time just how much her mother hated Nick.

"What did Nick ever do to you?" she asked, keeping her voice low. "Other than being born poor, of course."

"He stole you from me. He impregnated my little girl and drove her from my life." Vivian spun away, going to the window. "I lost years with you because of that man."

Clea followed, standing beside Vivian. Her mother gripped the edge of the windowsill.

"Nick didn't drive me away, Mom."

Her mother sucked in a breath. "Don't say it, Clea. Don't you dare." She kept her eyes on the street outside.

"All right, but I want you to understand. I was in love with Nick. Yes, he frightened me at first. Yes, he broke my heart. But when we were together he loved me unconditionally. You can't imagine how strange that was for me. He loved me for who I am. Nick told me once that he didn't want to change a thing about me. *Not a single thing.* Do you know what that meant to me? I had trouble understanding that at first, because nothing I did or said was ever good enough for you and dad."

Vivian turned to face her, her hand on her heart. "I love you, Clea." Her eyebrows drew together, as if she were in pain. "I only wanted what was best for you. I couldn't let you throw your life away. All I ever wanted was for you to marry well, for people to see that the Roses were as good as Bloomfields."

"But that's silly. Why do we care what people think?" Her mother's face contorted with pain. Clea reached for her, realizing that Vivian wasn't just being dramatic. Her color was off. Sweat beaded her brow. "Mom, what's wrong?"

Vivian crumpled, her weight sagging against Clea.

"Elizabeth," Clea shouted. She caught her mother in her arms, going down to the floor with her. "Call 911. Mom. Oh, God. Mom, can you hear me?" Clea's heart raced. She couldn't lose her mother, not now, like this.

"I love you, Clea," Vivian said, her voice weak.

"I love you too, Mom."

A slight smiled touched her mother's lips as her eyes fluttered closed.

* * *

Nick heard about Vivian Rose's attack by mid-afternoon. He'd have heard about it sooner, but he'd been in Bradley with Billy at the bank, filling out the loan papers, and meeting with the web designer he'd hired.

He'd come home in a great mood, ready to celebrate his first steps toward owning his own business, then old man Mullin had told him about Vivian. He couldn't help but feel her attack had something to do with him.

When several hours had passed and Clea still hadn't come home, he'd really started to worry. He'd called the hospital to check on Vivian's condition, but they wouldn't release any information to non-family members. He didn't dare go to the hospital; not only wouldn't Boomer want him there, Vivian wouldn't want him there either.

Frustrated and worried, he finally went to bed around ten o'clock. He hadn't been in bed more than a couple of minutes when he heard the slam of a car door. He got up and went to the window.

Boomer's BMW was parked at the curb. He watched as Boomer pulled John from the car and carried him upstairs, Clea following behind. John must have gone to sleep on the drive home. What would it feel like to carry his son in his arms? Would he be heavy and warm with sleep? The thought tortured him.

The lights went on in Clea's apartment. The lamp went on in John's room. Nick pictured Boomer putting his son to bed and the image turned his stomach. More than anything he wanted to go over to Clea's. He wanted to be the one to carry John to his room, put him to bed. He wanted to be the one to comfort Clea, to make her a cup of tea, to rub her back or hold her hand. Instead, he resisted the urge to go across the street. A confrontation with Boomer wouldn't do any of them any good.

The lamp in John's room went out. A few minutes later he heard the unmistakable sound of Boomer's car starting. Before the car pulled away from the curb Nick picked up the phone and punched in Clea's number.

"Hello," she said on the second ring.

"It's me."

"Oh, Nick." He could hear the dismay in her tone, and he prayed she hadn't gotten bad news.

"I heard about your mother. I've been going crazy waiting for you to get home. How is she?"

"They're keeping her overnight for observation. They aren't sure what's wrong yet. The doctor thinks it was a panic attack."

"That doesn't sound too bad," he said, relieved at the diagnosis.

"She collapsed in my arms this afternoon," Clea told him. "I've never been so frightened in my life. I thought she was having a heart attack. It was…"

She broke off, and Nick waited. "Are you all right?"

"Yes," she said, the word shaky. "I'm just tired. It's been a long day."

"Is John asleep?" he asked.

"Yes, he went out like a light on the way home."

"I'm coming over."

"No," she said unconvincingly. "Don't."

"Why not?"

"I'm afraid if I see you I'll crumble."

He heard the catch in her voice and made his decision. "You can crumble with me, Princess. That's what I'm here for. Unlock the door. I'm on my way."

* * *

Clea replaced the receiver. She had been doing fine until she'd heard Nick's voice on the other end of the line, so fine she'd sent Robert home without a second thought. Nick's offer of comfort was different. Just hearing his voice on the phone broke her will to resist him. She wanted him to come over, to make her feel better, even if it was just for a few minutes.

She unlatched the door and went onto the dark landing to meet him. She didn't flip on the light, and darkness surrounded her. He came up the enclosed stairwell, two steps at a time, and then she was in his arms.

Nick's leather jacket hung open and Clea buried her face against his T-shirt, the scent of fabric softener comforting. Her arms went around him, her hands sliding up the soft, worn jacket. This jacket felt like home to her, real. Nick's spicy scent wrapped around her and she drew strength from his body, a body she used to know so well.

"Are you okay?" he whispered against her hair.

"No." But she knew she would be, now that he was here.

One of his hands found its way into her hair. He pressed a kiss to the top of her head and an answering warmth flowed through her body. His lips brushed against her temple, the touch feather light. Clea tipped her head back. A low moan left her lips as his mouth grazed her cheek.

"This is wrong," she whispered, her heart not in her words. "I'm engaged."

"Break the engagement." His lips touched hers.

Clea opened her mouth to him, kissing him like a starved woman. Her hands fanned against his back. She held him to her, molded her body to his. She didn't want to think about today, or about her future. For now, she wanted to feel something other than fear and anxiety and emptiness.

His hands touched the bare skin under her sweater. With a feather-light touch his fingers moved up her back, to her bra. A single snap and he freed the lacy undergarment.

Clea's eyes closed as his hands found her breasts, his fingers teasing her nipples. A spiral of desire beat low in her belly, building into a raw lust she'd never experienced with anyone but Nick. He made her forget everything but him, the way he tasted, the way his skin felt under her fingers. She tugged his shirt from his jeans and slipped her hands underneath. Warm skin met her fingers, unforgettable skin. He pulled her sweater up. She slid his shirt up and leaned full into him, skin to skin. Her nipples hardened against his chest and this time he moaned.

"Mom?"

They broke apart, yanking their shirts down.

"Mom, where are you?" John called from inside the apartment.

"I'm out here, honey," Clea said, finding her voice.

John poked his head out the door. "It's dark. The light's not on." A click followed, and they were flooded with yellow light. John's eyes narrowed on Nick, his stare accusing as if he'd guessed what they'd been up to.

"Hi, John," Nick said, and Clea could hear the huskiness born from passion in his voice.

"Nick stopped by to see how Grandma is," she said, hoping John would buy the story.

"Why are you outside?" John asked suspiciously. "It's cold. You don't have your coat on."

He pointed at Clea's sweater, and she prayed he couldn't tell her bra was unhooked. She hadn't noticed the cold; in fact, her skin blazed. "Nick just got here." She turned to Nick and with false brightness in her voice, she said, "Would you like to come in?"

"Maybe for a few minutes."

Nick's hair was mussed, his lips stained by her lip-gloss. Could John see that? For that matter, how did she look? She closed the door behind Nick. "Excuse me for a minute."

Clea escaped to the bathroom to look in the mirror. The first thing she did was re-hook her bra. Her hair stuck up all over. The skin of her jaw held a red tint from being rubbed by Nick's whiskers. Her lips were puffy. She looked well-kissed. Would John notice?

Bending down, she splashed cold water on her face, dried off, and then quickly ran a brush through her hair. She couldn't allow herself to think about the wanton way she'd thrown herself at Nick. What must he think of her? More importantly, what did she think of herself? How could she marry Robert when she'd kissed Nick like that? Maybe she should call off the wedding. Thoughts of her mother, in the hospital, brought her to her senses. Stress over the wedding had put Vivian in the hospital. Clea couldn't call things off. It was too late.

Clea closed her eyes, willing away the turmoil in her mind and body. Why did everything have to be so confusing?

She returned to the living room, no closer to finding the answers. Nick and John sat at opposite ends of the sofa. Nick talked, but John wasn't responding. He sat with his arms folded across his chest, a closed look on his face. Her stomach turned. The door had been open a crack. How much had he seen before he'd called out to her?

"What are you two talking about?" Clea took a seat on the sofa close to John. She leaned forward to better see John, but he didn't reply.

"I was asking John about your mother," Nick said. "But he didn't have a whole lot of information."

"He didn't?" Clea raised one brow. "Well, my mother is spending the night in the hospital so she can have some additional tests done, just as a precaution. Dr. Martin thinks she's suffering from anxiety. She's been working too hard on the wedding. We all need to do what we can to help out. Grandma looked good when we left the hospital, didn't she, John?"

"I guess," came his noncommittal reply.

Clea glanced over at Nick. He shrugged.

"I should get you back to bed," she said to John.

"Okay," Nick said, the word holding a hint of resignation. He stood. "I should be going anyway. I just wanted to check on the two of you and make sure you were all right."

Clea came to her feet, relieved Nick was leaving. "Thank you for coming by. I'll see you out." She glanced at John, but he wouldn't meet her eyes.

Nick stepped outside. "Do you think he saw us?"

"Maybe."

"I'm sorry."

"Not half as sorry as I am. Good night, Nick." She shut the door before he could reply. Heaven help her, she liked kissing Nick too much. So much she'd forgotten that her son could discover them at any moment. And as much as that thought upset her, it upset her even more to think she could be so wrapped up in Nick and what she felt for him that she didn't even think once about the man she was going to marry.

What kind of woman did that make her?

CHAPTER ELEVEN

Nick couldn't sleep. Thoughts of kissing Clea filled his head. She'd felt wonderful in his arms, all soft skin and warm lips. He would have taken her there, in the stairwell, given half a chance. He'd been consumed by her and what she made him feel.

He groaned as his body roared to life once again. He could still smell her perfume. Could still taste the sweetness of her mouth, still feel the burn of her body against his.

Damn.

Throwing the covers back, he got out of bed and walked to the window. He pulled the curtain aside. The lights were out at Clea's. Was she in bed? Was she thinking about him, too? Or was she upset at John's near discovery of the two of them together? Had the boy seen them? Nick hoped not. He already had no idea how to get through to John; he sure didn't need another strike against him.

A movement across the street caught Nick's eye, drawing his line of vision to a white shape in the darkness. It took him a moment to focus. John. His son ran across the street and straight over to Nick's car.

Like a little thief, he crept around to the sidewalk side and knelt by the tire.

Nick didn't wait to see any more. He grabbed his jeans from the chair and tugged them on. He reached the sidewalk in record time. John had moved from the front tire to the rear of the car. His back to Nick, he stabbed the tire. The little devil! He was slashing the tires.

Nick came up behind him. "So, you're the one vandalizing my car."

John sprang up. "Ouch!" The knife fell to the sidewalk with a clatter.

He turned to run, but Nick caught a handful of his pajamas. "Not so fast. You and I need to talk."

"Let me go." John wiggled.

"If I let you go I'm going to follow you back across the street and you and I will have a little talk with your mother." John stopped wiggling. "Or you and I can go upstairs to my place and we can talk about this man to man."

"I don't want to talk to you," John said, his voice holding a slight wobble. "Let me go."

"All right." Nick kept his hand on John and started across the street. "Let's see what your mom has to say."

"No, wait."

"Wait?" Nick halted mid-stride.

"I don't want to talk to Mom. She'll kill me."

"You got that right." He turned back toward his place. "Come on. It's time we laid our cards on the table."

Nick let go of John, unsure if the boy would follow him. He'd climbed a few stairs before he heard the sound of John's boots behind him. Inside, Nick sighed with relief. If his son hadn't followed him, he had no idea what he would have done.

Once in the apartment, Nick shut the door and turned to look at John. His dark hair seemed even darker next to his pale skin. Eyes a deep ocean blue focused on him, wide with fright. Sticky blood covered his fingers.

"You cut yourself," Nick said calmly, but his heart raced. He'd had no idea John had been injured, and felt totally unprepared for the rush of concern filling him now. "Let me see the damage."

"I'll be all right." John sniffed.

"Don't get it on your pajamas. You'll never be able to explain the blood to your mother."

John held his hand away from his body.

"Come on." Nick walked into the bathroom and pulled out the small medicine kit that had been there as long as he could remember. "Let's see."

John held out his left hand. "The knife slipped."

A clean cut ran from his knuckle to the base of his thumb. The cut wasn't deep, more of a scratch really, but it was bleeding. Nick turned on the tap. When the water warmed, he put John's thumb under the spray.

"Ow," John said, but he didn't jerk his hand away.

"Is the water too hot?"

"No. It stings."

Nick added some liquid soap to the water and bit back a smile when John said, "Ow," again.

"It's clean." Nick shut the water off. He passed John a dry towel. While the boy dried off, Nick removed a couple of bandages from the old kit. The cut looked worse than it was, and two bandages covered the slice. When he finished he asked, "Does it hurt?"

John sniffed again, his eyes wary. "It's okay."

"What will you tell your mother when she asks about the cut?"

John cocked his head to the side. "What will you tell her?"

"I don't know. It depends." Nick watched John's face for a reaction.

"On what?" He touched the bandages, as if testing their strength.

"On what kind of agreement we reach."

John narrowed his eyes. "Agreement?"

"You'll need to find a way to pay for the damage you've done to my car. Aside from the tire, you've got the scratches to cover."

"I never said I scratched the car." John's lower lip jutted out in defiance.

For a split second Nick saw himself as a child, angry, scared, alone. God, he didn't want those agonizing emotions for his son. How could he break the cycle? Would being there for John be enough to keep the boy out of trouble? If his own father had been around would it have been enough for him to change the course of his life?

"You're in a lot of trouble, John," Nick told him. "This is how it starts, small crimes. Then, before you know it you're doing something even worse, maybe stealing, or lying to your mother. I'll be damned if I'll let you wind up like I did, wasting ten years of my life in prison. Because of my mistakes, I missed ten years of your life. You missed ten years of mine."

John hung his head. "What do I have to do?"

"You can work for me after school and on weekends."

"Work?" His head snapped up. "Doing what?"

"There's plenty to do around here, and I'll check with Mr. Mullin. If it's all right with him I'd like you to help repair The Boss."

"But I don't know how to do any of that." John's lips clamped together.

"I can teach you." Nick waited for his son's reaction, afraid to hope that John would agree.

"And you won't tell Mom about the stuff I've done?" John asked.

"I won't tell her," Nick promised, "but I think you should."

He shook his head. "No way. She'll kill me."

Nick grinned. "I don't think so. She loves you. This isn't the kind of secret you should keep from her. Think about it. Telling her is the right thing to do, and I'd like the confession to come from you, not me."

"I saw you kiss her," John blurted out, the combative tone back.

Nick sucked in his breath. No wonder John had acted out tonight. He wanted to tell John that everything would be all right, that nothing in his life would change, but in truth everything had changed already. Nick was back to stay, whether John liked it or not.

"I was comforting your mom." Nick chose his words carefully. "She had a bad day. Ask her about the kiss. Give her a chance to explain things to you."

"Yeah, right." John's eyes accused Nick of being a liar.

Nick wanted to pull his son into his arms and soothe the hurt away. John had seen something tonight he didn't understand, hell; Nick had been doing the kissing and he didn't understand how things were between Clea and himself. He hoped John wouldn't tell Robert, at least not until he had a chance to tell Clea that John had seen them together. "Let's get you back home before your mom notices you're gone."

John followed Nick to the door and together they left the apartment. He took his son across the street. When they reached the stairs, John motioned for Nick to follow him around back. Like a little monkey, John climbed up the fire escape to his bedroom window. At the window, he paused and looked at Nick hard before crawling inside. Was he wondering if Nick would keep his secret?

Well, let him wonder. The boy deserved to squirm a little after what he'd done to The Boss.

Nick started back across the deserted street. When he reached his car, he stopped to pick up the knife John had dropped on the sidewalk.

He'd gotten his first taste of parenting tonight. He had no idea if he'd handled things the right way or not. Time would tell, but until then he'd found a way to spend time with his son. The trick would be explaining John's sudden desire to be with him to Clea. She was a smart lady and would likely see through any deception. He hoped John would tell her the truth, so he wouldn't have to.

* * *

Clea felt like she was sliding on ice.

Every aspect of her life ran out of control and she had no idea how to make things right without upsetting everyone she loved.

John was barely speaking to her again. Her behavior with Nick last night had left her confused. Did he want to be with his dad or not? Was John as torn between Robert and Nick as she was? She could understand his emotions. They echoed her own. She didn't know what she wanted anymore. Thankfully, she hadn't seen Nick today, and didn't expect to. The snow had started again, signaling a busy day for him. The one bright spot in the day had been her mother's release from the hospital. She'd brought Vivian home a couple of hours ago.

"Are you comfortable, Mom?" Clea asked.

It hadn't been easy to talk her mother into staying with her, and it had been even harder to convince Vivian to stay in Clea's room. Her mother didn't want to impose by making Clea sleep on the couch, but Clea had insisted. Vivian would have rather had Clea up to her place, but Clea had to work and John had school. Her replacement at The Coffee House started today, and Clea needed to train her. It was easier for all of them if Vivian stayed in town for a day or two. That way Clea could be close by at all times.

"I'm fine." Vivian held her appointment book on her lap. She looked small and frail in Clea's bed, a warm quilt covering her legs. "Did you take care of everything I had planned for today?"

"Yes." Hoping to take some of the stress away from her mother, Clea had taken over the wedding plans. She had confirmed with the caterer and the florist while fighting the rising panic and doubt inside her. "Everything's in order."

"And the cake?" Vivian glanced up at her.

"Will be there. I changed one thing. Instead of the flowers being made of frosting, we are using real ones, the petals dipped in sugar."

"I don't know, Clea." Vivian frowned.

"They are edible flowers, Mom. They will look beautiful. Trust me." Clea smiled, but her heart wasn't in the action.

"All right." Vivian did look better today. The gray pallor had left her face and her cheeks bloomed with rosy color. Her eyes held their usual sparkle, not the dull, lifeless look they'd had in the hospital. Dr. Martin had released Vivian with the order to keep her stress level down. Clea hoped that was possible.

"Don't worry," Clea said. "Just relax. Dr. Martin told you to forget about the wedding plans. I have everything under control."

"How can I help but worry?" Vivian jotted something down in her book. "Oh! Did you let Elizabeth know which tiara and gloves you chose?"

"Yes. I chose the ones you liked."

"Excellent," Vivian said, with a bob of her head.

A knock sounded at the door.

"That's Robert." Clea left her mother to let Robert in. She pulled the door open.

"Hello, darling." Robert kissed her on the mouth. "Umm, you taste great."

"Hi." Clea smiled, happy to see him. She needed him. Robert always managed to steady her, to boost her confidence.

"Did your mother make it home okay?"

"Yes, I did," Vivian called from the bedroom. "I'm in here if you'd care to say hello."

Robert exchanged a smile with Clea before heading to the bedroom. Clea followed.

"How're you feeling, Vivian?" Robert placed a kiss on her mother's cheek.

"Better, now that you're here." Vivian's mouth turned up at the corners. "Clea assures me that all of my plans for the wedding are being taken care of, but I'll feel so much better if you keep an eye on her."

"Of course I will." He winked at Clea.

The phone rang.

"Excuse me," Clea said. She went into the kitchen to grab the phone. "Hello."

"Is this Ms. Rose?" a voice asked.

"Yes, it is," Clea replied.

"This is Marilyn King. I'm the principal at Bradley Elementary."

Clea's grip tightened on the phone. "What's wrong? Is it John?"

"I'm afraid John's been in a fight. He's all right, but this is the second time this week he's been involved in an altercation with another student. We consider fighting a serious offense at Bradley Elementary. I'm afraid I'm recommending that John be suspended from school for one day. Are you available to meet with me this afternoon? There are some things I'd like to discuss with you."

"Of course." A million questions rioted in Clea's head. "I'm on my way."

"Fine. I'll see you soon."

"Yes." The line went dead.

"John's in trouble?" Robert asked. He'd come out of the bedroom mid-conversation.

"He's been in a fight," Clea said, her wits returning. "I have to go. Will you stay with my mother?"

"Of course I will, but I hate to say I told you so, Clea. Like father, like son. John hasn't been himself since Nick's come back to town. Maybe now you'll listen to me and take steps to keep Nick from John's life."

An anger unlike anything she'd felt before threatened to strangle Clea. She refused to dignify Robert's comments with a response. Going to the bedroom door, she said, "I'm going to pick up John, Mother. I'm sure Robert with fill you in."

Before Vivian could ask any questions, Clea grabbed her purse and headed out the door.

At that moment, she didn't care about anyone or anything other than her son - a little boy who didn't understand why his world had turned upside down.

* * *

Nick opened the door to The Coffee House and stepped inside. The aroma of fresh brewed coffee filled his senses. He walked over to the bar counter and sat down. Mitzi chatted with a customer at the far end. When she spied him, she called, "Hey, Nick. I'll be right there. Just let me finish up here."

"Take your time," Nick said. He'd come here, hoping to find Clea and John. When John hadn't shown at the garage that afternoon, he'd had no idea what to do, how to enforce the consequences he'd given the boy. He'd been so sure John would honor his part of their bargain. Nick felt like a fool for believing John would show. His parenting skills were worse than he thought. He needed an expert parent's advice. He needed Clea's advice. He hoped Mitzi would know where she was.

While he waited for Mitzi, Nick looked around the shop. The counter top was an emerald green marble, beautiful and classy. The barstools at the counter were done in a matching shade of green leather. All around the shop were framed photos. Clea's photos? Nick scanned the pictures. Yes, her business cards were placed in the corners of each frame.

There were traditional shots of the canal, of the blue herons, of Port Bliss. Nick slid off the barstool and cruised the room, taking his time at each piece. There were photos where the people in the café looked like ghosts, their images transparent and haunting. There was a photo of an old woman's face, but the image had been split, cut in half, so part of her face was seen in profile. Clea had then painted part of the photo, using bright colors. The picture was unusual and creative, like Clea. Some of the photos looked modern to him, abstract, with the pieces of the photo cut apart and rearranged. Clea had talent. There was no doubt in his mind. He could see why she'd won the internship.

Nick made his way back to the counter, and climbed onto the barstool. More photos lined the wall above the coffee bar. A photo of John at the beach caught his eye. John played in the sand, his head bent.

"It's great, isn't it?" Mitzi said, joining him. She glanced up at the photo.

"Is it for sale?" Nick wanted that picture, no matter the price.

"Yes." Mitzi took the framed picture from the wall and passed it to him. "She never sells photos of John, but you can't see his face in this one. He's anonymous."

"Not to me," Nick said. "I'll take it." He turned the picture over. The tag read thirty-five dollars. He pulled his wallet from his back pocket.

"All right," Mitzi said, a knowing smile on her face. "Can I get you a drink?"

"I'll have a cup of coffee, black."

"What? No flavor of the day? It's mocha hazelnut today." She smiled.

Nick smiled back. "Just regular coffee."

Mitzi poured him a steaming cup. "How come you haven't been by before now? I expected you sooner."

"I didn't want to bother Clea at work."

Mitzi took a large chocolate chip cookie from a jar on the counter and handed it to him. "Here, on the house."

"Thanks." Nick chuckled. "Do you still have your sweet tooth, Mitzi?" Nick remembered all the runs they'd made for chocolate for Mitzi when they'd been in high school.

"I feed it every chance I get." She helped herself to a cookie. "Are you looking for Clea, or did you drop by to see me?"

"I'm looking for her. Any idea if she's home? I didn't want to knock on the door with Boomer's car parked out front."

"I think she's there. She brought her mother home from the hospital today. Vivian's upstairs, too."

Nick suppressed a groan. Boomer and Vivian. Is that why John hadn't shown today? Maybe he couldn't get away.

"Do you want me to call her? I can ask her to come down to the shop." Mitzi's eyebrows rose slightly as if to encourage him to say yes.

"Would you? It's important. I need to talk to Clea and I'd rather not upset everybody else in the process."

Mitzi smiled as she reached for the phone. She punched in Clea's number. "Robert? It's Mitzi. Is Clea there?"

She paused while Robert spoke. The conspiratorial smile slipped from her face. "Is he all right?" she asked.

Nick set his cookie down. His heart sped up. Something was wrong.

"Well, tell her to call me when she has a chance," Mitzi said. "Bye for now." She hung up.

"What's wrong?" Nick asked, afraid to hear the answer.

"John was in a fight at school. Clea had to go into Bradley to meet with the principal."

"Is John all right?" Nick asked.

"Robert didn't know. Apparently Clea didn't say much before she left."

"Damn it." Nick glanced down at the photo of John on the beach. The kid was drowning and Nick had no idea how to save him. "Ring me up, Mitzi."

"Okay, Nick."

Nick paid his tab.

"Do you want me to tell Clea you came by?" Mitzi asked her eyes filled with worry.

"No." Nick stood, replacing his wallet in his pocket. He picked up the picture. "I'll call her myself. Thanks for the coffee, the cookie, and the conversation."

"Anytime, Nick," Mitzi said, her tone warm. "Take care."

Nick walked from The Coffee House. He had no idea what to do next. Most likely Clea was already on her way back to town. He couldn't do anything until she got home, and even then it wouldn't be wise to contact her tonight, not with her mother and Robert at her place.

He was tired of being an outsider when it came to his own kid. He wanted to be there with Clea, to help her and John through this. He wanted Clea and John to know they could count on him.

But how did he make them believe in him the way he believed in them? The question drove Nick crazy.

CHAPTER TWELVE

Clea turned the television off and stood up, stretching. She'd hoped watching a show would help put her to sleep, but she felt more keyed up than ever. Seeing John at school in the principal's office had thrown all her own doubts into overdrive. She no longer knew what was best for John. The little boy had so much anger. One good thing had come from his fight today. They'd had the opportunity to speak with the school counselor, Mrs. Wilson.

Mrs. Wilson had suggested John might like to attend her anger management group. John had balked at first, but had finally agreed with some pressure from the principal. Mrs. Wilson had also suggested private family counseling for all of them, including Nick and Robert, pointing out that all of their lives had been changed by Nick's return. Everyone needed help adjusting, including and especially, Nick.

Clea sighed, walking over to the window. Nick's place was dark. She wanted to call him, share the details of today with him, details she'd withheld from Robert. She didn't want to ask herself why she hadn't told Robert about the family counseling. She'd intended to, but he'd had an "I told you so" look in his eyes when she'd returned from the school that had stopped her cold.

Clea turned away from the window. She wouldn't find any answers staring out into the darkness. Somewhere she had to find the strength to make the right choices for John. After today she wasn't sure about anything, not about leaving town, or about marrying Robert. It terrified her to think that she might make the wrong choice, the choice that would send John even farther away from her.

And she couldn't even begin to think about where Nick fit into her life.

Clea walked down the hall to do one last check on her mother and John before bedding down on the couch for the night. She peeked into her room. The sound of Vivian's deep, even breathing reassured her all was right with her mother. A smile on her lips, Clea closed the door and moved on to John's room. She opened the door and went to the bed. He looked lumpy and small under the blankets. She pulled the quilt away from his head, wanting to see his sweet face, but found herself looking at a pillow. Clea jerked the blankets back. The bed was empty.

Frantic, she searched the room. His coat was gone. His boots were missing.

"Mother!" she cried, running down the hall. "Mother."

"What is it?" Vivian asked, her voice groggy with sleep.

"John's missing. I need your help."

* * *

Nick's eyes opened in the darkness.

For a minute he thought he was back in his cell, but the dead quiet brought him back to reality with a snap. In prison the combination of concrete and steel caused a roar that never died. The constant clamor: the voices, the moaning, the screaming, bounced around, circling into a never-ending echo. Over time he'd learned to live with the noise. Once home, he'd had to learn all over again how to live with the silence.

But something had woken him. What?

A loud banging sounded at the door. "Nick, are you in there?"

Clea. The urgency in her voice shook the last remains of sleep from his mind and he bolted to the door, yanking it open.

"What's wrong?" he asked. Lines of worry creased her forehead. A frantic light danced in her eyes.

"Is John here?" she asked, pushing past him.

"John? Why would he be here?" Confused, he followed her. She glanced around the room, and then made a beeline for his bedroom.

"John," she called.

"He's not here." Realization dawned in Nick's sleep-fogged brain. A sick feeling seized his insides. "Is he missing?"

She ignored him, and went to Maude's room, trying the knob.

"No!" Nick cried, but she went in anyway. The last thing he wanted to do was to follow her in there.

When he reached her, she stood in the middle of chaos. She'd flipped the light on, exposing the room to their eyes.

Dirty, yellowed sheets twisted on the bed. Clothes littered the floor. The dresser drawers hung open, their contents spilling out. An ashtray on the bedside table overflowed with smoked butts. A box, filled with cheap costume jewelry sat on top of the dresser, the necklaces, bracelets, and rings a jumbled mass of rhinestones and plastic and metal.

On the bedside table sat several prescription bottles of medicine. And next to them, the ever-present bottle of vodka.

Nick's stomach lurched, and for the first time he felt the true impact of Maude's death.

He turned away. A kaleidoscope of memories flashed before him; Maude combing his hair, giving him money for school pictures, tucking him in, then later her drinking, her smoking, her male friends. Before the drinking, she'd been a good mother which made her downfall so hard to take. He'd loved her, he remembered now, and a long suppressed grief rose within him. Disgust or hate hadn't kept him out of this room since his return, grief and remorse had.

"Nick," Clea said softly.

"I don't want to be in here."

She walked out of the room and he followed, closing the door.

He went directly to the window and threw it open, needing to get the smell of his mother's perfume out of his system.

"I'm sorry," Clea said behind him, laying a gentle hand against his back. "I didn't think. I'm so worried about John. I thought he might be here. I've looked everywhere else."

He whirled around, pushing his mother from his mind. He could grieve later. Right now he had to focus on his son. "How long has he been missing?"

"I'm not sure. The last time I checked on him was around nine, nearly three hours ago." She headed for the door. "If he's not here, I need to go. I have to find him. It's cold outside."

"Wait a minute," he caught up to her. Had John sneaked out to do further damage to his car? The kid knew how to get in and out of the apartment without Clea finding out. If she discovered he was gone, and he knew it, he could be hiding. "Don't panic. I'm sure he's all right."

"He's not all right," she cried, her eyes wild. "He hasn't been all right for a long time."

Her words cut deep, leaving a scar he didn't think would ever heal.

Clea's fingers closed around his arm. "I didn't mean that the way it sounded. He was in a fight today, at school. He's been suspended. He's upset."

Had the combination of being caught in the act of vandalizing Nick's car and the suspension from school pushed John into running away?

"I'll help you find him." Nick sat down and pulled on his boots. "Come on." He shrugged into his waterproof jacket. "Let's find our son."

Together they hit the street. A glance at his car told him John hadn't been there.

"I don't know where he'd go," Clea said, a note of hysteria in her voice.

"Did you try his friend? What's his name? Toby?"

"Yes. Mother's at my place. She's called all his friends. I called Robert. He's not with him. That's when I thought maybe he'd gone to you."

He gave her a half smile. "Believe me, I wish he'd come to me, but I'm the last person he'd want to see. You don't think he'd try and get to Robert's on foot do you?"

"I don't know. Robert was with us all evening. John didn't ask him to stay. I don't think he'd try and go to him now."

"Is there anywhere else he'd go? A favorite place?"

Clea's forehead wrinkled. "I don't know. Wait. The fort. John and Toby have a fort. It's in the woods. I don't let John go there without an adult."

"You don't mean the fort up the hill behind the tavern? Billy and I used to go there when Mom brought her boyfriends home. The fort's an hour's walk from here."

"Yes," she said, her tone hopeful. "I'm sure it's the same one."

"That path is dangerous, even in the daylight." He couldn't allow himself to think of the danger John could be in, alone in the dark, the path slick with wet leaves and leftover snow.

"Oh, Nick," Clea said. "What if he's gone there?"

"I'm going to get Sheriff Kincade," Nick said. "If John's outside alone, I want as many people looking for him as possible. Go to your place and get flashlights, a blanket, maybe something warm for him to drink. We're going to find him. And then we'll figure out a way to make this right together."

* * *

Clea couldn't remember the last time she'd been this cold. Icy rain had started falling about twenty minutes ago, the drops stinging her cheeks. Her eyeballs even felt frozen. Wet ferns slapped at her legs, the moisture soaking her pants. Under her boots the frozen pine needles and leaves crunched, the sound mixing with their labored breathing.

Nick walked ahead of her. Their flashlights provided meager light this deep into the woods, and this far away from any town lights. She knew John had his flashlight, she'd checked his bedside table where he kept it, and found the flashlight missing. The knowledge gave her some relief, but the path was as bad as Nick had claimed, narrow, slippery, with a gully on the left side that scared Clea to death.

"John," she called for the hundredth time. "John, where are you?" She could hear the desperation in her words, feel it deep in the pit of her stomach.

"John," Nick shouted into the darkness. "John, can you hear me?"

She thanked God for Nick. He'd been her rock tonight. He'd taken charge with ease, helping to organize the search.

"How much farther is the fort?" Clea asked. They'd been walking for close to an hour. Her feet and hands had gone numb with cold. Just thinking about John, shivering alone made her move at a faster pace.

"It's got to be close. It didn't seem this far away when we were kids," Nick said.

He stopped. Clea almost ran into him.

"What?" She tried to peer around him to see what had caught his attention.

He bent down and picked something up, showing it to her.

John's flashlight.

Clea glanced wildly around. "John," she called. "Honey, where are you?"

Nick walked to the edge of the gully, shining his flashlight into the dark pit. She did the same.

"John are you here?" Nick asked. The beams of light played over the brush. "Look."

Clea followed the glow of his flashlight. At the edge of the path the pine needles had scattered, pieces of fern were ripped, as if John might have clutched at them, trying to save himself.

A strangled sob left Clea's lips. "Oh, my God. He's fallen. Nick, do something."

"John," Nick called again. "Can you hear me?"

"John," Clea echoed.

"Quiet," Nick said. "I need to listen."

Clea waited, the frantic beating of her own heart roaring in her ears. A horrifying silence filled the air. Then she heard him.

"Mom." His voice was far away, but strong.

"John," she returned. "I'm here, honey. Nick's coming down. Keep talking so he can find you."

"I'm coming, John." Nick pointed to the gully. "Shine your light down there so I can see. I need you to guide me to him. The brush is thick. Keep him talking so I can hear him." He reached for her hand, squeezing her fingers. "I'm going to get him."

Clea nodded. "I know. Now, go."

Nick left her, making his way down the side of the ravine. Twigs snapped, brush whispered. Clea held the light with shaking fingers, helping Nick find his way.

"Your dad's coming." She knew Nick would bring John to safety. She had no doubt of that. "Are you hurt, John?"

"My arm hurts. I can't get out," John said from below. "My boot is stuck in the mud."

"Keep talking, John," Nick said, shining his flashlight toward the sound of John's voice.

Clea kept her light on Nick until he disappeared, the thick foliage swallowing him up.

"Can you see him?" she yelled.

"John, talk to me," Nick said.

"I'm here. I can see your light," John said, excitement in his voice.

A dizzy relief filled Clea. She waited, her light on the last place she'd seen Nick.

"I see him," Nick called.

"Is he all right?" A rush of love for John brought tears to her eyes. Her baby was with his father.

"He looks okay," Nick replied. "I'm going to bring him up."

"All right."

She could hear Nick talking to John, but couldn't make out the conversation. The minutes ticked by with agonizing slowness. Below she could hear the rustle of the brush being disturbed, then she saw them. Nick had John on his back, piggyback style, with John's face visible over Nick's left shoulder. Clea used her flashlight to help light the way. When they were close enough, she held her hand out to Nick, helping to pull them to the path.

"Oh, John." She reached for her son, wanting to take him from Nick, needing to see for herself that he was all right.

"Careful," Nick warned. "He's bruised."

She helped Nick set John on the ground. Once there, Clea ran the beam of her flashlight all over him, checking him for possible fractures, but found none. A tear in his pant leg revealed a wicked scratch on his knee, but not much else. Relieved, she threw her arms around him, hugging him, kissing his tear-streaked face. "I was so scared. Don't you ever do that to me again, Johnathan Rose!"

"How far is the fort from here?" Nick asked John.

"Not far. I was almost there when I tripped." John's mouth puckered, as if he might cry. "I dropped my flashlight, and I couldn't see."

"It's all right," Clea said, her arm around him. "We're here with you." She glanced at Nick. "Should we try and take him back? It's cold and the rain is freezing."

John's teeth chattered.

"The fort is close, let's go there first and get him warmed up," Nick said. "You two stay here. I'll go ahead and take a look."

"All right, but hurry," Clea said. "John is frozen." Nick disappeared down the path. She had a thermos of hot chocolate in her backpack. She removed it, and poured her son a cup. "Here, drink this."

John nodded, taking the cup from her.

While he drank, she covered him with a blanket. Next she tried to call her mom, but the phone didn't pick up the signal this deep in the woods.

"Are you feeling better?" she asked.

"Um hum." He took another sip of the cocoa.

"Why would you come here, in the night?" She wanted to understand what had driven him from home. "What you did was so dangerous."

Before he could reply, Nick returned. "The fort is just ahead. It's dry inside. Let's go."

Clea took the cup from John. Nick bent to help the boy up. She waited for John to protest, to tell Nick to leave him alone, but John didn't speak. The three of them walked to the fort in silence.

She'd envisioned a small, crude lean-to, but the fort looked solid, with four walls and a roof. The inside had to be about ten by ten.

"There's a door." Nick nodded his head toward the entrance.

Clea held the door open so Nick could help John inside. Nick turned, holding his hand out to help her. "Come on."

Clea took his hand and let Nick pull her in. Once inside, she checked on John. He sat on a mattress in the far corner. She shined her flashlight around the interior, surprised to find the fort filled with so many things. A rug covered the floor. There was a small table. In the center sat a red plastic lantern. Nick had already spied the lantern. He turned the switch and filmy white light filled the room.

"Where did all this stuff come from?" Clea asked.

"Toby's mom," John said. "She lets us leave it here."

"I see." She glanced at Nick. "The boys come here with Toby's dad. It's their camping place."

"I used to come here with Billy," Nick told John. Clea could hear the nostalgia in his words.

"I know," John admitted.

"How do you know?" Clea asked, curious.

"Dad's name is carved on the wall."

She'd never heard John call Nick "Dad" before. Had Nick noticed? Yes. Nick only had eyes for John.

Clea went to the wall. Behind her, she heard Nick follow. *Nick Lombard.* She touched the carved letters. Below Nick's name, John had carved his. *John Rose.* What did it mean to John to play in the same fort his father had played in? Had he felt a connection to his father here while Nick had been in prison? Is that why John loved the fort so much?

Nick reached out, his own fingers touching the carved letters. "It's still here."

"Yes." She went to join John on the mattress. He appeared scared and small, huddled close to the wall. Clea put her arm around him. "How's your knee?"

"It's okay."

Clea examined the tear in his jeans. The wound no longer bled. Clea pulled the first aid kit from her backpack. Instead of removing his pants, she tore the fabric covering his knee open wider to give her access to the cut.

"Does your shoulder hurt?"

"A little," John said.

"Are you cold?" she asked, as she cleaned the injury. Inside the fort the rain didn't hit them, and the wind couldn't touch them, but the air was freezing.

"Yes."

Nick took his jacket off and handed it to Clea. "Cover him with this. It will keep him warm."

"No, Nick, you'll freeze," Clea protested.

"I've got a sweatshirt on," Nick said. "I want my son to be warm."

She could see how important it was to Nick to take care of John. She took the coat from him and removed the blanket from John's shoulders. She could feel the heat from Nick's body still in the coat as she slipped John into the jacket. "Is that better?" she asked.

"Um hum." John slumped back against the wall, tired and dirty and cold.

She glanced at Nick. "How long are we going to stay here? Everyone is probably frantic by now."

"Let's wait and see if the rain lets up," Nick said. "Did you try to call?"

"Yes, but my phone doesn't work."

Nick rubbed his hands together. He had to be freezing.

She tossed Nick the blanket. "Come over here and sit beside us. We can all share this blanket to keep warm."

Nick came and sat on the other side of John. They held their son between them, warming him with their bodies. Nick hadn't said much since finding John. Clea wondered what he was thinking.

"Do you want to tell me why you ran away?" Clea asked.

"No." John stared down at his lap.

"We're going to have to talk about it, honey. Something is

bothering you. It's not good to hold it inside."

John's head jerked up. "I saw you kiss him."

"Who?" Clea asked, her stomach flipping over.

"He saw us kissing," Nick said.

"Oh, no," Clea moaned, understanding.

"I told him you were upset," Nick said. "That I was comforting you."

Clea met Nick's eyes over the top of John's head. "You two have talked recently?"

"Last night," Nick said.

"When? At the apartment when I was in the bathroom?"

John exchanged a look with Nick, but kept his mouth clamped shut. When he didn't respond, she said, "Someone tell me what's going on."

A heavy silence filled the small fort.

"John," Clea prompted.

"He's ruining everything!" John cried. He tried to scoot away from them, but there wasn't anywhere to go in the small fort.

"How is Nick ruining everything?" Clea asked, trying to understand.

"He kissed you. He likes you. What about Robert?"

"Oh, John." Clea wanted to cry for her son. How could she explain her feelings for Nick to him when she didn't understand them herself? "Is that why you ran away, because you saw me kissing Nick? Is that why you got into the fight at school today?"

"No."

"Then why, honey?" she said, desperate for him to talk to her.

"You'll be mad at me," John said, his voice tiny and small.

"I promise I'll try and understand." Clea touched his arm in a gesture of comfort.

"I did some things to The Boss." He glanced at Nick, who nodded his head in encouragement.

"What kinds of things?" Clea asked, not sure she wanted to hear any more.

"I scratched the paint. And I shot at the windows with my BB gun."

Nick groaned. "You shot at the windows?"

"Yes. And…" John said.

"Dear Lord, there's more?" Clea asked, horrified.

John nodded. "I slashed one of the tires. I wanted to cut them all, but Nick caught me last night."

A pent up sigh left Clea's lips. "I see." She glanced at Nick. Compassion and something else - pride, shined in his eyes as he looked at John. "Then what happened?"

"John and I had a talk," Nick said. "We came to an understanding."

"You did?"

"I told him he could work off the damage. I wanted him to tell you, and he did." Nick made eye contact with John. "I'm proud of you. You did the right thing telling her."

"Yeah, right," John said, but he didn't sound convinced.

"He was supposed to start at the garage after school today, but he didn't show. I know why now," Nick said. "Is that why you ran tonight, John? Were you afraid I was going to tell your mother when you didn't show up after school?"

"I don't care what you do," John said.

Clea closed her eyes, willing herself to be calm. Would working with Nick be good for John? It would force them to spend time together. Was Nick onto something with this idea, or would working for Nick anger John more?

Clea chose to side with Nick. John was out of control. She needed Nick's support and help with him. "I'm with Nick on this one, John," she said. "I'll expect you to work with him after school until you work off the damages. Your father loves you. And he loves that car. What you did must have really hurt him. It's time for you to start thinking about Nick's feelings. He's tried to make things right with you. You need to give him a chance."

"Mom," he moaned in protest.

"I want to say one more thing," Clea said, cutting him off. "I understand why you vandalized the car, but I'm still bothered. There are other ways to express emotions. I wish you had come to me to talk about your feelings for Nick. I know things aren't the way you want them, but that doesn't excuse your behavior."

John didn't reply.

"Vandalism isn't the answer. Running away isn't the answer." Clea hugged him to her, his body stiff. "We need to work through all the changes together. You, me, Nick, and Robert."

"Why? You're just going to take me away anyway," John cried. "Robert will be my dad, not Nick."

"That's not true," Clea said. "Nick will always be your dad.

Robert will be your step-father. You'll have two dads."

"It doesn't matter where you live, John," Nick said. "I intend to be part of your life wherever you go."

John leveled a stare on Nick. John wanted to believe Nick; she could see the naked hope in his eyes. How could she make him understand that Nick would be there for him? And she did finally believe Nick would be there. He loved John. She'd seen that love a thousand different times as they'd searched for their son tonight. Nick wasn't going to give up on John. Nick had always gone after what he wanted, and to her knowledge he'd succeeded. He'd won her once. She had no doubt he'd win his son.

Nick went to the door and peered out. "The rain stopped. Do you want to start back?"

"Yes." She rubbed John's back. "Can you make it?"

"I'll carry him," Nick said.

"I can walk." John sat up straighter, the look of defiance back on his face.

"All right." Nick took Clea's hand, helping her to her feet.

"Thank you," she said. At the door, she turned and mouthed for Nick's ears alone, "For everything."

CHAPTER THIRTEEN

Nick glanced at the clock. Three fifty-five. His stomach sank. He'd heard John's school bus drive by twenty minutes ago. He'd hoped that after their talk at the fort last night John would show today. He never realized he'd be this disappointed when he didn't.

Taking a rag from his back pocket, Nick wiped his hands. His shift working for Mullin had ended at three-thirty. He usually looked forward to this time of day, the time when he could work on his own projects. He'd contracted the work on a '53 Chevy Bel Air this morning. The car had arrived earlier and sat waiting for him in the bay. The owner wanted a full restoration from the mohair that lined the roof to the chrome bumpers. A classic car like this one would look damn good in his portfolio. When he finished, he hoped Clea would photograph it for him. He was eager to get started, yet one dark cloud hung over his satisfaction - John.

John had barely looked at him last night when he'd left him at Clea's. All his glances had gone to Robert, who'd met them at the door. Robert's excitement at seeing John faded quickly when he'd noticed Nick. Reaching for John, Robert had snatched the boy from Nick's arms. He'd wanted to retaliate, to take John back from Robert, but somehow he'd managed to hold his anger in check.

Clea's mother had been there, too. Vivian had hurled

accusations at him like sharp stones, telling Nick that this was all his fault. Not wanting to hear any more, he'd stormed out. To his disappointment, Clea hadn't come after him. He had no idea what she was thinking. Did she blame him, too?

"Hi."

Nick turned at the sound of her voice. She stood in the doorway. Her hair looked windblown, sexy. No matter how many times he saw her, Clea's beauty always caught him off guard, and it took him a minute to recover his senses. "Hi." John stood beside her. "Hi, John."

John didn't reply.

"John's come to work off his debt," Clea said, her tone up-beat. "I'm sorry we're a little late. I wanted to make sure John had a snack first."

"It's okay." Nick gestured for them to move inside. "Come in."

Clea walked directly to the '53. "That's an old car."

"I know it's not much to look at now, but when I finish the restoration, it'll be a real beauty."

She stepped closer to take a better look.

"I've got two more lined up after this," Nick told her. "The web page is working. In fact, I could use another bay, but Mullin will only rent me this one." Nick smiled. It felt great to know his business plan was working. It felt even better to share the news with Clea.

"I knew you'd succeed," Clea said, and he could hear the sincerity in her voice, see it in her eyes. She ran her fingers over the roof of the Bel Air. "I like the colors."

"Root beer and cream," Nick said, telling her the names of the colors.

She smiled. "I like that. It sounds delicious." Clea touched John's arm. "What do you think of the car?"

"It's okay." John kept his head down, his focus on his tennis shoes.

Wanting to get John's attention, Nick pulled the door open. "Get in. See how much room it has? They don't make cars like this anymore."

"No," Clea agreed. "Go ahead, John."

A frown on his face, John got in the car. "It smells funny."

"Like dust and mold." Nick grinned. "It's old. It's supposed to smell that way."

"Well, I'll leave you two alone to get to work," Clea said, backing away. "I'll be back at six to pick him up."

"I can bring him by," Nick offered.

A skeptical look crossed her face. "I suppose that would be all right."

"Okay." Nick gave her a wave. "Go on, we'll be fine." He said the words with a confidence he didn't feel. He had no idea if John would respond to him, or if he could handle his own son. Squashing his doubts, Nick said, "John and I have plenty of work to do."

"Bye, John," Clea said.

"Bye." John popped the glove box open and looked inside with interest.

Nick leaned into the car, dipping his head to avoid hitting the frame. "Ready to get started?"

"I don't know what to do," John said, the words petulant. He touched a chrome tissue box, which was mounted under the dash. "What's this?"

"It holds a box of tissue." Nick reached inside the car, tapping the box. "Look, it swings out so you can take a tissue."

"Cool." John glanced at him. Nick could see the wonder in his eyes, that familiar excitement he too felt when looking at an old car. John had the same car bug Nick did. Cars were a common interest for them, one Nick intended to exploit if it helped him get closer to his son.

Nick smiled. John glanced away. Nick ignored his frustration, refusing to give in to it. It wasn't going to be easy to win his son, but he would never give up trying.

* * *

"I can't believe you just took your son over to that filthy garage and left him there," Vivian said.

Clea stood at the kitchen counter chopping carrots for a salad. The blade bit into the carrots with more force than necessary. If she didn't rein in her annoyance over her mother's questions, she'd cut her fingers off.

"John is fine, Mom. He needs to be responsible for his actions. He's lucky Nick is giving him the chance to pay for the damages instead of calling the police."

"The police!" Vivian's voice rose. "It's Nick's fault John did those things to his silly car. If Nick had stayed away, John would be the happy little boy he's always been."

Clea sighed. She scooped the carrots into the bowl. "I don't think John's been happy for a long time, Mom. The counselor seemed to think his anger started a long time ago, but Nick's return caused John's emotions to snowball. We need to talk about Nick with John. Nick can't be a dirty little secret, Mom. He's John's father."

"Oh for God's sake." Vivian pressed her fingers to her temples. "He's a sperm donor. He hasn't shown any interest in John up to this point."

"You're wrong." Clea came around the counter and took a seat on the sofa, next to Vivian. "Nick wrote me. He sent me money every month he was in prison, but I sent the money back. I didn't open the letters. I denied John his father. Do you see that? I'm to blame for this mess, not Nick."

"That's not true, Clea. You were trying to protect your son," Vivian said.

"No, Mom." Clea's hand went to her heart. "I was trying to protect myself. Nick hurt me. I loved him so much. Maybe I still do." It felt liberating to say the words out loud, voicing thoughts she'd left trapped inside her for ten years.

Vivian blanched. "You don't know what you're saying. Nick will never amount to anything. People like us don't fall in love with people like him."

"People like us?" Clea repeated, wishing she could make Vivian understand. "There aren't any rules when it comes to loving someone."

"I won't listen to this." Vivian stood, the blanket covering her legs dropped to the floor.

"Sit down, Mom." She didn't want her mother to get upset, to add to the stress she already felt, but Clea couldn't pretend anymore. Something was happening between her and Nick. Something she needed to explore before marrying Robert, or taking John away.

A knock sounded at the door. Clea glanced at her watch. Five forty-five. Nick and John were early. "That's probably John. Can we let this drop for now? I don't want him upset."

Vivian sat down, her mouth pinched.

Clea went to the door and pulled it open. Robert and his parents stood on the landing, none of them smiling. A feeling foreboding came over her.

"Hi," she said, unable to keep the surprise from her tone. She'd expected Robert, but not Ellen and James Bloomfield.

"Hello, darling." Robert kissed her cheek.

"Come in." Clea pulled the door open wide. "Hello, Senator. Ellen."

"Good evening, Clea," Ellen Bloomfield said, as she passed in a cloud of expensive perfume. Impeccably dressed in a navy pants suit, a brightly patterned scarf at her throat, Ellen exuded cool sophistication. In fact, Ellen was always a little on the cool side, even when it came to her family. She never showed too much emotion. Clea hadn't realized until now how much that bothered her.

"Clea, nice to see you," Senator Bloomfield greeted, giving Clea's hand a warm squeeze. "I hope we're not interrupting."

"No, of course not. I was just making dinner. I'm always glad to see you. Is there a reason for this visit?"

"I called them here," Vivian said from her perch on the sofa. "We need to discuss things with you, Clea. You haven't been thinking clearly since that man returned to town."

"That man?" Clea repeated, feeling like a horse being led to slaughter. "You mean Nick? John's father."

A slight hiss escaped from Ellen. The senator cleared his throat.

"Darling, we don't mean to gang up on you," Robert said, his tone placating. "We're worried about you, and especially about John. You just don't seem to be making the best decisions now."

"Nick Lombard is a criminal," Ellen said. She fingered a large ruby ring on her right hand. "Do you really want him around John?"

"Why don't you just say it?" Clea said. "Nick killed Danny. That's what this is about, isn't it? What happened to Danny has nothing to do with John. Nick loves John. If you saw them together, you'd know it. Last night Nick showed me how much he loves his son. He kept me from falling apart, when I knew he wanted to fall apart, too. I can't exclude Nick from my life because he makes all of you uncomfortable."

"You're not in your right mind." Vivian pressed her lips together before shooting a pleading look at Robert.

"Excuse me?" Clea said, her temper shooting up. She didn't like being ganged up on. Every instinct she had told her to protect Nick and John. "Are you implying I'm crazy for letting Nick into my life?"

"Well, you haven't been yourself." Robert came to her and took her hand. "I know things will be better once we leave town, but don't you think it's best if we nip things in the bud right now? Aren't things confusing enough for John? Why add Nick to the mix?"

"It's too late," Clea cried. "Nick is back to stay. No one is asking any of you to like it. In fact, and I'm sorry for saying so," she looked at the Bloomfields, "it's not really any of your business."

Ellen gasped. Senator Bloomfield turned away, walking over to the window. Thankfully, he'd kept silent so far.

"Clea Rose!" her mother said. "Apologize at once."

"No," the senator said. "She's right. It isn't any of our business."

"It most certainly is," Vivian replied.

Clea pulled her hand from Robert's. "I know you don't like Nick, Mom, and I'm sorry, but I have to think of John. He needs Nick in his life, even after we go to New York. He will need his father forever. Can any of you accept that?"

The door burst open, and John ran through, Nick behind him.

John skidded to a stop when he saw the group. "Hey, why is everyone here?" he asked, surprised. A streak of grease marred his right cheek. His shirt was untucked, his hair wild.

Clea saw the worry in Nick's eyes. "They stopped by to see if you were all right," Clea lied. "Everyone was worried about you last night." It was the reason they should have come by, and it saddened her that they hadn't asked about John once.

"I'm okay," he said, sounding skeptical.

"Why are they together?" Robert asked, his focus on Nick. "What's happening here?"

"John is working with Nick at the garage," Clea explained.

"What!" Robert strode to Nick. "I told you to stay away from Clea and John."

"Robert," Senator Bloomfield warned. "Stay out of it."

"I won't stay out of it," Robert cried, his voice rising. "He killed my brother. I don't want him around Clea or John."

"That's not really your choice, Boomer," Nick said quietly.

"The hell it isn't!" Robert took a menacing step toward Nick.

"Stop it." Clea stepped between the two men, halting Robert's progress. She cast a worried glance at John. His eyes were wide with horror.

"Shut up," John shouted, covering his ears with his hands. "Stop it. Stop yelling at my dad. I hate all of you." John ran from the room, slamming his bedroom door.

"Son of a bitch," Nick muttered with a shake of his head. "I'm sorry, Princess." He walked from the apartment.

Clea started after him, but Robert grabbed her arm.

"Where do you think you're going?" he asked. "Don't you dare run after him."

Clea yanked her arm free. She'd never felt more confused, yet she couldn't let Nick go, not like this. Stepping outside, she called, "Nick, wait."

He'd already started down the stairs, but he stopped and waited for her to catch up.

"I didn't know they'd be here," she said. "Robert had no right to speak to you that way. I'm so sorry." The hard look was back in Nick's eyes. The urge to reach out and touch him almost overpowered her, but she fought the feeling, not wanting to make things worse. Changing the subject, she asked, "How did it go with John?"

"Fine."

He said the word through clenched teeth. Clea could feel his anger, and she couldn't blame him for being mad. He'd been attacked in her apartment.

"John's a quick study," he said. "I think he liked working on the car, even though he'd never admit it to me."

"I'm glad it went well." She nodded toward the apartment. "Don't let them get to you."

"I won't if you won't." He gave her a wry smile.

Clea smiled back. Her mind screamed danger. It felt so good to be on the same side with him.

Robert came out onto the landing. "Clea, we're waiting for you."

"I'm coming." She turned back to Nick. "John will be there tomorrow."

"I know he will." Nick continued on down the stairs. Clea watched until he left her view.

"Are you coming?" Robert called, his tone impatient.

"In a minute."

Robert stormed back into the apartment. The door banged

shut.

Clea stared out at the street below. The cold numbed her cheeks, but she needed a minute to clear her head before facing Port Bliss' elite again.

She didn't like to be bossed around. For too many years she'd done things the way her mother wanted her to. She never realized it before, but she'd become a puppet, with everyone pulling her strings. Was she strong enough to break away from her mother, from the social pressure Vivian and the Bloomfields put on her?

So many important decisions weighed her down. If she made the wrong choices, John would be hurt. Before Nick's return everything had seemed so clear, but the future had grown muddy and messy. Inside her apartment a roomful of people waited to convince her to cut Nick from her life. Could she really choose between her mother and Nick?

She thought of John, alone in his room, angry, upset. Her son needed her to be strong. Sighing, Clea climbed the stairs to her apartment.

* * *

Nick had just crawled into bed when he heard a knock on the door. Sitting up, he ran a hand through his hair. The clock glowed eleven-thirty. He had no idea who would come over this late at night. Billy hit the sheets early. Clea would be home in bed. That left Robert.

Nick yanked on his pants. The last thing he wanted was another confrontation with Boomer Bloomfield. By the time he reached the door, he'd worked up enough anger to snap off Boomer's head. He unlatched the door and yanked it open.

"Yeah," he snarled. Instead of Boomer he found himself looking into Clea's startled eyes. "Clea," he said, softening his tone. "Is everything all right? Is it John?"

"No, he's fine." Rain dotted her hat, and soaked her coat. "I couldn't sleep. May I come in?"

"Sure." He pulled the door wider and she walked past him into the apartment.

She looked around the small room, at the pitiful kitchen, the tired furniture, the faded photographs. He remembered bringing her here when they were teenagers. The place had been a mess. The apartment had reeked of alcohol and cigarettes. He'd wanted to die at the pity he'd seen in her eyes, and he prayed he wouldn't see that same pity now.

"You've done a lot with the place." She removed her hat and gloves, setting them on the kitchen table. "Is that my photo?" She walked over to the wall where he'd hung the picture of John he'd purchased at The Coffee House. "Did you buy this?"

"Yes. I hope you don't mind."

"Of course I don't. I'll refund your money. I don't want you to pay for pictures of John." She faced him. "I have others I can give you, if you want them."

Her words touched him. "I'd like that. Let me take your coat."

She unbuttoned the coat and he helped her shrug out of it. The wool felt wet and heavy, as if she'd walked in the rain a long time. She rubbed her hands together, blowing on them to warm her fingers.

Nick caught her cold hands in his warm ones. "You're ice cold."

"I've been walking."

He rubbed her hands, trying to restore her circulation, wondering what was wrong, fearing the news wouldn't be good. Had Boomer, Vivian, and the Bloomfields managed to convince Clea to cut him from her life? His gut tightened.

"I needed to think tonight, Nick," she said.

"About what?" He didn't see pity in her eyes as he'd feared. Instead he saw questions.

"I'm going to be married." She gave him a slight smile. "I should be happy, but instead I'm all mixed up. Things are a mess. My son is angry with everyone. My mother and Robert are putting all kinds of pressure on me. The only thing going halfway right is my career, and even that isn't perfect, because I don't think John wants to leave Port Bliss. I keep asking myself why?"

"Why what?" he asked, not sure he understood anything she'd just said.

"Why I'm not happy." All signs of a smile slipped from her lips and she turned her face up to his, the honesty in her eyes touching him in a way her hands could not.

"The answer to that is simple." Nick pulled her toward him until a thin slice of air separated their bodies. "You're marrying the wrong man."

"Am I, Nick?" she asked, the words a whisper. "I don't think I am. Robert is the right man in many ways."

"Not in the ways that count."

She moved away from him and went to the window. "We can't base a relationship on sex. When the sex is over, what would we have left?" Confusion filled her eyes.

"Are you saying what I feel for you is just sex?" Nick asked, his heart hammering in his chest. "Because if that's what you think, you're dead wrong."

"I think what I feel for you is lust," she said. "Pure lust. It's what I felt for you ten years ago - an uncontrollable passion that clouded my good judgment. I don't want that to happen again. It took me years to recover, to refocus on what was truly important to me, John and my photography."

"Are you saying the time you spent with me was a mistake?" His throat closed around the words.

"I don't know." She rammed her fingers through her hair. "Maybe. Yes."

Her words cut deep, extinguishing the spark of hope he'd felt for their future. "Why are you here, Clea?" He'd never been good enough for her. After ten years, nothing had changed. She was still listening to her family, still doing what they wanted her to do. She was still a coward.

"I just wanted to be clear about everything before I marry Robert. I want you to understand why we can never have a relationship. We're too different."

"We're not so different. We're more alike than you think."

She shook her head, but she couldn't find the words to dispute him.

"You're afraid," Nick said. "You're afraid of what you feel for me, just like you were afraid ten years ago. You're afraid to tell your mother and Robert what you really want. You came here tonight to make sure I didn't tempt you anymore. Well, I have news for you. You wanted me then, and you want me now."

"No." Clea backed away from him. "I didn't want you. I knew it was wrong."

"But, baby, it felt so good."

Clea clamped her mouth shut and made a beeline for her coat. Before she reached the door, he caught her arm.

"Why did you really come here?" he asked, his temper rising along with his desire for her. "Was it for sex? Did you want to see if you could resist me?"

For a split second passion darkened her eyes, a passion he

wanted to ignite.

"No, Nick." Her protest came out weak and unconvincing.

He backed her up against the wall, one hand on each side of her head. At the base of her throat, her pulse beating wildly, fanning his desire for her.

"Did you come for one last fling?" Nick asked, knowing his words hurt her. He wanted her to feel the same pain he did.

"No." Her chest rose and fell with each breath she took.

"Then what, Clea? Why did you come?" He whispered the words close to her ear and she shivered. "Tell me why you're here." He touched her ear with his tongue. She tasted as sweet as honey. He wanted more. He wanted all of her. He'd been crazy in love with her from the beginning. If she wanted to end things with him, she never should have come over. She wouldn't win. Not here, not alone with him.

"I thought I could make you understand." She moaned when he sucked her earlobe. "I thought I owed you that much."

"Understand what?"

"That I can't be with you."

"You're with me right now." He grazed her neck with his lips, kissing her jaw, her mouth. She moaned again, setting him ablaze with desire. The stiffest erection he'd ever had strained against his jeans and he moved against her, wanting the relief only she could give him.

He wanted to take what was his, and he claimed her mouth in a fiery kiss, bringing a moan from deep in her throat. Surrendering, she melted against him. She opened her lips and her tongue met his. Impatient hands moved up his bare chest, to his shoulders, her nails digging into his flesh. He needed more, wanted everything.

Reaching behind her, he lifted her up, and she wound her legs around his waist. He thrust against her, and even with their clothing between them he knew he would lose control soon. It had been too damn long for him and she felt too good.

"Say you want me, Princess," he said, doing a slow grind against her. "Tell me."

"I want you, Nick," she said against his mouth. "God help me, I want you."

Her declaration sent a shot of satisfaction straight to his soul. He kissed her cheek and tasted the salt of tears. Reality intruded and he paused to look at her. "You're crying."

"I don't know what to do." Her eyes glittered with the tears of her confusion.

The sadness in her voice ripped into him, making him feel like a heel.

"I want you," she admitted. "No one sets me on fire like you do, Nick, but I have to marry Robert. I don't know how to stop the wedding. I can't disappoint everyone. I feel like such a failure. Even if I could end things, I'm leaving town. There's no happy ending here, Nick. Not for any of us. I'm mixed up. And poor John, he's caught in the middle of this mess."

She sounded saner than ever to him. "Tell Boomer you don't want to marry him."

"I can't stop the wedding. It's too late. Do you realize how many people are involved in this wedding, how much money my mother has sunk into it? And worse, Robert has given up his job to come with me. How do I tell him I can't marry him?"

"I'll tell him for you."

She shook her head. "No."

He let go of her legs and her body slid down his until her feet touched the floor.

Clea wiped her tears with her sleeve. "There's a lot at stake. Things you don't understand. My son is angry. My mother's health is failing, and Robert can't take one more disappointment."

"It's all about them," Nick said. "Put yourself first for once."

"I tried, but I can't." Her words held a hopelessness that tore at him.

"I'm just supposed to watch it happen?" Nick asked, unable to keep the bitterness from his voice. "You've just admitted to me you don't want the marriage. What am I supposed to do? How do I put out the fire that does a slow burn in my gut whenever I think about you? That flame keeps me alive. I'm not willing to be miserable the rest of my life because of some misguided loyalty you feel to a man who doesn't begin to deserve you. We belong together, and you know it. You have to call the wedding off before it's too late."

Clea backed away from him. "I never should have come here. It's not fair to you. I'm sorry, Nick."

She put her coat on. He didn't want her to go, not like this with things unresolved between them. "I love you, Clea."

Tears filled her eyes.

And then she was gone.

Nick stared at the door, wondering what had just happened. Clea had all but told him she didn't want to marry Robert, but she still intended to go through with the wedding. This was insane. This was wonderful.

Whether she realized it or not, she'd just given him hope.

CHAPTER FOURTEEN

Clea let herself into her apartment, her hands shaking on the knob. What had she done? Why had she gone to Nick's? She'd wanted him to take her, right there, against the wall. Never in her life had she wanted anything more. A part of her had hoped he would make love to her despite her protests. Had she wanted to use him as her excuse to call off the marriage? She wasn't being any fairer to Nick than she was to Robert. A hot rush of shame stained her cheeks. Both men deserved better.

Taking off her coat, she hung it on the rack near the door. She took a step and the lamp beside the sofa flared to life.

"Where have you been?" Vivian asked.

Guilt washed through her. "You should be in bed, Mom."

"I asked you a question, Clea." Vivian sighed, long and heavy. "Don't bother to answer. You've been with him. I could see it when you were a teenager, and I can see it now."

"I don't want to talk." She needed time to think.

"You're getting married," Vivian said tightly. "How can you cheat on Robert?"

"I didn't cheat on him." Or had she? She'd kissed Nick. She'd allowed him to take liberties with her, and she'd barely given Robert a thought. In fact, sex with Robert had dried up since Nick's return. Somehow, she'd managed to come up with one excuse after another to avoid being intimate with Robert.

"Robert deserves better than this," Vivian said. "What're you doing? You're about to become the daughter-in-law of a United

States senator. Doesn't that mean something to you Clea? It should. You have a chance to enter the inner circle, and Robert is your ticket inside. Why would you want to squander such an opportunity? Why?"

Clea's stomach turned. "Is this about what I want, or about what you want, Mom? Because if you knew anything about me, you'd know that I don't care about running with the rich and the beautiful. That's your dream, not mine. I care about John, and what's best for him."

"Robert is best for John," her mother interrupted.

"Is he? Is he better than John's real father?" Clea crossed her arms over her chest, hugging herself. "You weren't there tonight when I had to explain to John why everyone is against his father. John might be angry with Nick, but he loves him. Can't you see that?"

"No. John's a little boy. He doesn't know what's best for him." Vivian's eyes blazed. "Nick Lombard will never amount to anything. He'll always be poor, always be a loser."

"How do you know? No one has given Nick a chance before. He's smart. He's determined. He's even started his own car restoration business. Did you know he earned his AA in prison, as well as a stack of certifications in the automotive field?"

"From a mail-order university? Why, that means nothing."

"It means everything, Mom," Clea said, frustration eating at her. "Why can't you see that? Nick's a hard worker. He's ambitious, every bit as ambitious as Robert."

"He's done it again." Vivian frowned. "He's managed to convince you that he is the right man for you. I won't let you throw your life away on him. Think about Robert. Think about the Graceland Mitchell Internship. Are you ready to give up your dreams for a man who has brought you nothing but grief and heartache?"

At the mention of the internship Clea's heart skipped a beat. Would she give up the chance to study with Graceland Mitchell for Nick and John? She didn't know, but she did know one thing; even if she and Nick never got back together, she couldn't make a life with Robert, not when she could kiss Nick with such abandon. No matter the cost, she had to follow her heart. A strange freedom filled her. The time had come for her to make her own choices.

"I'm going to bed." Clea turned to leave.

"We're not done with this discussion, Clea Rose."

"We are for now." Clea went into the bathroom and closed the door. Tonight her life had taken a new twist. Tomorrow she would talk to Robert. She couldn't marry him. He didn't turn her inside out. She didn't crave the sight of him. Her skin didn't tingle when he touched her. The signs were all there; she'd just been too blind to see them.

She wasn't in love with Robert. She doubted she ever had been. To marry him now would be grossly unfair. He'd be trapped in a loveless marriage. She couldn't do that to him.

The thought of building a relationship with Nick terrified her. If she made the choice to pursue a relationship with him, she'd be working without a net. Her mother wouldn't support her decision. For the first time, Clea would be totally alone, personally and financially. Could she do it? Could she trust her instincts and let her heart lead her? The thought of making it on her own terrified her, but she'd never felt more in control. And she liked it.

* * *

"Hey, Nick." Billy walked into the garage through the open bay door.

"What's up?" Nick came around the Bel Air. It was Billy's day off, and Nick hadn't expected to see him at the garage. Right away he noticed his brother's frown. Something was wrong.

"I have bad news." Billy held an envelope in his hand.

"What kind of news?" A rock had landed in Nick's stomach.

"It's about the loan. This came from the bank." He passed Nick the envelope.

Nick's hopes and dreams crashed down around him, leaving behind a bitter disappointment. He'd wanted the loan to go through. Securing the warehouse would have allowed him to accelerate the business. "I don't need to open it. They said no."

Billy nodded. "They wanted a bigger down payment."

"I knew it." He thrust the envelope back at Billy. "Why did I let you talk me into it? I knew we didn't have enough cash between us."

"We'll find another way," Billy said. "This business was meant to be."

Nick went over to the pop machine, fed it some coins and hit the cola button. He grabbed his soda, twisted off the top and took a long drink.

"We'll try another bank," Billy said optimistically.

"Changing banks isn't going to help."

"I could sell my trailer," Billy offered. "That would get us some cash."

"No." Nick took another sip of his soda. "There has to be another way. I'm not giving up. I can't. Not now. I've made promises to my son. I want to build something for him he can be proud of."

A slow grin lit Billy's face. "That's great, Nick. Maybe we can sell off some of Mom's stuff."

Nick frowned. "Be realistic. Maude didn't own anything of value. Certainly nothing that can bring us the kind of cash we need."

"I guess not." Billy's smile faded. His shoulders slumped.

Nick finished off his soda, chucking the bottle into a nearby recycling bin. "I need to get back to work."

"I think I might have a solution to your problems," Mr. Mullin said.

Nick and Billy both turned to face their boss. Nick hadn't realized Mr. Mullin had overheard his conversation with Billy. The older man had been in his office most of the afternoon, glued to his computer.

"What kind of solution?" Nick asked, exchanging a glance with Billy.

"I've been watching you, Nick," Mr. Mullin said. "You are a fine mechanic. I think you probably know as much about cars as I do, maybe more. I've read your business plan. Your ideas are sound. I'm already seeing them at work." He nodded to the Bel Air. "You know I love this place, but I'm getting too damn old to run it. I want to retire. If you boys are interested, we may be able to work out a deal."

Nick couldn't believe what he was hearing. Mullin wanted a deal? No one had ever given him a break before. His first instinct told him not to trust this good fortune. Why would Mullin want to help him?

"A deal?" Billy grinned. "Of course we're interested. Right, Nick?"

"I don't know," he said, unable to keep the skepticism from his voice.

Mr. Mullin walked to him, placing a gnarled hand on Nick's

shoulder. "Nick, I've known you since you were a boy. I gave you your first job, and I sure as hell never believed you killed the Bloomfield boy in cold blood. I never had sons of my own. You and Billy are the closest thing I've got to children. I'd like the garage to go to someone I like and respect. Why don't the three of us sit down tomorrow morning and talk about this?"

Sincerity shone in the old man's eyes. Did he really see Billy and Nick as sons? Until this moment Nick never realized how much he respected Mr. Mullin, how much the old man had done for him and Billy over the years. How could he have been so blind? Had there been other people in Port Bliss who had pulled for him, despite the evidence being stacked against him? He thought of Mitzi. She'd been on his side. And Sheriff Kincade, he'd been giving Nick advice his entire life. Damn. Why hadn't he seen it sooner? He'd spent so much time wallowing in self-pity he hadn't noticed that some of the people in the town had supported him.

"All right. Let's talk." Nick's excitement rose. He extended his hand, and Mr. Mullin shook it.

The old man smiled, his eyes crinkling in the corners. After he let go of Nick's hand, he turned to Billy, shaking his hand.

"We'll talk tomorrow," Mr. Mullin promised.

"You bet," Billy agreed.

Mr. Mullin chuckled as he went back into his office, closing the door behind him.

"Can you believe it?" Billy asked. "He wants to make a deal with us."

"If he's talking about selling us the place, we still have to come up with the cash," Nick reminded him, giving himself and Billy a reality check.

"Still." Billy looked beyond Nick to the open door of the garage. Nick followed his brother's stare, surprised to see John.

"Hey, John," Billy greeted. "What brings you here? You coming to visit Nick?"

"Sorta," John said.

Nick's heart froze. He couldn't forget the look on John's face yesterday when he'd said he hated them all. What had Clea said to John? How much of Nick's twisted relationship with Boomer had been explained to him?

"Where's your mom?" Nick asked.

"She let me come alone." John hovered in the doorway, as if he were afraid to come in. "She said she'd be by at six to pick me up."

By sending John alone was Clea trying to avoid him? After last night, Nick wouldn't blame her. They'd both said and done things they shouldn't have.

"I'll leave you two alone then." Billy headed toward the door. "I've got plans to make. See ya, John." He touched John's shoulder as he passed the boy. "Talk to you later, Nick."

"I'll call you when I get home," Nick said, walking to meet his son. "I'm glad to see you, John. We have a lot of work to do today."

"On The Boss or the Bel Air?" John asked.

"I'm putting you to work on The Boss. I was about to apply the final coat of paint to the door. I need your help."

John had gone over to the bay where The Boss was parked. He ran a small hand over the side of the shiny yellow car.

"It's a smooth paint job," Nick said, coming to stand beside him. "The best I've seen."

"Yeah."

An idea flashed in Nick's mind. "You want to go for a ride?"

"Really?" John tilted his head to better see him.

"Sure." Instead of punishment, maybe what John needed was a little fun. "I'm off work. Let's go."

He opened the passenger door, and his son climbed in. Nick shut the door and told him to buckle up before rounding the car and sliding into the driver's seat. The smell of leather filled him making him remember his youth. With a twist of the key the engine roared to life and he backed out of the garage, his son beside him.

And inside Nick a foreign pride began to grow. Pride for his son, who'd kept his word to work off his debt, and pride for the life Nick now had, and dreams he hoped would come true.

Only one thing was missing as he pulled out of the garage.

Clea.

He wanted a life with her and John. He'd been too passive, letting her have all the power. The time had come to trust his instincts. As a teenager he'd courted Clea his way and won. He'd known then she was off limits, and he hadn't cared. He'd gone after her, using every trick he had. What was to stop him from doing the same thing now? Nothing. Absolutely nothing.

* * *

Clea let herself into the apartment, glad to have some time to herself.

She'd been afraid John wouldn't want to go to the garage today after his outburst yesterday afternoon, but he'd come home from school today, had his snack, and then announced he was going to the garage. She'd offered to take him, but he'd wanted to go alone. He'd had an anger management session with the school counselor, Mrs. Wilson, today. Had the woman managed to help John? Clea had talked with the counselor afterward. Mrs. Wilson said things had gone well. John had talked about his anger toward both Nick and Robert, different kinds of anger. The counselor had worked with him on some solutions to defusing his emotions and on how to make better choices.

His progress pleased Clea, and she prayed he wouldn't backslide when she talked to him about breaking things off with Robert.

She'd been useless at The Coffee House today, unable to keep her mind on her work. All day long she'd done nothing but think about Robert, about ending their engagement. She'd called him first thing that morning, asking to see him, but he'd been busy. He'd promised to come by as soon as he was free. Waiting all day to see him had set her nerves on edge.

Robert wouldn't take the news well, and she dreaded telling him. The end of their engagement wasn't his fault, and she hoped she could make him understand that. She could see now her feelings for Nick had never died. She had no idea where they would go from here, but she couldn't marry Robert, no matter what she felt for Nick. She still intended to go to New York. A change of scenery would be good for her and for John. She didn't want to think about where that would leave her with Nick.

A knock sounded at the door.

Her stomach flipped over. Robert. She answered the door.

"Hello, darling." Robert embraced her. "What's so urgent I had to run right over?"

Clea pulled out of his arms. "Sit down. We need to talk."

"I don't like the sound of this. You're scaring me, Clea." His eyes held a wild, knowing look. She'd seen that same look in his eyes when they'd been teenagers, when she'd broken things off with him before.

"Sit down, please." She swept her hand toward the sofa.

"No." The word came out harsh.

Clea winced.

"I don't want to sit down." His chin came up. "Tell me what's going on."

A lump of tears formed in her throat. She didn't want to hurt him. "There's no good way to say this. I can't marry you. I'm so very sorry."

"No. Not again." He turned away from her and rammed his fingers through his hair. "That son of a bitch. Has he touched you?"

"Robert, no," she said sadly. "Let me explain."

"Don't bother. I've heard it all before." His hair stuck up. His eyes sparked with anger. "I'll kill him. This time I swear I'll kill him."

He started for the door. Clea grabbed his arm. "Stop. I'm the one you should be angry at. Me."

Robert pushed past her.

"Listen to me," she said. "I'm not ending things because Nick came back to town. I've thought about us a lot. I love you. You're a good man. You deserve someone who'll love you completely. That someone isn't me."

His face crumpled. Clea's chest tightened painfully.

"I love you enough for both of us, don't you see that?" He reached for her, his hands closing around her upper arms. "I'd do anything for you. Anything."

"I'm sorry, Robert." Never had she meant any words more. Tears filled her eyes, and she let them run unchecked down her cheeks.

"What am I supposed to do?" Robert asked, his fingers tightening on her arms. His features changed, contorted with anger.

"I don't know."

"I've resigned my job. We have money down for caterers, a florist, and a six-piece band."

"I'll take care of everything." She whispered the words, knowing they would anger him even more.

"I think I'm going to be sick." Robert thrust her away from him with enough force Clea stumbled back. "I knew he would get to you. Have you been sleeping with him?"

"No."

"But he's kissed you. I saw the grease on your face that day, and I knew he had put his hands on you. I knew then, but I didn't care. You belonged to me."

"Oh, Robert."

"Shut up." A savage light lit his eyes. He pressed his fingers to his temples. "I can't think. God, it's just like that night I saw you with him at Lookout Point."

In two strides he had her, his fingers holding her head prisoner. He took her mouth, forcing a kiss on her she didn't want. When she didn't respond, he let her go.

Clea touched her mouth, her fingers shaking.

"This isn't over." Robert flung the door open and strode out.

Quickly, Clea went to the door, closing, then locking it. She leaned against the wood, her tears coming hot and thick against her cheeks.

She deserved every bit of Robert's anger. She'd made him promises of love and commitment, and she'd broken them. For the first time she understood how Nick must have felt the day he'd sent her away, and a new compassion for him unfolded within her.

Clea pushed away from the door, wiping her eyes on the sleeve of her sweater. She needed to do something constructive, something to take her mind off the hurt she'd caused Robert. Taking her coat from the hook, she pulled it on. On the way out she grabbed her camera bag. She had no idea where she was going, only that she needed to forget.

CHAPTER FIFTEEN

It was Nick's lucky day.

Having his son in the car with him satisfied him in a way nothing else could. Nick turned the corner, going by The Coffee House. He hoped to coax Clea into going for a ride with them. To his delight, she stood on the sidewalk as if she waited for them.

"There's your mom," he said to John.

Nick pulled the Mustang over to the curb, and rolled down the passenger window.

"Hey, gorgeous, want to go for a ride?" he asked, smiling.

Clea walked to the curb, dipping her head to see into the car. "I thought you two were working."

Her eyes were red, puffy. Had she been crying? He glanced at John. Had he noticed Clea's eyes? He wanted to ask what was wrong, but held his tongue. Instead he said, "Come on. It's a beautiful day. The sun is out. Let's show our son what this car can do."

He could read the indecision in her eyes. Something was desperately wrong, and his gut told him it had to do with Robert.

"Do you want me to go?" she asked John.

"Sure." John shrugged, as if it didn't matter.

"Come on," Nick coaxed. "The engine's all warmed up."

His words brought a reluctant smile to her lips. "All right. Maybe taking a drive is just the thing I need, but first let me get a shot of the two of you in the car."

She removed her camera from the bag. Stepping back, she

focused the lens. Clea snapped several pictures, each one from a slightly different angle. He loved watching her work, loved the way her forehead wrinkled as she concentrated on the shot.

"Okay. I'm done." She put the camera back in the bag.

Nick opened the door for her. "Hop in back, John." He helped Clea unlatch the seat. John climbed in back.

"I haven't been in The Boss since I was a teenager," Clea said. "It still smells the same, like leather rubbed with coconut oil and grease."

"Some things never change," Nick said with a wink. "Buckle up, Princess."

The minute Clea put her seat belt on, Nick punched the gas, the tires screeching against the pavement.

"Nick, for heaven's sake," she cried in protest, but Nick could read the excitement on her face.

He pressed his foot to the accelerator and a straight shot of adrenaline went through him. The familiar feeling of being in his car with his best girl came rushing back.

"Slow down!" Clea said, the words ending in a squeal of delight.

The sad look had left her eyes, and that pleased him.

"Go faster," John urged from the back seat.

"John," Clea reprimanded. "Don't encourage him."

"Oh, come on. Don't pretend you don't like it, Clea," Nick chided. "I know you do. I can remember one time when…"

"Nick." Clea cut him off. "I don't think John needs to hear any of our stories."

"Aw, come on, Mom." John grabbed the back of Clea's seat with his hand, scooting forward as far as he could while still remaining in his seat belt. "Tell me, Dad."

"A bunch of us used to race," Nick said. "Out on Deer Road. Deer Road got its name from the deer that crossed the road at all hours of the day and night. That made racing there really dangerous. You never knew when a deer would run in front of your car. If that happened, it could mean sudden death."

"Oh, Nick." Clea groaned. "I don't think John needs to hear this story."

He remembered one night on Deer Road vividly. He had raced Danny Bloomfield and won. The victory had been especially sweet because Danny seemed to get a twisted pleasure from harassing him. Their rivalry had started long before Clea's family had moved to Port Bliss. After that race he'd driven Clea down to the beach and they'd made out in The Boss until the windows were covered in steam. They'd nearly made love that night, and probably would have if Danny and Robert hadn't driven up beside them, drunk as skunks, their car full of girls.

The Bloomfield brothers had given Nick a hard time the entire summer, following him, challenging him to races, making trouble for him. He'd understood why Robert hadn't liked him, but he'd never understood Danny's hatred, a hatred that ultimately had cost him his life.

"What happened?" John asked.

"I raced The Boss and won," Nick said.

"Cool."

"The best part was I managed to avoid a deer and still win the race."

Clea turned to look at John over her shoulder. "It wasn't cool. It was dangerous. Nick could have been killed. And if I ever catch you doing something so foolish, you'll be grounded for life and won't be driving until you're thirty."

Nick laughed. "I'm afraid I have to agree with your mother on that, John. What I did was stupid and reckless. I hope you'll have more sense than I did."

"Let's change the subject," Clea said. "The Boss looks great, Nick. I'd love to photograph the car for you, inside and out."

"Really?" Her offer surprised and delighted him. "I was going to ask you if you'd do that for me." He smiled. "I want to keep a portfolio of every car the Lombard brothers restore."

"I'd love to take the photos," she said. "You do nice work, Nick."

"Billy did most of the work on The Boss. The Mustang's in mint condition from the 302 under the hood to the AM/8-track player in the dash." He pushed the tape in and Aerosmith's *Sweet Emotion* filled the air.

The song took Nick back to the night John had been conceived. They'd parked at Lookout Point above the lake, making love in The Boss. The night had started out with so much promise, but had ended in tragedy.

"It's a beautiful car." Clea's fingers caressed the leather seat. "I'll bet it's worth a lot of money."

"Yeah, I guess it is." He reached over and gave Clea's hand a squeeze.

"Can we go faster, Dad?" John asked.

"Oh, no. Like father, like son." Clea glanced at Nick, a warning look in her eyes. She let go of Nick's hand. "Nick Lombard, don't you dare. Your son is in the car. And put both hands back on the steering wheel."

"Hang on." Nick laughed as he pressed the accelerator to the floor.

The car shot forward. Clea clutched the seat. But just as quickly, he slowed the Mustang. Clea tossed him a scathing look.

"I'm just showing the boy what the car can do, Princess."

"Why do you call Mom 'Princess'?" John asked.

"Because that's what she is to me," Nick said. "A beautiful princess. And when she went out on a date with me, I felt like the luckiest man alive."

"Yuck," John said with disgust.

Nick smiled and reached for Clea's hand. In that second a flash of pain filled her eyes. Something had happened today. Had she finally broken her engagement? He longed to ask her, but couldn't in front of John. For now the questions would burn inside him until they were alone.

* * *

By the time Clea got dinner on the table she'd pulled herself together. She felt better about ending the engagement. She had Nick to thank for her change of heart. He'd been wonderful today. Spending time with Nick and John had been the perfect antidote for her sadness. Nick had given her a glimpse of her future, and she'd needed that today.

Clea fed John a quick meal of macaroni and cheese and salad. When he finished, she helped him with his homework, then drew him a bath. The sounds of water sloshing calmed her nerves. She had to tell John about the broken engagement, tonight, before he heard it from someone else.

The gurgle of draining water met her ears. A few minutes later, John came out of the bathroom, dressed in his pajamas.

"Can I play video games?" He plopped down next to her on the sofa.

"In a minute. I have something I want to tell you."

"What?"

He leaned back against the cushions. His fresh scrubbed face tugged at her heartstrings. She didn't want to cause him more pain, but didn't know how to avoid it.

"It's about Robert."

John sat up, his eyes instantly guarded.

"I'm not going to marry him. I'm sorry, honey." Clea braced herself for the worst.

"I knew it!" John jumped up, but he didn't run. His hands knotted into fists at his sides.

"Honey." She reached for him, but he backed away.

"Are you going to marry Dad?" he asked.

She hadn't expected that question. She had no idea what answer he wanted to hear or what the answer to that question was. "I'm not going to marry anyone right now. I think you and I need some time to adjust."

"Are we still going to New York?" John asked.

"Yes. It's a great opportunity for us."

"I don't want to go." John ran to his bedroom, slamming the door.

Clea followed. He lay face down on his bed. "John." She sat down beside him, rubbing his back. "I know this is confusing for you. It's confusing for me, too. I love Robert, but I'm not in love with him the way two adults should be if they're going to get married. It's not fair to marry someone when you don't love them with your whole heart and soul."

"Do you love Dad?"

"That's what I need to find out," Clea told him honestly. "But no matter what happens between me and Nick, your father loves you. He will always be in our lives."

"Will he come to New York with us?"

"He can't. He has certain rules he has to follow under the terms of his parole."

"Then I don't want to go." He buried his face more deeply into the pillow.

Clea's hand stilled on John's back. Did John want to be with Nick? If so, could she really take him away? She had no idea what to do next. "Let me think about things, John. I think we can find a way to work things out with Nick. Does that make you feel better?"

He sniffed.

"Come on. Get up. I'll play video games with you."

"You will?" He sat up, wiping the tears away.

Her heart broke for him. "We've had a rough day. Playing games won't make everything all right, but I think we both need a distraction, don't you?"

He nodded. Clea reached for his hand, pulling him from the bed. "Come on, I'll race you to the sofa."

* * *

Nick walked into the garage. He'd gone home after he'd dropped Clea and John off and had some dinner. Restless, he'd decided to come back to the garage and work for a while. Even now he couldn't forget the haunted look in Clea's eyes when he'd picked her up this afternoon. The time they'd spent together today had been bittersweet. He felt certain she'd ended things with Boomer, and while that pleased him, he didn't like to see her hurting. He longed for the chance to pull her into his arms and tell her everything would be all right, but he sensed Clea wouldn't have accepted his comfort. She needed time, but how much?

"Hey, Nick." Billy sat on the bench outside Mullin's office, a can of soda in his hand. His coveralls were streaked with grease.

"Hey, yourself," Nick replied. "I didn't think you'd still be here."

"Where have you been?" Billy asked. "I missed you earlier."

"I took my son and Clea for a ride in The Boss."

Billy frowned.

"You got a problem with that?" Nick asked, wondering at Billy's change in mood.

"You know I want you to have John in your life, but why Clea? The woman is trouble on great legs. You don't need her, Nick. Can't it just be the Lombard brothers?"

"Are you serious?" He'd never given Billy's feelings for Clea any thought at all. To discover that Billy didn't want her around was a shock. "You want to explain yourself?"

"She got between us before, and look what happened," Billy said. "You lost your focus. After you met Clea you didn't have much time for me. I needed you, Nick."

Shock washed through him. "I went to prison for you," Nick said. "What did you want me to do?"

"I don't know." Billy stood up, pacing over to the Bel Air. "She's not one of us."

"Why does it have to be us and them?"

"That's just the way it is."

"Bullshit." Betrayal washed through Nick. He'd expected this kind of comment from Vivian Rose and the Bloomfields, but not from his own brother. "Don't you think I'm good enough for Clea?"

"I don't think she's good enough for you," Billy said. "She's a spoiled rich girl. If you keep chasing after her you're going to get us run right out of this town."

Nick grabbed his brother by the front of his shirt. "That's enough. I love her. I want her in my life. I'm not afraid of the people in this town."

Billy jerked away. "Then you're a fool, Nick. The lake people are rich and they're mean."

"What happened to you, Billy?" Nick asked, suddenly afraid he really didn't know his brother at all.

"I killed a man." His eyes closed in anguish. "I can't forget. Every day I replay the moment I hit him. Every day you spent in prison ate at me until I didn't want to live. I should have been in prison. *Me.* Not you. For ten years my life has been about you. Every choice I made I made with you in mind. I don't know where you leave off and I begin. Hell, I'm not even sure I want to stay in this town."

"Then go," Nick said in a whisper. "Go. You don't have to stay for me."

"I owe you, don't you see?" Tears filled his brother's eyes. "I have to stay for you."

"No, you don't. You don't owe me anything. I made the decision to go to prison for you. I didn't give you a choice. I'm sorry, man." Nick walked to Billy. "I'm so sorry." He embraced his brother. Billy hugged him back, a hug born of desperation and heartache. He might have kept Billy out of prison, but his brother had been living in a prison of his own making; Nick had just been too blind to see it until now.

"Don't stay in Port Bliss for me, Billy. Only stay if you want to. Live your life."

"It's not over for me." Billy pulled away to look at Nick. "It will never be over for me." He walked from the garage his head down, his shoulders slumped.

Nick hoped Billy was wrong. He couldn't bear to think he'd screwed up both their lives by going to prison.

Would he ever do the right thing?

Yes, he had to. Prison had forced him to focus on the things that were truly important to him. He knew what he had to do. He glanced over at The Boss. Without stopping to think he went into the office and booted up Mullin's computer. He connected to the Internet and typed in the web address for a well-known classic car sales website.

If Billy Lombard wanted freedom, Nick would give it to him.

CHAPTER SIXTEEN

Nick knocked on Clea's door at seven sharp.

The past twenty-four hours were catching up with him, leaving him drained and tired. After Billy's revelations last night, Nick had done nothing but think about his brother's feelings. He'd had no idea Billy didn't like Clea. He couldn't help but think he'd failed his brother. A profound sadness had stayed with Nick all day.

Then, when John had shown up at the garage this afternoon, he'd given Nick a note from Clea, asking him to come by around seven. Nick's mood had instantly improved. He hoped Clea had broken her engagement to Boomer and was ready to tell him about it.

After spending time with Clea and John yesterday Nick knew he wanted more days like that. He just had to find a way to get around Clea's internship. Giving the internship up wasn't an option. Clea had to go. Talent like hers shouldn't be squandered. Yet, he couldn't follow her to New York. His business had just begun to take off. He didn't want to give up, especially after Mr. Mullin had made the offer to sell him the garage. Instead, he wanted to work harder. He wanted to provide for Clea and for John.

He knocked again.

The door whipped open. "Hi, Nick."

Clea's hair was wet, as if she'd just come from the shower. Loose, the tresses flowed past her shoulders to settle on the swell of her breasts. A soft pink sweater hugged her curves to her waist, where gray woolen pants took over, running down the length of her legs. Her feet were bare, showing him her brightly painted red toenails. Red. The sight of those bare toes sent a straight shot of lust to his gut.

"I'm sorry. I'm running late." She smiled, showing him her perfect white teeth. "I haven't had time to dry my hair. Come in." She pulled the door open wider and he went inside.

The smell of cinnamon lingered in the air, yet the kitchen was neat and tidy, leaving him to guess she'd eaten earlier.

"Where's John?" He tossed his jacket on the dining room chair.

"He's staying overnight at Toby's." Clea ran a hand over her hair. "Let me go and dry my hair and throw on some makeup. I'll be right back."

"Don't," Nick said, still trying to digest the news that they were alone, and she had invited him over. He reached out and touched her hair. "You don't need makeup. You're beautiful just the way you are. And I like your hair curly, the way it was in school. Don't straighten it. Leave it."

She didn't move. "I haven't worn my hair curly for years." Her tongue came out to wet her lips, upping his desire he for her.

"What am I doing here, Clea?" he asked. "Because this is looking like an invitation to something more than conversation."

She spun away from him, giving him a great view of her back and her bottom, round and inviting inside her form-fitting pants.

"I broke the engagement." She turned. Clear green eyes stared at him, honest and wide. "I couldn't marry him. I thought I wanted to. Robert is safe, steady. But I just couldn't go through with it."

"I knew it." Her admission filled him with a rush of happiness, yet he knew what breaking the engagement had cost her.

"I didn't say anything yesterday, because I wanted to tell John first. I told him last night."

"How did he take the news? Is he okay?" John had seemed fine at the garage this afternoon, but the kid was good at holding his emotions in.

"I've explained things to him, but he has questions, most of them about us and where we go from here."

"Where do we go?" he asked, afraid to hope.

"I don't know, Nick, but I owe you an apology."

"For what?"

"Where do I start?" She gave him a weak smile. "For the other night when I came to your place. You were right. I did go there hoping you'd try and seduce me. I realize now I was looking for an excuse to end things with Boomer. I was wrong to put you in the middle of my problems. I'm ashamed of my behavior."

"Forget it." He didn't want her apology. He understood about the other night, understood the driving need to find answers in her arms, just as she had looked for answers in his.

"I don't know what happens next," she said. "But I asked you over tonight to share something with you." She pointed to the window.

An easel stood near the window. "What's this?" He walked over to the picture resting there. His heart skipped a beat when he realized it was a framed photograph of John and himself in The Boss. Clea had managed to capture them perfectly, from their smiles to the smooth paint job on the car. "This is wonderful."

"It's a gift, for you." She went to the hall closet and opened the door, removing what looked like several photo albums, as well as a couple of large leather-bound portfolios. "There's more."

Curious, Nick helped her. She placed the albums and portfolios on the floor.

"Sit down." She dropped to the carpet and opened one of the portfolios, turning the cover aside.

Nick went down on his knees. It was a picture of John as a baby. Unable to help himself, he reached out, tracing the line of the infant's cheek. God, he was beautiful with a head of dark hair. Although the photo was done taken in black and white, Clea had colored the eyes a startling blue. Nick glanced up at her, but couldn't find any words to describe what he felt.

"I took this when he was just three weeks old," she said. "He had the softest skin, and I wanted to capture that. I wasn't as good with lighting then as I am now, but every time I look at this I remember how soft he felt, how good he smelled. I colored the eyes in later, because I couldn't get over the shade of blue. He has your eyes Nick."

"He's beautiful," Nick said, his chest tight with emotion.

She turned the page. "This is John at about eight months. He's crawling, and getting into absolutely everything. As you can see, he's chubbier."

John had grown bigger. Clea had captured him in mid-crawl. A priceless moment, a moment he wished he'd been a part of.

"Let's see, what's next? I took so many pictures, it's hard to remember." She turned the page, revealing a portrait of Clea, John nursing at her breast. Dressed in white, she looked like an angel. Her hair curled wildly over her shoulders, one lock captured in John's chubby fist. This was the Clea Nick remembered. The wild hair, the younger face. John stared up at her. Nick could see the love in John's eyes, and in Clea's eyes as she returned the baby's stare.

"I used a tripod and a timer for this shot. I've always liked this one," she said wistfully. "John would die of embarrassment now if he were to see it. I nursed him until he was about eighteen months old." She smiled. "I loved holding him close, his cheek against my breast. The connection between us was strongest when he nursed. I fell so in love with him during those precious moments. There's nothing like it, Nick."

A whirlwind of emotions swept through Nick with the force of a tornado. Regret for the time he missed with Clea and John, mixed with an overwhelming love for them. Because of the love he felt for Clea, a baby had been born. His son. Their child. In this instant he knew he would never let anyone or anything take them away from him again.

"It's the most beautiful picture I've ever seen," he said, wishing he'd been there to witness the special closeness in person. "You've given me a gift."

Her smile widened. "I wanted to give you John's childhood. I took these pictures for you, Nick. I made a mistake when I returned your letters. I shut you out of John's life. You'll never know how much I regret that now."

The unfamiliar sting of tears touched his eyes. He couldn't remember a time when he'd cried, not when he'd gone to prison, not when Maude had died. His heart swelled with unchecked love for Clea and for his son. Never would he have imagined that she'd even thought of him while he'd been in prison. And to find out she'd not only thought of him, but had photographed a history of their son's childhood for him. His heart soared.

"There are more," she said, breaking the comfortable silence that had settled between them. She showed him pictures of John's first steps, of his first day of school, of his sixth birthday party. Nick reveled in the photographs, committing them to memory. The photos were more than just images committed to paper, each picture captured a moment of history, of a life he'd missed. Clea had given him those moments back. He could see the love she felt for John with each picture she'd taken. She had a remarkable talent she couldn't waste here in Port Bliss.

"I can see why you won the internship," Nick said with awe. "Why don't you have these displayed?"

She shook her head. "I couldn't. It hurt to look at them with you gone."

"Clea."

"The pictures are so personal, so private." She gave him a small smile. "You're the only one I wanted to share them with."

He reached for her, taking her face in his hands, her skin smooth under his rough fingers. While in prison he'd tried to remember the way she felt, the way she tasted, but nothing he'd imagined prepared him for the reality of Clea in the flesh. She felt a million times softer, smelled a million times better. The scent of watermelon tempted his nose as he lowered his mouth to hers. He didn't kiss her, but kept his mouth a fraction away, savoring her, anticipating the kiss. Her eyes closed, her lips parted slightly, her breath soft and sweet between them. With a feather touch he moved his mouth across hers, the motion a tease of the kiss to come.

"Kiss me, Nick," she pleaded. "If you don't kiss me soon, I'll die."

Her words fanned his desire, and he couldn't hold back any longer. Lips as sweet as summer fruit met his, bringing to life the spark of desire low in his belly. Nick took her mouth, doing all the things he'd dreamed of while in prison. In his fantasies, he'd made love to her in every way imaginable. He'd forgotten the heat of her mouth and how wild it made him. He sucked her tongue, then mated with it, savoring the texture, the taste of her, deepening the kiss until she moaned low in her throat. She pressed her body to his, her hands in his hair, her breasts flattened against his chest, the mounds burning into him. He couldn't get enough of her, needed more, wanted more.

Together they fell back onto the carpet until his body covered hers. "You belong to me," he whispered against her lips. "Only to me." His fingers slid into her hair, still damp, but feather soft against his skin.

"I do belong to you, Nick. I've never stopped wanting you."

Her words blazed through him, his erection straining against his jeans. He wanted to be inside her, feel her hot and wet around him. "I want you naked, Princess. Now."

Desire filled her green eyes, making them shine with promise.

Nick rolled from her and pulled Clea to a sitting position. With frantic fingers they removed each other's clothing, until nothing separated them but air. Nick yanked his wallet from his pants pocket and removed a condom. There would be no unplanned pregnancy this time.

"You'll have to help me," he said, his hands shaking. "I don't think I can get the damn thing open. God knows, I haven't had much practice using one, but this time I want you protected."

Clea gave him a seductive smile and took the package from his fingers. "I'm not an expert either, but..." She tore the wrapper open. "I think it goes like this."

Nick shut his eyes as she placed the condom on him, rolling the protection down. By the time she finished, he was having trouble holding onto what little self-control he had left. She ran her hands up his arms, over his shoulders.

"Do you want to move to the bedroom?" he asked, thinking of her comfort.

"No." She held her arms out to him.

Slowly, so slowly, he lowered Clea down to the carpet.

"You're so beautiful." He touched her nipple with the back of his hand. Her breasts were round and fuller than he remembered, the nipples pink and sweet.

She reached for him, guiding his mouth to her breast. Nick licked her nipple, the swollen nub sending a shock wave of pleasure through him. If he was dreaming he didn't want to wake up.

"Oh, Nick," she moaned, her fingers twisting in his hair.

He sucked her nipple into his mouth, rolling his tongue over the tip, sucking, then rolling again, until she cried out, arching her back. Gently, he trailed his hand over her smooth stomach, threading his fingers through her triangle of honey curls. The softness fed his desire. When his fingers slipped inside of her, the slick wetness closing around him, he had to grit his teeth, so great was the rush of pure lust that shot through him.

"I want to touch you," she said, her hand closing around his most male part. Her voice was husky with desire, desire he'd put there. Again, lust jolted him, taking him closer to the edge.

"It's been too long for me," he whispered, knowing he couldn't hang on much longer. He couldn't remember if she'd climaxed the last time they'd been together, but he was sure as hell going to make sure she did this time.

His fingers moved inside her, urging her toward release. Clea moved against him, her cries of pleasure filling the air. For every movement he made, she stroked him with equal fever.

"You feel so good," Nick whispered against her breast, his tongue making a lazy circle around her nipple. "You can't imagine how many times I've made love to you in my mind, but it never felt like this."

"Oh, Nick," she cried. "Oh." Her back arched, her fingers tightening around him as she found release.

Nick didn't wait a moment longer. Her legs parted and he moved between them, looking deep into her eyes. Clea locked her legs around his waist, and he dove into her. A low moan escaped her lips and he wondered if he'd hurt her, but when he saw her face, lips parted, eyes closed, he knew the sound signaled her desire. Slowly, he pulled out, the pleasure almost more than he could bear.

Clea's hands found his hips. She pulled him back to her, urging him to continue with her hands. And he did. With each thrust his need to possess her completely increased. Nothing had ever felt this good: her skin against his, her hair, her taste. A roar filled his ears, a pulsing he couldn't control. Her nails dug into his back and he knew she was slipping over the edge again. This time he went with her.

Powerful waves of pleasure crashed through him, one on top of the other, until he couldn't think, only feel. When he finally opened his eyes, he found Clea watching him. She smoothed the hair from his eyes, a satisfied smile on her face.

"You okay?" he asked, knowing he'd taken her like a man possessed, and maybe he had been. He'd wanted to make her his, and he had. The thought pleased him.

"I'm better than okay." Her smile widened. "I don't remember sex being quite that intense the last time we were together. I didn't know I could feel so much."

Nick grinned. He couldn't remember the last time he'd been this satisfied or optimistic. "The night is young, Princess." He kissed her. "And we have ten years to make up for."

* * *

Clea came awake slowly, and before she opened her eyes she smiled. Sometime during the night they'd moved to her bed. Without looking, she knew Nick slept beside her. His scent, a mix of clean soap and sex, filled her head. Heat radiated from his skin, warming her. She didn't want to move, didn't want to come back to reality. Last night, Nick had made her his, again and again. His passion had consumed her to the point where she could think of nothing but him. After so many years of missing him, thinking about him, she'd wanted to do all the things to him she'd dreamed about, and she'd managed to knock quite a few of those things off her list.

"Why are you smiling?"

Clea opened her eyes. "I thought you were asleep. How long have you been watching me?"

"For a while." He reached over and wound a curl around his finger. "Why are you smiling?"

"Why do you think?" She smiled again. Last night had been the stuff of dreams.

"How much time do we have before reality intrudes?" He gathered her close, until their bodies touched everywhere.

"Enough." She ran her fingers over Nick's cheek, then kissed him. "I don't want to think about being a parent yet, or about going to work. Right now I just want to feel like your lover."

Nick gave a low growl, rolling to his back, pulling her on top of him until she straddled his body. "What did you have in mind?" His hands found her waist, moving lower to cup her bottom.

"This." She leaned forward to lick his nipple. "And this." Her tongue found its way to Nick's other nipple. "You're not the only one with fantasies."

"I think you're a naughty girl." Nick grinned.

"That's what people say," Clea said, returning his grin. He was so handsome. His blue eyes blazed with desire. And his mouth, just looking at him, naked and in her bed, gave her a sexual meltdown. "And imagine what they'd say if they found out I did this." She took a condom from the bedside table, making quick work of getting the protection in place. There was no denying Nick wanted her, the evidence of his desire felt hard and smooth under her fingers.

Clea lifted herself up, then sank down on him, taking his length into her. She moved against him, and Nick closed his eyes, his face taut with pleasure. Clea moved, up, down, around, fueling her own desire, using Nick to bring her pleasure in a way she never dreamed possible. He felt so good, and if she moved just right, sparks of pleasure exploded within her.

A moan left Nick's lips. Clea leaned forward and kissed his mouth without breaking the rhythm between them.

She wanted to please him, to make him as crazy for her as she was for him. Clea rode him. His face told her everything. She could see his pleasure rising with the creasing of his brow, the arch of his neck against the pillow, the parting of his lips as he moved with her, his hands clutching her hips. Watching him was as powerful an aphrodisiac as being touched by him.

Suddenly, his eyes opened and she was startled by the sexual prowess she saw there. He sat up, their faces so close together she could feel his breath against her lips.

"I want to watch you," he whispered, the words husky with need. "Look at me."

Clea's hands found his shoulders and she held on as he moved her against him faster and faster, his gaze locked with hers. On the brink of climax, she closed her eyes.

"Look at me," he commanded.

She did. As she found her release, he found his, and she could see his pleasure in his eyes because it mirrored her own. Her soul melded to his and an incredible feeling of peace came over her, making her want to cry with happiness, the experience so powerful it left her breathless.

CHAPTER SEVENTEEN

"Tell me about the night Danny was killed," Clea asked.

Nick propped himself up on one elbow. He'd just made love to her for the second time that morning. Soon, reality would crash in around them. He wanted to use the time they had left to savor Clea, enjoy her.

The last thing he wanted to do was talk about Danny Bloomfield.

He'd been dreading this conversation. After last night he knew he couldn't lie to her anymore. He owed her the truth, but at what cost to Billy?

Clea lay beside him on her back, her head turned to the side against the pillow to look up at him. Earlier, she'd brushed her hair, trying to restore order, but she'd failed. Soft golden curls spilled across the pillow and over her shoulders. Anyone who saw her now would guess what she'd been up to all night, and it pleased him to no end to know he was responsible for the serene smile on her face.

"I don't want to talk about that now," Nick said. "In fact, I don't want to talk at all." He smiled and reached over to brush the curls from her forehead.

"I need to talk about it, Nick." She captured his hand and intertwined her fingers with his. "I was shut out of the whole thing. One minute we were making love, the next you were arrested."

He glanced away from her. The truth would set him free, but the truth would harm his brother. A deep loyalty for both Clea and

Billy warred inside him. No matter which path he took, someone would come out the loser.

"Tell me, Nick," she said again. "I want to understand."

"You know what happened." He brought her fingers to his lips and kissed them.

"Was there really a gun, like you said at the trial? Was it self-defense?"

"Yes," he confirmed, telling her the one thing he was certain of. Their relationship was new and fragile. He didn't want anything to crack their newfound closeness, and telling her the truth was sure to do just that. He wanted to tell her, but not now when everything felt right between them.

"But no gun was ever found. How do you explain that?" Her eyes held a thousand questions.

"I don't know. I can't. I've had a lot of time to think, and I can only come to one conclusion. Someone else was there that night, someone who wanted me to go to jail for murder. There's only one person I can think of who hated me that much."

"No, Nick." Clea shook her head, and he could see the understanding in her eyes. "Not Robert. That's what you're thinking, isn't it? Why would he do that? Danny was his brother. That would mean Robert took the gun, and then left Danny there alone. He wouldn't do that. No matter how much he hated you, he would never leave his brother alone to die. Besides, he had an alibi. His mother confirmed Robert had been home asleep."

"Robert wanted you," Nick said. "He saw a way to get me out of the picture. I can't prove it, but I know he took the gun."

"But that would mean his mother lied." Clea struggled to understand all he'd told her. "Why would she do that?"

"Maybe she believed he was home," Nick said. "Or maybe she knew Robert had something to do with Danny's death, but she couldn't bear the thought of losing him, too. Where do you suppose the gun came from? My guess is it belonged to the senator. He claimed no guns were missing, but I'm not convinced. I'm not sure about anything anymore."

"Oh, Nick." Her fingers grazed his jaw, her touch tender.

"If the gun had been found, my sentence would have been much lighter, or I may not have gone to prison at all. It *was* self-defense."

His gut tightened to an ache born of fear. He let go of her hand

and rolled on his side, their faces just inches apart. He could no longer put off telling her. If he wanted to keep Clea, he had to come clean, tell her all of it, and pray she'd understand why he'd made the choices he had.

"Tell me what happened," Clea said. "Please."

Compassion filled her eyes, but would the emotion harden to hatred when she knew the truth? It was a chance Nick had to take if they were going to have a future together.

"I'm not sure exactly why things happened the way they did that night," he said. "After I took you home, I picked up Billy. He'd been over at that girl's house, you know, what was her name?"

"Mary," Clea supplied. "I remember. She lived near my house."

"Yeah, Mary." Nick had thought about that twist of fate many times. If he hadn't picked up Billy that night, would Danny be dead now? There were so many ifs - and no way of knowing how things would have turned out. "We hadn't gone far, when Danny's car came up behind us. He bumped the back of The Boss. Lookout Point was just ahead. I pulled over, and he followed. The confrontation between us was a long time coming."

"I know." Clea's fingers tightened around his. "They were brutal to you, to us. They taunted you about the lakeside robberies all summer, trying to blame you. It was as if they wanted the entire town to hate you as much as they did."

He'd never given a lot of thought to how Clea had seen things that summer. Had she been as harassed as he had?

"When I broke my engagement to Robert," Clea said, "he said something that bothered me. He said he'd seen us together at Lookout Point. Could that have had something to do with the irrational way Danny behaved?"

"Maybe," Nick said. Robert Bloomfield had an obsession with Clea she still didn't understand, even after all this time. "I've had a lot of time to think about the choices I made that night. Some of the choices I regret, others I don't."

A flicker of surprise crossed Clea's features. "What kind of choices?"

He frowned. "For the most part it happened like I said. Danny forced my car off the road. He got out of his car. I got out of mine. I didn't realize until it was too late that he had a gun. He held it on me, talking crazy, saying he'd had enough of me, that I didn't deserve to be born. I knew he was drunk, and that's what scared me. Danny Bloomfield was a mean drunk. I'd seen him that way more than once, and I know you have, too."

Clea nodded. "But where was Billy?"

Nick braced himself for Clea's reaction to the news he was about to give her. "Billy didn't get out of the car right away. I don't think Danny realized Billy was with me. I had a bat in the car."

Nick broke off, reliving the moment. Over the years he'd had so many nightmares about that night, about seeing Danny fall, seeing the blood. Images like that didn't erase, not even with time.

"Go on," Clea urged.

"Danny said he was going to kill me. I called him a coward and told him to go ahead and pull the trigger. But before he did, Billy hit him from behind with the bat. Danny lost his balance and fell, hitting his head on a rock."

"Wait," Clea said her brow wrinkling. "You said Billy hit Danny."

"Yes."

A storm of emotions passed over Clea's features, everything from disbelief to betrayal. Nick knew the exact moment when she realized that the last ten years had been built on lies.

"No! Damn you!" Clea threw the covers back and pulled on her robe. "You lied? You didn't hit Danny? Billy did?"

Nick winced.

Clea paced over to the door, her agitation obvious. "I spent the last ten years alone. You've admitted to me that you never wanted to push me away, that you thought it was for the best. Well, maybe that was best for you, but not for me. You've been calling the shots, Nick, and that's not fair. If we are going to have any kind of future together, I want the entire truth and I want it now."

Nick climbed out of bed and pulled on his jeans. When he finally got up the nerve to face her, the wounded look in her eyes nearly killed him.

"Nick," Clea said, her hand at her throat.

"Billy hit Danny." The admission lifted a giant weight from his chest. "It wasn't me. I didn't kill anyone."

The sentence hung in the air between them and before Clea even said a word he could feel her withdrawing from him.

"You said you wanted the truth," he reminded her, taking a step toward her. Around him, his dreams were falling away.

"No." She backed away. "I've changed my mind. I don't want to hear anymore." She held a hand up, as if to ward him off.

"Damn it, listen to me," Nick said. She turned her face away, her lower lip between her teeth. "I had to take the blame. This was my fight, not Billy's. Danny had been after me for years. Billy just got caught in the middle. He was a kid who happened to be in my car when Danny Bloomfield came looking for me."

Clea didn't speak. She stood still, so still he couldn't even see the rise and fall of her chest.

"I left Billy with Danny and I went to call the police. When I came back, Billy was gone and so was the gun. The police arrived. I told them I hit Danny. By the time Billy came to his senses and returned to the scene of the accident, it was too late. I'd already been placed under arrest. Billy tried to speak up, but I wouldn't let him. I told him to shut up and he did."

"Did Billy do something with the gun?" Clea asked.

"No. He remembered seeing the gun on the ground, but swore he didn't touch it."

"But why?" Clea asked, the words raw. "Why would Billy let you take the blame?"

"I didn't give him a choice." Nick paced the length of the room. "He was smart. Everyone knew he'd get a scholarship for college, and he did. I wanted him to have his life. I was nothing, Clea. I got into trouble. I was seventeen. I never thought they'd try me as an adult."

"But you both saw the gun."

"And it didn't make a damned bit of difference. The jury convicted me of manslaughter anyway. Danny Bloomfield was dead. Someone had to take the blame. There was no evidence that Danny had a gun. No one believed the Lombard brothers."

"I did." Her belief tore at his soul. "I believed in you, in us." Tears spilled over her cheeks. "I would have done anything for you, and you threw me away. You could have been free. You could have been there for your son. You wouldn't be strangers now. Do you even realize what you gave up? Do you?"

"Yes," he replied, remembering the photo history of their son. He crossed the room, his hands closing over her arms. His insides heaved with pain, with regret. "I thought about my choices every day."

"Yet you chose to go to prison. Damn you." Clea's palms hit his chest. "I'm so angry right now. Every time I think about how alone

I felt, how terrified..." She broke off, her words dying away.

"Clea." He reached for her again, wanting to soothe her anger, but not knowing how.

"No." She stepped out of his reach, wiping her tears on the sleeve of her robe. "Just go, Nick. Leave me alone. I need to think."

"What are you going to do?" he asked, hating himself even more for asking. "Will you go to the police about Billy?"

She shot him a scathing look. "This isn't about Billy. It's about you and me."

"I spent my childhood taking care of Billy," he said. "It's what I had to do. God knows Maude couldn't take care of him. I didn't think that night. I reacted in the only way I knew how. I protected him, just like I always had. Can you understand that? I didn't know what else to do. I'm sorry."

She turned away from him, and he finished dressing. The silence in the room pressed down on him, and told him more than her words could have. He'd taken a risk telling her, but now that he had he wasn't about to give up on her, or on them. At the door, he took one last look at her.

"I love you, Princess," he said. "I may have made bad choices then, but I would never choose anyone or anything over you and John now. I've changed. You gave me a gift last night. I'll never forget that. Never."

He walked from the room, from her apartment, and out into the rain. Once again he'd made a mess out of things. But this time, he would prove himself worthy. In some ways he felt that the worst was behind him. There were no more secrets between them. Last night Clea had shown him the depth of her feelings. Feelings that strong didn't die an easy death.

* * *

Clea sank down on the bed. Her fingers touched the pillow Nick had reclined against just minutes before. She could still see the indent of his head. Picking up the pillow, she brought it to her nose and inhaled. The fabric smelled like him. A painful ache filled her chest. She loved him. She loved him so much it made his betrayal hurt even more.

His confession had taken her totally by surprise. Never had she suspected Billy. Yet, it made sense. She'd always known how much Nick adored his brother. But to go to prison for him? She still couldn't believe it.

She squeezed the pillow.

Where did they go from here?

Last night had been incredible. Nick's tenderness and fierceness had made her come alive in every sense of the word. For the first time in a long time, she looked forward to the future. She didn't want to lose that feeling again. She didn't want to let him slip through her fingers, yet she'd pushed him away, allowing him to think she didn't want him.

Had she done it on purpose, giving herself an excuse to go through with her move to New York?

Clea dropped the pillow on the bed.

Nothing stood in her way. She could go to New York, but did she want to? Was she doing the right thing for John?

Clea came off the bed. What role had Robert played that night? Was he as guilty as anyone? Could she really have been so duped by the man she almost married? The thought turned her stomach and made her anger burn, making her question every choice she'd ever made.

The lies had gone on for ten years. Before she could have complete closure on the past, she needed to hear from Robert about his part in Danny's death.

And she felt certain he had one.

If she'd learned anything today, she'd learned she did trust Nick. He could have continued lying to her, and she would have been none the wiser. Instead, he'd chosen to tell her the truth, risking their fragile relationship. Ten years ago Nick had lied for noble reasons. Had Robert lied for spite and revenge? If so, there was no contest between the two men, and maybe deep down Robert had known all along he couldn't compete with Nick when it came to what really mattered, integrity and loyalty.

While she wasn't ready to forgive Nick just yet, she was beginning to understand why he had protected Billy. Nick possessed honor.

Did she want to leave him behind and start over in New York?

No.

She had no idea where they would go from here, but she wanted Nick in her life. And as soon as she cleared the air with Robert, she intended to find Nick and tell him so.

* * *

Nick had an offer on The Boss twenty-four hours after he posted the car online. He'd asked thirty thousand, but had settled for twenty-seven five. The buyer had agreed to meet him in Tacoma to make the exchange.

Under the terms of the contract Mr. Mullin had drawn up, Nick had his down payment for Mullin's Garage without any financial help from Billy. After the conversation he'd had with his brother the other day, he didn't want Billy to feel obligated to stay in Port Bliss. Billy had his own demons to fight, and he needed the freedom to fight them.

Nick would be fine on his own. Buying the garage gave him all the space he needed. He could hire another custom man and a mechanic with the money he would pull in from the cars he had lined up. With hard work, he felt confident he could take care of John and Clea in the style they deserved.

After seeing her photographs last night he couldn't let her give up New York. She needed to go. Talent like hers should be recognized. It was no surprise she'd won the internship.

She'd been so angry with him this morning. Her eyes had held all the betrayal he'd known she would feel, but he wasn't giving up on her, or their son. He loved them both. He couldn't bear to live without them. There were no more secrets left between Clea and himself. After what they'd been through, they could get through anything, even a separation while she followed the dream she'd put off for ten years because of him.

Nick paced his apartment. The time had come to get his life in order. He glanced at Maude's bedroom door. The end of the month was this weekend. The apartment would no longer belong to him. He couldn't put off cleaning things out.

Billy had promised to come by and help, but so far he was a no show. Steeling himself for the worst, Nick pushed the bedroom door open.

The scent of Maude's perfume assaulted him and his stomach rolled. But it was more than the smell of perfume, the stench of sickness lingered in the room. Nick turned away, taking a gulp of air from outside the bedroom.

He focused on the mother she had been before the drinking. That mother would have come to see him in prison. He never realized how much he'd hoped she'd visit him. Wanting her love, even after years of neglect made him feel weak. Yet, he knew he didn't hate her, not anymore. Somewhere along the way he'd begun to understand her choices. John had helped him see Maude as the woman she'd been before the drinking, the caring mother who had loved her boys. She'd tried with John, and that meant something to Nick whether he wanted it to or not. For the first time, he wished he'd come home before she'd died. He'd never have closure with her, and that saddened him.

Nick shook off his memories, picked up a couple of boxes he'd set near the door, and walked into her room. Looking around at the mess, he had no idea where to start. He planned to throw everything away. He started with the vodka.

Into the box it went, followed by her pills, her ashtray, butts and all. A kind of inner peace came over him as he worked, a cleansing. Having Maude as a mother had been rotten luck. Not his fault. Maybe she'd done the best she could after the divorce from his father. Nick stripped the bed, tossing the sheets into the box, leaving the mattress bare. Stained and dirty, the mattress looked as sad as he felt. Unable to stand the sight of it, he flipped the mattress over, intending to haul it from the room and onto the landing.

The shine of silver caught his eye, a key, hidden between the mattress and the box spring. Nick picked up the key, wondering what it opened. He glanced around the room.

Maude's jewelry box didn't need a key, the contents spilled out everywhere. None of the dresser drawers had locks. Going to the closet, he pulled the door open. Maude's faded dresses hung in a jumbled row, as untidy as the rest of the room. Her shoes lay in a pile on the closet floor.

Nick looked higher. The small closet shelf was packed tight with shoeboxes and assorted junk. He pulled down a box, and lifted the lid, finding report cards for Billy and Nick, as well as Mother's Day cards they'd made Maude, and assorted other children's art projects. Why had she kept this stuff? Maude had always seemed tough. Had it been a façade? He was coming to realize his mother had a small soft spot for her boys, a soft spot she'd also had for John. He didn't know what to think anymore. He tossed the box aside, going onto the next one.

He found boxes filled with scarves, gloves, and even old hair clips. Junk. Maude had more junk than anyone he knew. He continued removing Maude's things from the shelf until nothing remained. There was no box that fit a key. He wasn't sure he wanted to find a secret box anyway. A shroud of sadness had settled over him. He didn't know how much more he could take.

Maude's dresser still waited to be emptied. Cursing Billy for not showing up to help with this loathsome task, Nick yanked a drawer open. Maude's underthings lay in a tangle. He yanked the drawer out, and turned it upside down, dumping the contents into the box. Something solid fell from the drawer. A metal box.

A small metal box with a silver lock. He took the key from his pocket. Did he even want to open it? What did Maude have that she felt she had to lock up?

Nick left the bedroom and placed the box on the kitchen table. Taking a deep breath, he inserted the key and lifted the lid. There wasn't much. A bankbook and an envelope. Nick opened the envelope. Inside were photos. Slowly, he removed the faded pictures.

Maude with a young Senator Bloomfield. Maude kissing the senator, drinking with him. Shit. Disbelief shot through him. What the hell was his mother doing with the senator? Maude looked younger, a lot younger, in the photos. She'd always been a looker, that had been her problem. Nick flipped one of the photos over and looked for a date seeing the year he'd been born.

Nick picked up the bankbook. Starting with the month of Nick's birth Maude had made neat entries, five hundred dollars each month. There were also deductions for school pictures, shoes, clothing, and even attorney's fees. He'd always wondered how Maude had paid for his attorney. Nick flipped to the last page. The last deposit had been made on his eighteenth birthday.

Child support. Holy shit.

Nick dropped the bankbook into the box. His stomach rolled. Was Senator Bloomfield his father? It would explain everything. Had Danny known? Did that explain his hatred for Nick?

A sharp rap sounded at the door. Billy entered. "Hey, Nick. Sorry I'm late." He paused, getting a good look at Nick. "What's wrong, man?"

Nick couldn't reply. He didn't know what to say to Billy. How did his tell his brother that in the space of an hour he'd discovered they didn't share the same father?

Billy looked from Nick to the box. "What do you have there?" His brow wrinkled with concern as he picked up the bankbook. He flipped to the last page, disbelief on his face. "There's over seventy-five thousand dollars here. What is this?"

"I don't know."

"You're scaring me, Nick." Billy studied him. "You look like you're going to be sick." Billy picked up the photos, going through them. "Maude and the senator? No way."

Nick needed air. Going to the window, he swung it open, and closing his eyes he inhaled.

"There's a lot of money here, Nick, and your name is written in the front of the book."

Nick grabbed the book from his brother. He didn't want one penny of Senator Bloomfield's hush money. He couldn't even begin to think about why Maude hadn't used more of the money to clothe and feed her kids. Maybe the thought of payment to keep quiet about her son had sickened her as much as it sickened him. Is that why she'd been such a drunk? Had her bad taste in men been her undoing? For the first time he felt compassion for his mother. Had she really loved her sons before her addiction to booze got in the way?

"Is he my father, too?" Billy asked, an aching note in his voice. "The account only lists your name."

"I don't think so. The photos are dated. I think Hank Lombard is your father. Mom must have married him when she found out she was pregnant with me."

Nick turned away. For ten years he'd wanted answers to his questions about the night Danny was killed. He finally had the power to get those answers.

Bankbook in hand, he started for the door.

"Where are you going?" Billy asked.

"I'm going to see the senator. I want the truth from his lips."

"Jesus, Nick. If it's true, Danny and Robert are your brothers." Billy flopped down onto the kitchen chair. "I killed your brother."

So many secrets, so many lies.

It was time for the truth.

CHAPTER EIGHTEEN

"Clea, hello," Ellen Bloomfield said. She kept one slim hand on the oak door, using the door as a shield to keep Clea from entering the house. Robert's mother wore a soft blue sweater and black slacks. Pearls encircled her throat and dotted her earlobes. Ellen Bloomfield had a strength; a polished look and attitude that even Vivian couldn't match.

"I'm sorry to intrude," Clea apologized. After Nick's confession she'd wasted no time driving up to the lake to see Robert. Her confrontation with Nick had left her with questions only Robert could answer. She hated to think she'd been deceived by her fiancé, but the more Clea thought about Nick's version of that night ten years ago, the more she suspected Robert did have something to hide. "I need to speak to Robert." She knew he was there. His BMW was parked in the driveway.

"I see," she said, the words frozen and unforgiving. A gust of wind picked up, blowing a lock of Ellen's impeccably styled hair across her cheek. She let go of the door to set the strands back into place. A second gust of wind caught the door, blowing it open, giving Clea a clear view inside.

Robert stood in the hallway, a glass of liquor in his hand. His clothing appeared as neat as she'd expect, but there was a slight droop to his eyes that told her he'd been drinking for some time.

A pang of pity for him shot through her, but just as quickly she pushed the emotion away. If he'd done all she suspected him of doing, he didn't deserve her concern.

"What're you doing here?" His eyes held the light of hope.

"I need to talk to you, alone." She glanced at his mother.

"All right." He drained the liquor in a single gulp, then set the empty glass down on the hall table. "Let's go down to the boat house where we can have some privacy."

"It's cold," Clea said, stating the obvious. She didn't want to be totally alone with him, not when he'd been drinking. There were too many old hurts between them, and she couldn't forget Robert's anger when she'd broken their engagement. He'd been enraged, and he hadn't had a drop of alcohol then.

"You asked for privacy." Robert slipped his coat on. "Besides, the boathouse is heated." He walked past her, leaving Clea no choice but to follow if she wanted to talk to him.

Once inside the boathouse, he flipped on the light. While the boathouse did have an attached garage to house the boats, the part they stood in was more of a beach house, a place to change into swimsuits and host lakeside barbecues. Wicker furniture with plump floral cushions filled the room, giving it an inviting, homey feel.

"Why are you here?" Robert asked. "Let me guess. You've come to your senses and come to beg my forgiveness." A wry smile twisted his lips as he shrugged out of his coat, tossing the garment on a nearby chair.

The light of hope had left his eyes, and in its place Clea now saw a meanness that sparked her fear. "How drunk are you? Maybe I should come back later."

He laughed, the sound brittle and angry. "I plan to stay drunk for a while, Clea. Maybe days."

"Oh, Boomer." She hated seeing him this way, hated knowing she'd caused his pain.

He reached for her, hauling her roughly against him. "Did you come here to torment me? God, I can smell your perfume."

"Let me go." Clea twisted out of his grasp. "I came here because I have questions."

"Well, I have questions, too," Robert said, his eyes filled with agony. "I want to know why you always choose him."

"I love Nick." She'd never said those words out loud, even to Nick, and it felt right to say them now. Suddenly, her life zoomed into sharp focus. She did love Nick, no matter his past. But to really be free, she wanted to know the truth about that night, a truth she suspected only Robert knew. "Let's go back to the house." She turned to leave.

"Not so fast." Robert caught her by the arm. "You'll leave when I say you can leave."

"What?" She tried to yank her arm free, but he held tight. "You're drunk, Robert. Let me go. It was a mistake for me to come here." A wild look entered his eyes, sending panic through Clea.

"You're not going to call the shots this time." Robert hooked an arm around her waist, dragging her body up against his.

The smell of Scotch filled her nostrils, sickening her. Clea turned her head to the side to avoid his breath. "This is crazy. Let go of me."

"Lombard is right about one thing. You are a princess," Robert sneered, his breath hot on her cheek. "I could have made you my queen."

His lips grazed the side of her face. Clea yanked her head back, struggling to be free of him, but he held on tight.

"I love you," he said. "I've always loved you. Everything I've ever done, I did for you."

"What do you mean?" Clea asked. "What have you done for me, Robert?" She forced herself to look into his eyes, eyes filled with pain and something else? Anger? Remorse? Revenge?

"I have secrets, Clea," Robert said thickly. One of his hands twisted in her hair. "I can't share my secrets with anyone and it's killing me."

"What kind of secrets?" Clea asked, keeping her tone calm. "Tell me your secrets, Robert."

"Why should I?" he said. "You'll just tell Lombard."

"Do your secrets have something to do with Nick?"

"I hate him," Robert said with enough heat to wither a spring leaf. He closed his eyes, a tortured expression on his face. "He's taken everything away from me."

A deep pity for him filled Clea. "Not everything," Clea said in a small voice.

"He took my brother. He took you and John. And he took…"

"What? What did he take, Robert?" Clea asked, frustrated. Robert's hand moved painfully in her hair. She cried out.

"He has no right," Robert said. "He's not a Bloomfield. He's just white trash. He ruined everything. You belong to me, Clea."

"Robert, you're hurting me," Clea gasped. It had been a mistake to talk to him alone. For the first time she understood the depth of his feelings for her.

Robert's mouth crashed down over hers. Clea twisted her head, and bringing her knee up, she kicked Robert between his legs. Then she was free. She turned to run, but Robert caught her ankle, bringing her to the ground with him. Bigger and stronger, he pinned her under him.

Clea screamed.

* * *

Nick rounded the corner at sixty miles per hour. The Boss roared under him, as angry and charged up as he was. Every part of him rebelled against the possibility of Senator Bloomfield being his father. He didn't want to believe it, and wouldn't until he heard it from the man himself.

One more curve and he'd be there. The Mustang slid into the curve. The car fishtailed. Taking the next left, he floored it, barreling down the hill to the Bloomfields'. When he hit the driveway he slammed on the brakes, leaving black tire marks down the center of the senator's pristine driveway. Before he climbed out of the car the senator and his wife were at the front door.

Nick fixated on the senator. Grabbing the bankbook from the passenger seat, he exited the car, slamming the door.

"What's going on here?" Senator Bloomfield called from the porch. His mouth set in a grim line, he walked to meet Nick. "Just what the hell do you think you're doing driving like that?"

"You tell me." Nick tossed him the bankbook. He stared at the senator hard, looking for some resemblance between them, but other than their height, he didn't see anything. Nick's coloring came from his mother. The senator was blond, while Nick's hair was jet black. The senator's eyes were green, where Nick's were blue. Could this all be some mistake, some cruel joke?

The senator opened the book and scanned the contents. When he looked at Nick again, his skin had lost some of its color, and Nick knew this was no joke. This was real.

"Go inside," Senator Bloomfield said to his wife.

"What's this about, James?" Mrs. Bloomfield asked. When he didn't reply, she sent a fearful glance Nick's way.

Nick locked his sight on the senator, issuing a silent dare for his father to tell his wife the truth.

"Go inside, Ellen," Senator Bloomfield said calmly, but Nick didn't miss the beads of sweat on the old man's forehead.

"I'm calling the sheriff." She whirled away, heading back to the house, leaving the two men in the driveway.

Nick glared at the senator, too upset to speak.

"I'm sorry," Senator Bloomfield said.

The hardness left the senator's eyes, and in its place was a regret that stirred up every bitter memory Nick had of growing up fatherless. "You're sorry?" Nick asked, incredulous. "That's it?"

"I don't know what you want me to say." He held the bankbook out to Nick. "This belongs to you."

"I don't want your money." Years of frustration and heartache festered inside Nick. He wanted to lash out, but his body refused to move, to react.

"I wanted to do right by you," the senator said, "but you have to understand what it was like for me. I had a family. What your mother and I had was a one-night stand. I was at the lake, alone, lonely. I went to the tavern to have a drink and I met Maude. She was such a beauty. I drank too much, and the rest is history. It was a night of bad judgment on my part. I've always regretted it, and I'm sorry you had to pay for my mistake."

"I'm sorry, too," Nick said unable to keep the sarcasm from his voice. "Sorry I had to be your dirty little secret."

Senator Bloomfield grimaced, his hand coming up to rub his arm. "I want you to know something, Nick. Your mother loved you. She came to me months ago when you were up for parole. I think she knew she was sick and didn't have much time. She threatened to expose our connection if I didn't manage to keep Robert away from the parole hearing. I did as she asked, even though you took the life of my firstborn son. I owed you that much, if nothing else."

Nick couldn't begin to digest everything he'd just been told. His mother *had* helped him? John had been right. Why now, after all this time? The senator had done as Maude had asked, even while believing Nick to be Danny's murderer. Somewhere deep inside did he give a damn for Nick, the son he could never acknowledge? What a web of lies the senator had become tangled in. How did the man live with himself day after day?

"What do you want?" Senator Bloomfield glanced toward the house. "I've given you a considerable amount of money. You could rebuild your life, or use the money to set up a trust for my grandson. Or is it my career you want to ruin?"

Nick didn't care about any of those things. He didn't want justice. He didn't want to profit from the information. He just wanted peace and he couldn't have that until he knew the truth about that night ten years ago. "What about Robert?" Nick asked. "Does he know about me?"

"No, of course not. I've never spoken about my time with Maude to anyone, even my wife."

"Maybe you weren't as careful at covering up your secret as you thought you were," Nick said.

The senator frowned. "What do you mean?"

A scream came from the yard. Nick looked past the senator toward the direction of the scream and he saw Mitzi's car. In his haze of anger he hadn't noticed the Audi parked behind Boomer's BMW. "Is Clea here?" he asked, knowing Clea had been using Mitzi's car while her Honda was in the shop.

"She's in the boathouse with Robert."

Nick didn't wait to hear any more. He charged past the senator. His heart hammered in his ears as he ran, his thoughts on Clea. Throwing the door open, he skidded to a stop. Boomer lay on Clea, covering her body from Nick's view.

"Let her go you son of a bitch," Nick ground out.

"Nick," Clea cried, her voice muffled.

"I said let her go." Nick's hands closed over Robert's arm and pant leg. He yanked the man from Clea, tossing him in the air as if he weighed no more than a feather. The sound of splintering wood filled the room as Robert landed on one of the wicker chairs, sending it toppling over backwards.

Nick followed Robert, lifting him off the floor by the front of his shirt. The smell of Scotch on Robert's breath repulsed him. "I've had just about enough of you," Nick said through gritted teeth.

"Stop it," Senator Bloomfield yelled from the doorway. "That's enough!"

"I want the truth about the night Danny was killed and I want it *now*, brother."

Nick heard Clea gasp. He hadn't meant to blurt it out that way, but bitterness and resentment had dulled his thinking.

"For God's sake," Senator Bloomfield said. "He doesn't know."

"Nick," Clea said from behind him. "Please. Robert's drunk. He doesn't know what he's doing."

"When are you going to quit defending him, and see him for the conniving son of a bitch he is?" Nick said to her.

"Stop this," the senator cried.

"Tell me." Nick shook Robert. "You knew we shared a father, didn't you? You knew that night."

"You can't be my brother," Robert mumbled. A lock of hair fell over his eyes and he seemed to have trouble focusing. "Danny told me, but I didn't believe him."

"Danny? Did he tell you that night? How long did he know? Is that why he hounded me?" Nick asked, his fingers tightening on Robert's shirtfront.

"I went to Danny," Robert spat out, tossing his head back to get the hair out of his eyes. "I saw some canceled checks with Maude's name on them. I tried to call you," Robert said to the senator, his eyes filled with accusations, "but you didn't return my calls."

"Dear God," Senator Bloomfield said.

The fight left Robert's body. He slumped against Nick. Tears filled Robert's eyes. Suddenly, Nick didn't want to go on with the conversation. So many lies. So many people hurt. He let go of Robert and he slid to the floor, a pitiful heap of wounded man.

"I don't understand," Clea said, coming to stand beside Nick. "What does this mean?"

Nick searched her face for signs of injury, but didn't see anything. "It means that Boomer and I are half-brothers."

"What!" Clea exclaimed. "No. Oh, Nick."

Robert's head jerked up. "It's always been poor Nick, hasn't it? I've never understood it. He has nothing. His mother was the town whore, but you loved him in spite of everything. He's always had everything I ever wanted. And when I found out he even had a part of my father…"

"What?" Senator Bloomfield asked, coming forward. "What did you do, Robert?"

"I told Danny, but he already knew. He'd known about Nick for years; that's why he hated him so much." Robert laughed, the sound demented and sad. "Danny was the only person who understood me."

The senator turned away, bringing his hands up to his temples as if to press away the pain, the grief, the sorrow.

Nick closed his eyes. He felt Clea's touch on his arm, could hear the gentle intake of her breath. "And that night. Why did Danny come after me?"

"I saw you with Nick," Robert said brokenly, his eyes on Clea. "At Lookout Point. You were in his car, wrapped all over him. Seeing you with him made me vomit. I went home and got drunk, and when Danny came home, I told him Nick raped you. Something inside Danny snapped. He went crazy." Robert turned to Nick. "He said he would take care of you once and for all. Danny already hated you. He knew the combination to the gun safe. He took a pistol and we went after you."

"You were there that night," Nick said.

"Oh, Robert." Clea's hand tightened on Nick's arm. "You knew it wasn't rape. You set Nick up."

"I wanted to kill you myself, Lombard." Robert pushed his hands into his hair. "But I was too drunk."

"That's when Danny ran my car off the road," Nick said, his voice strangely devoid of emotion. A numbing, disconnected feeling settled over him. A movement near the door caught Nick's eye. He glanced over. Billy and Sheriff Kincade stood in the open doorway. How much had the Sheriff heard?

"I don't remember much," Robert said, the words broken. "I stayed in the car, but everything was spinning and I had to lie down. I knew Danny had the gun. I wanted the pain to end. I covered my ears and shut my eyes, waiting for the gunshot, but it didn't come. I didn't look up until it was over and Danny was on the ground."

A small measure of relief filled Nick when he realized that Robert hadn't seen Billy hit Danny. Billy's secret was still safe. Robert had been too drunk, his head down.

"Then everything happened so fast," Robert continued. "You got in the car and drove off. Billy ran into the woods. I crept out of the car and went to Danny, but he wasn't breathing. That damn gun was lying there on the ground. My only thought was to protect Danny. I could hear the sirens. Before they arrived, I took the gun and ran."

"And the lakeside robberies?" Nick asked. "Were you responsible for those, too?"

"No, it was Danny. He wanted to set you up. I didn't have anything to do with those crimes."

Nick turned away. His stomach rebelled. He had expected to

feel hatred for Robert, but instead he felt sorry for him. In his own way, Robert had suffered every bit as much as Nick or Billy had for that night. Robert's words to his brother had prompted the confrontation. They'd all been victims of something bigger than themselves. The true blame lay with the senator. His secrets had cost them all so much. His secret had ultimately taken the life of his firstborn.

"And your mother," Nick said, remembering Robert's alibi. "She covered for you, didn't she?"

"Yes, but she didn't know she did. I sneaked into the house, wiped the gun clean, and put it back in the safe. After that, I crawled into bed." Robert sobbed quietly, his own secret now set free. "Mother assumed I'd been home the entire time."

"There's just one thing wrong with the story," Billy said.

"No," Nick warned. "It's over. Let it go."

"I can't, Nick." Billy came toward him.

"Let the boy speak," Sheriff Kincade said.

"Don't you see what keeping the secret has done to me?" Billy glanced at the sheriff. "I've already told Sheriff Kincade that I'm the one who hit Danny." He walked to the senator. "I didn't mean to kill him. He was going to shoot Nick. I had to stop him. It was an accident. Forgive me."

Senator Bloomfield clutched his chest. "Oh, dear God. What have I done?"

Nick could see the pain in Billy's eyes, hear the torment in his voice. He'd made a mistake. All this time he'd thought he'd been protecting Billy, giving him a better life, but instead Billy had been slowly dying inside. The truth was out, but would it set Billy free?

"You hit Danny?" Robert asked in a stunned whisper. He pointed an accusing finger at his father. "This is your fault. If you'd just kept your pants zipped, none of this would have happened. Billy might have swung the bat, but you killed Danny. Your secret killed him."

The senator recoiled, his skin a strange shade of gray. Sweat dotted his brow and neck, wetting his shirtfront. His hand clutched frantically at his chest. "I'm sorry," he said. "Please forgive me."

The senator's eyes closed. His knees buckled, and he pitched over, landing with a thump on the cold linoleum of the boathouse floor.

* * *

A cold March sun shone over the crowd of mourners at the Port Bliss Cemetery. Under their feet a carpet of freshly mowed spring grass scented the air. Overhead a seagull stretched its wings, a brilliant white against the indigo sky.

At the graveside of Senator Bloomfield, Clea sat with John next to her, Nick on his other side. Although John had thought of the senator as his grandfather, it had been a shock for John to learn the truth. Clea had explained Nick's parentage to John, but she knew John had questions, questions she'd hoped Nick would help answer, but he'd been upset and distant since the senator's death. She'd struggled over letting John attend the funeral, but he'd asked to come, and she hadn't wanted to deny him the chance to say good-bye.

Clea glanced over at Nick. His jaw was tensed. Clean-shaven and dressed in a black suit, he looked vulnerable, yet so hard and bitter. She longed to pull him into her arms and give him comfort, but she'd tried that when the senator had died; Nick had pulled away, leaving Clea heartbroken and confused all over again. Would the timing ever be right for them?

In the space of a few weeks Nick had lost his mother and his father, parents who were strangers to him. Clea knew their deaths were as painful for him as they would have been had they been close. He'd withdrawn from her since the boathouse. His rejection of the comfort she wanted to give him stung, but a part of her could understand it. He'd suffered a life altering shock when he'd learned that the senator was his father.

She had no idea how to make things better between them before she left for New York. Her things were packed, her tickets purchased. She should be happy, but inside she mourned for Nick. She didn't want to leave him behind, but he hadn't asked her to stay.

She looked over at Robert. He sat a few rows ahead of them, his head bowed, his expression hidden. He'd been arrested after his confession. Free on bail, he faced charges of concealing evidence, but because the crime was committed when he was a juvenile it seemed doubtful he'd serve any jail time.

To Robert's left sat his mother. A black veil covered Ellen Bloomfield's face, hiding her grief from the small group gathered here. Shamed by her husband's infidelity and her son's part in

Danny's death, she'd kept the service small and private. She hadn't spoken to Nick, but she hadn't stopped him from attending the funeral. Maybe Ellen realized they'd all lost too much already.

Clea tried to focus on the eulogy, but her mind kept straying to Nick and Robert and Billy. She had no illusions that Nick and Robert would ever be friends, but she hoped they wouldn't remain enemies. Billy had his own demons to face. He'd gone in for questioning, but no formal charges had been filed. She knew Nick worried about his brother, but the time had come for Billy to figure things out on his own. It was the only way he'd ever be free of his haunting past.

The service concluded and everyone stood. Immediately Robert and his mother were whisked away by a waiting limousine. Clea stood and took John's hand.

"Are you ready to go?" she asked Nick.

"In a minute," he said, his voice hoarse with emotion. "You two go on."

Clea didn't want to leave him, but she smiled at John and they walked to the car. When they reached the car, they waited outside in the sunshine for Nick. He left the senator's grave and walked a few yards away to where Maude was buried. He stayed at Maude's grave so long Clea began to worry.

"When's he going to come?" John asked.

"I don't know. I think he's saying good-bye to his mother," Clea said, her heart aching for Nick. "I'm sure he just needs a few more minutes."

John continued to study his father, and Clea couldn't begin to imagine what her son was thinking. Could he even wrap his mind around the fact that Senator Bloomfield had been Nick's father? She'd explained Danny's death to him, telling him about Billy and Robert's parts in that night. John understood that Nick hadn't killed Danny, that he'd gone to prison to protect his brother. She'd expected him to be angry with Robert, but instead John had withdrawn into himself, increasing her worry over taking him to New York.

John pushed away from her, walking toward Nick. Clea started to call for him to come back, but decided against it.

When John reached his father's side, Nick turned and looked down at his son. John said something, but Clea couldn't hear him. Then the boy reached for Nick's hand. They stood together, holding hands, John and Nick, father and son. Clea's eyes filled with tears.

Maybe they needed each other more than they let on. How could she take John away from his father? Did she even want to make the move permanent, or did she want to come back to Port Bliss after the internship ended?

She'd waited for Nick to ask her to stay. Maybe she'd waited too long. If she wanted Nick she had to fight for him this time. And she intended to do just that.

CHAPTER NINETEEN

Nick pulled into the parking lot at the Tacoma Dome and turned off the Mustang's engine. He glanced over at John. The boy had been silent during the ride to Tacoma. So much had happened the past week. He had no idea how to talk to John about the senator's death or about his own plans for the future. How much could the kid really understand? Time was running out.

Nick glanced at the rearview mirror, watching Billy as he pulled into the parking lot.

"This is it," Nick said, his tone light. "Our last ride in The Boss."

"Do you really have to sell the car?" John asked. He fiddled with his seatbelt buckle.

"I want to sell the car," Nick told him. "The money I get from The Boss will be my down payment on the garage. I'll have my own business. I'll be able to take care of you and your mom."

"How can you? We'll be in New York. You can't take care of us there."

"I wanted to talk to you about that."

John cocked his head to the side. "What about it?"

"I have some ideas I want to run past you." He took a breath, praying John wouldn't shoot his plans down.

"What kind of ideas?" John shifted on the seat to better view Nick.

"I love you, John. And I love your mother. I want to marry Clea, but I wanted to ask your permission first. It's important to me that you approve." He paused, his heart beating so hard he thought it might come right out of his chest.

John didn't reply. He glanced away, out the window.

Nick's heart sank.

"How can you marry us if you live in Port Bliss?" John asked, his voice small.

"I've got a couple of different plans in place, but I need to talk to your mom about them first. You have to trust me. We will all be together. I promise," Nick said. "Do I have your permission to ask her to marry me?"

"I guess."

Nick could see the hope in his son's eyes. For the first time since he'd come home, Nick could feel a bond between them, a small bond, but one he felt certain he could build on.

Nick gave John a smile of encouragement. "Everything is going to be all right, John."

John's teeth sunk into his lower lip. "Things will never be the same. Robert's in trouble. Billy's in trouble. Senator Bloomfield is dead."

"Robert and Billy will be fine," Nick said. "I know you're sad about the senator. I'm sad too, and that's okay, but we have to move forward. We have so many years to make up. I want to spend the rest of my life making you and your mother happy. It's all I've ever wanted."

John nodded. Nick reached over and squeezed his son's hand. John didn't pull away. For one sweet moment he felt a connection to John, the kind of connection he'd always wanted to have with his son.

The sound of an approaching car pulled their attention away from each other. Billy drove up beside them, rolling his window down. Nick opened his window.

"He's not here yet?" Billy asked, referring to the buyer.

"No," Nick said. "Park your car. We're going to go on one last ride before he gets here." Nick turned to John. "What do you say, John? Let's take one last wild ride."

* * *

Clea ran the packing tape across the top of the box. She took a look around the apartment. Tears pricked her eyes. All her things were boxed up and ready to be moved into storage. Everything was happening too fast. She couldn't get her breath, didn't know what to do. Yesterday, Mitzi told Clea that she'd rented the apartment. It was what Clea had wanted, but it made the move seem final. Her home here would belong to someone else. She kept telling herself she would still have her half ownership of The Coffee House. She could come back to Port Bliss whenever she wanted. Focusing on her dream should be a priority, but Clea knew in her heart her dream was no longer her photography.

Nick's return had changed everything. Making love with him had changed her. She didn't want to live without him, or raise John without him. She loved him too much.

Port Bliss was her home. Her mother was here. Her son's friends were here. Nick was here. More than anything she wanted to stay, to be a family. But if Nick didn't ask her to stay, if he didn't want to be with her and John, did she want to come back? It was so confusing. She couldn't leave town with things unfinished between them. Nick had called her a coward once, and maybe she had been, but not any longer. Somehow, she'd fallen for Nick all over again, and this time she intended to hang onto him with both hands.

The sound of a car pulling up out front brought her to the window. She watched as John and Nick got out of Billy's car. When they were clear, Billy drove off. Nick had asked to spend some time with John today. While she thought it was a good idea, she'd been surprised when John had agreed. Something had happened between the two of them at the funeral. They'd made a connection in spite of the sorrow and anger they both felt.

Clea turned as they came into the apartment. "Hi," she said, smiling. Just seeing Nick in her apartment made her feel better, lighter. She'd missed him this week.

"Hi," Nick said softly and there was something in his tone that told her they'd be okay.

"Mom, is it okay if I go over to Toby's now?" John asked, running by her and into his room.

"Yes." She had a million questions for Nick, but first she had to deal with John. She followed John to his room, surprised that he didn't seem upset like she'd feared. "Toby called when you were out. I think he has a surprise for you."

"I'll walk him over," Nick said, joining them, "then I'll be back."

John flew out of his room, his backpack slung over his arm.

"What do you have there?" Clea asked.

"Stuff I want to show Toby," John answered on his way to the door.

"Did you remember the card?" Clea asked. She'd gotten Toby a phone card so he could call John whenever he wanted to.

John gave her an exasperated smile. "Yes, it's inside."

"All right then." She went to the door. "Call me when you are ready to be picked up."

"I will." John exchanged a glance with Nick, a glance that said they had a secret. She wanted to question them both, but instead she let John go.

The door closed behind them. She could hear John's chatter as he walked down the stairs. In a minute, Nick would return. It was their last chance to talk, to be together for a long time. Tears filled Clea's eyes and she bit down on her lip to stop the flow. What if Nick didn't say the words she wanted to hear? No, she refused to think negatively. If Nick turned her down this time, it wouldn't be for lack of trying on her part. From the beginning they were destined to be together. Fate wouldn't be so cruel as to pull them apart again.

* * *

Nick paused outside of Clea's apartment door. Inside she waited for him. They had a lot to discuss and not much time to do it. He wasn't a praying man, but right now he prayed for things to work out between them. He knew she thought he'd withdrawn from her, but he hadn't. He'd needed every minute of the past few days to set his plans into motion. The senator's death had slowed things a little and sent him into a tailspin of self-doubt. The funeral had been tough, but after the service concluded he'd known it wasn't just his father he had to make peace with. He'd gone over to Maude's grave and made peace with his mother. An incredible sorrow had filled him, making him question every choice he'd ever made, then John had joined him, taking Nick's hand, telling him it was okay to be sad. John's words and caring touch had pulled Nick out of his funk, and made him more determined than ever to get his family back.

Nick took a deep breath, then turned the knob, letting himself into the apartment. Clea stood at the window, her back to him. Was she upset? Could he blame her if she was? He went to her, his hands spanning her waist. She didn't flinch, didn't push him away as he'd feared she might. Instead she relaxed against him. Her surrender sent a shot of pleasure through him. They hadn't been alone since the night they'd made love. There was still so much unsaid between them, but he vowed to say everything tonight.

"Are you all right?" he asked. Her summer scent filled him and he kissed the smooth skin of her neck. For the first time he felt truly free to kiss her, to love her the way he wanted to. There were no more secrets left between them.

"I should be asking you that," she replied a catch in her voice.

"I'm going to be fine, Princess. In fact, I'm going to be better than fine."

She turned in the circle of his arms.

He wanted to kiss her fears away. His mouth lowered to hers.

"Wait." Her hands landed on his chest.

"I don't want to wait anymore," he said. "I need you. I want you. I love you."

He expected desire to fill her eyes, but instead he saw a resolve there.

"No," she said, putting some distance between them. "I can't. I need to know where we stand."

"All right." He understood her need for answers. "We're standing in my new apartment."

"What?" Her brows drew together in confusion.

"The lease was up at Maude's. I knew this place was up for rent. I went to Mitzi and rented it." He waited for her reaction.

"You can't be serious?" she said incredulously.

"Why not?"

"I don't know." She spun away from him, but he could hear the confusion in her tone, see it in her body language.

This wasn't the reaction he'd expected. He was going about things all wrong. She was pulling away from him and that was the last thing he wanted. "I wanted to leave the door open."

"For what?" she asked in a small voice.

"For you and John."

"Are you saying you want us to stay?"

"Hell, yes, I want you to stay," he answered, suddenly realizing that she hadn't understood his motives for taking the apartment, "but I'm not going to let you."

She turned to face him and he could see the angst in her eyes, the wanting. "What if I want to stay?"

He smiled. "No way." He cupped her face in his hands. "You have to go, at least for now. This is important. You have incredible talent. I didn't say anything sooner, but I've been working on things."

"What kinds of things?" she asked her tone hopeful now.

"I sold The Boss today." He kept the regret from his voice and looked straight into her eyes. The Boss had been a part of him for years, a part he didn't need anymore.

She started to speak, to protest, but he covered her lips with his fingers. "I wanted to, for us. Billy, John, and I drove to Tacoma today to deliver the Mustang to the new owner. I want to use the money as a down payment for Mullin's. Mr. Mullin has offered to sell the garage to me. Thanks to my website, I already have four vintage car restorations lined up. There's big money in this business. You won't lack for anything, Princess. I promise. I want to take Mullin's offer, but it depends on you."

"On me?"

"If you want me. If you want to make a life with me here."

She gave him the most brilliant smile he'd ever seen. A smile he felt all over his body.

"Of course I want you. I've always wanted you." She brought her hands up to grasp his forearms. "I love you, Nick Lombard. I always have."

Nick didn't give her a chance to reach for him. He claimed her mouth in a kiss of liquid fire. Every emotion he felt for her went into his kiss. He needed to show her how much he loved her. With a growl, he picked her up and bore her to the bedroom, but he didn't lay her down on the bed. Instead, he released her, letting her body slide down his until her feet hit the floor.

For one exquisite moment they stared into each other's eyes, the effect shattering.

Then Clea yanked his t-shirt from his jeans, bringing it up, over his head, tossing it to the floor where it landed with a whisper.

She went for his fly next, but Nick grabbed her hands. If she touched him, he'd go up in flames, and he wasn't ready to do that yet, not until she felt the same passion and desire he did. Grasping the hem of her sweater, he pulled it over her head. Her hair floated like a cloud around them and he couldn't get her jeans off fast enough. He yanked his own pants off with an urgency she couldn't mistake for anything other than what it was - pure lust.

Together they fell onto the bed. Clea's bra hit the floor. Her panties followed, the lace light and airy in his hands. The satin of her skin slid under his. And then he was inside her. A contented purr left her lips, and he kissed her, over and over, so deep and so consuming he couldn't think, only feel her around him, against him, until she climaxed, crying out. She tightened around him and he found his own release, the feeling so intense he thought he must have gone to heaven.

The sound of their ragged breathing filled the room. A sheen of moisture covered their bodies, so great was the heat between them.

Nick pulled back to stare down at her. "Damn." His mouth moved against hers. "Marry me. Today, tomorrow, whenever you want. Just say you'll do it."

"I want to, but I have to talk to John first." Love sparkled in her eyes.

"I already have. I asked him today. He wasn't as excited as I wanted him to be, but he said it was okay if I asked you. I'm asking, Princess. Say yes."

"Yes."

He sealed the proposal with a kiss.

"I love you, Nick," she said.

"And I love you." He rolled to his side, taking her with him. "I'll be here for you in any way you want. I'll wait here, or I'll come with you to New York if that's what you want. My parole has been lifted. I'm free to come and go as I please. Or I can keep John with me, here in Port Bliss. I know my relationship with John is still new, but if he wants to stay, he's welcome. I'll take care of him for you while you do your internship. I love him as much as you do."

"I know you do." Clea stroked his jaw, her touch gentle and soft. "I want to live here, Nick. I want my son to still have his best friend. We can talk to John together, and ask him what he wants. I'll go to New York, but I'll come back to you. A part of me has never given up hope that we'd be together one day. You are my dream, Nick, for myself and for John. My photography takes second place next to the love I feel for you. Love is everything. Family is everything."

Family was everything. For the first time in his life he felt like he had it all. In Clea's arms he'd found the love of his life. He had a chance with his son. He had his family back.

And that made Nick smile.

JOLEEN JAMES

Award-winning author Joleen James became an Indie author with the launch of her contemporary novel *Falling For Nick*. Since that time, she has released her second and third novels, *Under A Harvest Moon* and *Hometown Star*.

When she's not busy writing, Joleen enjoys spending time with her family at her lakeside home in the beautiful Pacific Northwest. You can find Joleen James at www.joleenjames.com and on Facebook and Twitter.

19868117R00118

Made in the USA
Charleston, SC
15 June 2013